# iMULA

## RICHARD SATTERLIE

2008 Silver medal IPPY award-winning author of
*Something Bad*

2009 Silver medal IPPY award-winning author of
*Agnes Hahn*

Medallion Press, Inc.
Printed in USA

*Accolades for*
**AGNES HAHN** *by Richard Satterlie*

"It's one of those books that you will decide on just one more chapter before you turn the light out (for the eighth time that night)."

–L.E. Lester, *Eternal Night*

"Agnes will hook readers who get inside her head and learn her value system is structured around good and bad people as she perceives them. Although others like psychologist Dr. Leahy, Detective Bransome, and reporter Powers are fully developed characters, the insightful discerning glimpse at the title protagonist makes for a strong tale."

–Harriet Klausner, *Midwest Book Review*

". . . a deftly plotted, ingeniously crafted, and elegantly written suspense thriller."

–CountGore.com

# IMOLA

## RICHARD SATTERLIE

# DEDICATION:

To my wife Tricia and my children, Alison, Jake and Erin.

Published 2009 by Medallion Press, Inc.

The MEDALLION PRESS LOGO
is a registered trademark of Medallion Press, Inc.

Typeset in Adobe Garamond Pro
Printed in the United States of America

ISBN: 978-193475504-4

10 9 8 7 6 5 4 3 2 1
First Edition

## ACKNOWLEDGEMENTS:

I thank Tricia and Alison for being my primary readers. Thanks also go to the crew at AW for all of their help over the last few years. Finally, I appreciate all of the help provided by Helen and all of the other good people at Medallion Press.

# CHAPTER 1

My name is Agnes Hahn. I'm a serial killer, emasculator of men. And I'm not. I've seen the pictures, heard the descriptions. If the voice isn't real, like they've told me, then how can the actions be real?

We have cable television here at Imola, but they don't let us watch what we want. Figure that. At home, I liked to watch those real doctor shows—actual surgery. The only thing that bothered me was the initial incision. The first slice of the sharp scalpel through fresh skin gave me a sick feeling in my stomach. It made my fingers curl into fists and my toes grip the soles of my shoes. I always had to look away. That's why I don't understand how I could have cut all of those men. Dr. Leahy says they were hurt by my hands, but, she says, my hands weren't controlled by my mind. How can that be? I know my hands, and my hands couldn't cut through skin.

Once the skin was opened in the TV shows, I was fascinated by the surgeries. The human body is a remarkable machine. The most incredible thing is the way the body heals itself after such an invasion. It can be opened and a piece removed, and if properly stitched, it will heal like nothing happened. Too bad the same can't be done to the mind. It's easy to find the junction between the small and large intestine, locate the appendix, and cut it out. But one can't remove a few brain cells and expect a bad memory to go away forever. Not without removing a lot of other memories.

For me, it's impossible to forget small parts of the past without forgetting all of the past. Same thing for remembering. Now, Dr. Leahy wants me to remember things I don't like to remember. About Lilin. About our father. What he did to her. She wants to know about specific things that happened, but more than that comes back. She wants a bucket of water, but wave after wave crashes on the beach to fill that tiny bucket. She says it will help me. Helping shouldn't hurt.

*Hurt her back.*

# CHAPTER 2

Agnes spun in her chair. Jingling footsteps echoed in the women's hall, coming closer, the pace fast. Shoe bells meant only one person—Milo.

The skeletal man bobbed toward Agnes, the bells barely keeping up with his pace. He bent toward her and shoved something into the breast pocket of her hospital-issue jumpsuit. A long finger pressed to his mouth. "Shhh."

Agnes turned in her chair to follow Milo's arc through the Day Room.

Near the opposite wall, he leaned close to the green, fake leather seat cushion of an armchair and puffed air from his mouth, rotating his head around to clean the entire seat. He paused, blew a full breath on the center of the cushion, and swiveled his behind onto the seat. A chuckle escaped his taut lips.

Agnes glanced around the room. The lengthening shadows of the massive oak trees penetrated the high windows and decorated the interior wall of the Day Room, the only hint of life on the outside. The windows were little more than a source of natural light, too high to see anything but a narrow swatch of sky and the very tops of the gnarled oaks. Agnes kicked at the leg of a chair. Everything was intended to exude a calming influence on her and her fellow residents, from the serene green walls and seamless linoleum floors, to these narrow slits of natural light that projected the first oak shadows on the east wall in midafternoon. Those shadows would grow up the wall like vines, then dissolve as the sun ran through the changing colors of the sunset.

Residents? They were patients to the staff, but really prisoners to the legal system, and each ruling group independently worked hard to produce the calm.

But how can life without horizons be calming? A high window ledge is no more a physical horizon than the dull existence of psychological incarceration is to one's emotional outlook. The absence of the horizon on a rolling sea is the best trigger of seasickness, yet no one associated with Imola seemed capable of comprehending the analogy of a missing horizon with rolling emotions, in terms of the maintenance of mental health. It was a wonder the residents themselves weren't as green as the walls. Agnes kicked the chair leg again.

She glanced around the room. All of the men and women sat quietly in scattered chairs, oblivious to Milo's movements. Several of them faced the television on the far left wall, barely blinking at the flickering light of a cartoon.

Did any of them see what he had done? See what he had put in her pocket? No one reacted, but that was the way here. She wanted to look in the pocket, but Milo had given the "shush" sign. With so little privacy, such things had to be respected.

Her eyes swung to the right, to the two hallways that opened from the main room. The one on the left sprouted the men's rooms; the one on the right, the women's. The two hallways reminded her of a pair of naked tree branches with parallel sets of blossom buds, each bud a room for one of the residents. Would she ever get to see a real tree wake up after a winter pause and burst out in bloom again? How long would her winter pause last here in Imola?

A new commotion built in the right-hand hall, punctuated by the swelling squeals of regulation shoes on linoleum, pushed to a trot. Agnes turned her head and flopped back in her chair. The sounds came from the nurse's station, at the end of the women's hall.

Nurse Reginald barged into the Day Room. "Where is he?" She spotted Milo and sprinted to his chair. "Where are they? Where did you put them?"

Milo shrugged.

"Stand up." Nurse Reginald's round face glowed

crimson, enhanced by the ultra-white of her starched uniform. "Turn your pockets inside out."

Milo rose in slow motion, unfolding his six foot three, rail-thin frame in time-lapse jerks. His hands crept into his pockets, diving to their depths with magician-like deliberation. In a single decelerating motion, his hands pulled back from the pockets, tugging the liners inside out like floppy rabbit ears. He held his arms out straight, parallel to the floor. His shadow formed a cross that bent from the floor up onto the east wall of the Day Room, dwarfing the tangled mass of phantom branches. A grin inched across his face.

Nurse Reginald stepped close and patted his hip and chest pockets, then down his legs, up his torso, and back down his back. She stood away. "Okay. I know where they are." She grabbed his crotch, hard.

Milo flinched, but maintained his scarecrow posture. A flickering scowl spun into another grin.

"Damn it, where are they?"

Milo shrugged.

"You took them. I know it. I want them back. Now. Or you'll go in lockdown."

Agnes crossed her arms across her stomach just below the breast pocket that held Milo's prize. Lockdown wasn't a punishment for him. He spent most of his time in his room anyway.

Her frown mutated to a grimace. That would leave

Stuart Guerin as the only other interactive male in the wing, and he was no bargain. Fortunately, Stuart spent a good part of his day in his room as well. She scanned the Day Room. The other four men on the floor were medicated to a point just this side of a vegetative state. She didn't even know their names. Two sat and stared all day. The other two rocked back and forth until they fell asleep, hunched in sitting positions that nearly defied gravity. A major plus—it let the girls have the run of the Day Room for most of each day.

The Imola annex, though modern and progressive, wasn't supposed to have co-ed wings like this. But Agnes read the newspapers, listened to the complaints of the staff members, and asked lots of questions. Some were even answered. Evidently, a paltry budget further withered by three rounds of annual budget cuts had altered the organization of the hospital from functionally coordinated to crisis shuffled. Patients were housed based on their level of required care, the severity of their behavioral peculiarities, and the nature of their criminal activities. Gender fell low on the ward assignment priority list. Supposedly, there was a complex formula used to determine placement, but to Agnes the formula came in the shape of a dartboard.

Criminally insane wasn't a politically correct tag anymore. She knew all of her ward-mates had been arrested and tried for a crime, or crimes. And they all had been sentenced to Imola rather than jail or prison. They all had problems that required therapy. Most of them, anyway. Here, the rallying cry wasn't of unrecognized innocence, but of undiagnosed sanity. Unfortunately, it was obvious medication was doled out more to maintain order than to correct chemical imbalances, and group and individual counseling sessions came and went in unpredictable waves for those with interactive minds.

Agnes felt lucky. She had the regular services of Dr. April Leahy of Santa Rosa, one private session per week. She wasn't sure why the good doctor made the drive all the way over to Napa and worked for free. But she was grateful. Dr. Leahy seemed to be particularly competent. Best of all, Dr. Leahy had been with Agnes from the beginning. From the first arrest of what is now called the menstrual murders. When Lilin showed up to pull Agnes into the horrendous acts. It was also one of the best times of Agnes's life—when Jason showed up.

Then again, maybe Dr. Leahy was doing all of this because of Jason. Agnes stiffened in her chair. This was the only subject that made her think Dr. Leahy wasn't such a great doctor. Jason didn't come to see Dr. Leahy. Maybe the doc wasn't so perceptive. She didn't even realize who Jason came to visit.

Agnes tightened her crossed arms and felt something poke her left forearm. Milo's spoils. But she didn't want to look. That was Milo's business.

"I'm going to give you to the count of ten to give them

to me," Nurse Reginald said to Milo. She stomped her right foot in time with her backward count. "Ten . . . nine . . . eight . . ."

Milo's grin widened, his body frozen in place. His chest didn't even move with his breathing.

Agnes stood and walked around behind Nurse Reginald. She smiled at Milo.

". . . three . . . two . . ."

One of Milo's eyelids twitched. His version of a wink?

Nurse Reginald stomped her foot twice more. "God damn it." She spun around and rushed down the women's hall, a string of unintelligible words flailing in her wake.

Milo tiptoed over to Agnes and nodded.

She pushed her chest out toward him and turned so he could reach into the pocket. His hand barely touched cloth as it slid in, then out with his prize.

Agnes stared at the object and shook her head. "You need reading glasses?"

He shrugged, smiled, and turned toward the men's hall. The bells on his shoes rang in triumph all the way to his room.

# CHAPTER 3

The days passed in bunches, sometimes dragging on forever, sometimes over in a blink. To Agnes, time was marked by Dr. Leahy's weekly visits—the days had lost their formal names. They were called "one day until Dr. Leahy," "two days until . . ." "three days . . ." and so on. What day of the outside week did she visit? Thursday? Sunday? It didn't matter. Not in Imola.

Agnes straightened in her chair and turned her right ear toward the door of the Day Room. It was the only connection to the outside world—the passageway for visitors and visiting therapists. Every time the door opened, a breath of the outside world wafted in, only to be terminated by the hiss of the gas cylinder of the door closer, and the clunk of the automatic lock.

Agnes tilted her head like a curious dog. There she

was. Dr. Leahy. If Agnes listened carefully, she could tell it was the doctor. The double tap of each heeled shoe on the tiled hallway was like the gait of a tap dancer: two sounds from each foot strike.

Agnes slumped in the chair and gripped the armrests.

Dr. Leahy leaned back a little when she walked, so her weight shifted forward slowly. Tip-tap. Maybe it would sound different if she didn't wear those shoes with the big, blocky heels.

*You know why she does it.*

Agnes nodded.

It pushed her breasts out. And gave them a bounce when she walked. She wanted everyone to look at her breasts.

Dr. April Leahy pushed open the self-closing door of the Day Room and tip-tapped along the far wall. Agnes's eyes followed her. The doctor's shoulder-length auburn hair flowed behind her, exposing her ears and dangling earrings, each a single, thin bar that widened at the apex to accommodate a diamond. At least half a carat each.

She slid her soft sided, leather attaché onto a table at the far right of the Day Room and opened it, fishing inside. "Hi, Agnes. Are you ready?" Her jaw hinged against her ever-present piece of gum.

Agnes leaned forward and rested her elbows on her knees. She didn't like to walk over too soon. It wasn't because the sessions were unpleasant. She just didn't like to give in to Dr. Leahy right away. And she didn't know why.

*You know why.*

"Agnes?"

Agnes scanned Dr. Leahy from head to toe.

Brown and orange today. She always wore a suit: tight fitting, with a coordinated blouse, also snug. Seventeen meetings now, and she hadn't duplicated an outfit yet. But they weren't really that different.

Agnes looked down at her own jumpsuit. She could get the same variability if she rolled up the sleeves one day, cuffed the legs another day, changed the level of the zipper, and then varied the combination.

But Dr. Leahy's clothes were way different if she knew Jason was visiting. Then the skirts were higher—upper thigh—and the blouse was low cut, showing cleavage. Her walk changed, too. The tip-tap went to tip-TAP. It made her cleavage sway as well as jiggle.

Dr. Leahy didn't talk the same way when Jason was around either. She was more animated, and she laughed a lot. Not laughed. Giggled. She giggled when he was around. She didn't giggle when it was just the two women.

*She's fucking him.*

Agnes balled her hands into fists and ground her molars together.

Dr. Leahy must have thought Jason came to see her. Why else would she bounce her breasts and giggle? But she was wrong. He didn't come to see her.

*She is fucking him.*

Dr. Leahy shifted her weight onto her left leg and tapped a pencil on the table. "Come on, Agnes. I haven't got all day." She cradled her attaché in the crook of her arm and tip-tapped into the small conference room midway along the far wall of the Day Room. She turned. "Now, Agnes."

A slight hint of a smile tugged on Agnes's lips as she stood. She tried to duplicate the tip-tap walk, but her hospital-issue sneakers squished with each step. She squeezed through the door and stood next to her chair. "Good morning, Dr. Leahy. How was your week?"

Dr. Leahy sat. "You can call me April, you know."

April. Her parents probably named her for the optimism of spring, and she fulfilled their prenatal hopes and expectations. MD, psychiatrist. Not one of those newly graduated, strange-talking psychologists who fingered imaginary Freudian pipes when they pontificated. Imola was sprinkled with them, and their apprentice-level salaries. Agnes smiled as she slid onto the chair opposite her private doctor.

Dr. Leahy touched her pencil tip to a steno tablet. Her jaw relaxed, the gum apparently shoved into some secret pocket in her mouth. "I'd like to review a little, if you don't mind."

She always started the same way: her review was a review.

Dr. Leahy crossed her legs. "We made excellent

progress last time. Remember?"

There was nothing else to do in here but remember. "Yes."

"So you remember that your twin sister died when she was four years old?"

"Her name is Lilin."

"Yes, I know." Dr. Leahy wiggled in her chair and fingered her tablet and pencil. "Do you remember anything else about her?"

"Not much."

"Can you remember your time with her? Were they happy times?"

Her memories from her childhood were mostly nonexistent, but since Dr. Leahy had been coming around, asking questions, probing her past, little parts were coming back to her. Times with Lilin. Laughing. Playing. But there was something eerie in that background. Something big. Something dark.

"Agnes? Were there happy times?"

"Some."

"What were the happy times?"

"Playing together."

Dr. Leahy wrote a few sentences. "Do you remember anything about your father?"

"Yes." A large door. Closed. "Vague memories."

"Happy memories?"

"I don't know. Just that he was there."

Dr. Leahy wrote without looking at the tablet, except for an occasional glance. "I know your mother passed away too soon for you to have memories of her, but do you remember if another woman was in the house with you and your sister?"

"Lilin. Her name is Lilin."

"Sorry. Was there another woman?"

"No. I don't remember a woman."

Dr. Leahy's hand danced on the tablet. "What was your house like?"

"I don't know. Just a house." *Not a home. Not like in Mendocino, with Gert and Ella.*

"Do you remember anything in it?"

Agnes rubbed her face with her hands. "I remember some toys."

"What kind of toys?"

"Blocks. A train."

*Two trains.*

Agnes frowned. "Two trains."

"Anything else?"

"Not really."

"Any dolls? All little girls have dolls."

"No!"

Dr. Leahy jumped. "Why did you answer like that?"

Something wasn't right. Pictures flashed in her mind. Pictures of a doll. But it wasn't smiling. Was it real?

"Agnes?"

"I don't know."

"You didn't have a doll?"

Agnes's gaze drifted to the ceiling. She paused. Her heart pounded; bubbles of sweat traced her hairline.

Dr. Leahy leaned forward.

Agnes sensed the closeness, but it was momentary—then she felt like she was drifting away. She felt her body relax, lose all animation, like it was just a shell. "I think I did have a doll." Her own voice seemed to echo, like it was almost mechanical, from somewhere in the distance.

The pencil scratched at the tablet. "Can you picture the doll?"

"I think so."

"Did you play with it?"

"No."

"Why not?"

"Lilin took it."

"What did she do with it?"

*Hurt it.*

Agnes didn't answer. She was sliding back, a little too fast. She felt her eyes well with tears.

"Agnes. What did Lilin do with your doll? Do you remember?"

"Yes." Barely audible.

"What did she do with it?"

Agnes took a deep breath and let it out fast. A flash of memory. A closed door, opening. "She took it into the bad room."

Dr. Leahy uncrossed her legs and sat up straight so fast her pencil tip drew a line across the tablet. "Agnes. What's the bad room?"

The tickle of tears rolled on Agnes's cheeks. She could feel her mouth move, but no sounds came out.

Dr. Leahy sat back into the chair and rubbed her chin with her thumb. "When Lilin took your doll into the bad room, did you try to get it back?"

"Yes."

"Did you follow her into the bad room?"

"Yes."

"What did she do to the doll?"

*Hurt it.*

"She hurt it."

"How did she hurt it?"

No answer. Agnes didn't move. The room was bright, like her eyes were wide open, staring through the opposite wall, to an open door in the distance. She tried, but she couldn't close her eyes—not even to blink.

"Agnes?"

The door swung wide. "Oh no."

"Agnes. What is it? What's happening?"

*Agnes. Stop him.*

"Him!"

"Who's him? Is there someone else in the bad room?"

*Help me.*

Tears again, with sobs.

"Is it your father?"

*Agnes. Please.*

A deep breath. A large figure hovered. Speaking in incomprehensible words. A feeling of panic pierced her, but as soon as it penetrated, it swirled away, like it was being pulled down a drain. Then, an overwhelming sense of calm. "I'm not Agnes."

Dr. Leahy leaned forward again, pushing against the table. She stared into Agnes's eyes. "Who are you?"

"I'm No One."

# CHAPTER 4

Jason Powers knocked on the door of the second floor apartment. The building was not yet a flophouse, but it had great potential. It was difficult to tell the paint color on the walls of the hallways and stairwell. Where the paint wasn't peeling, it was smudged with who-knows-what, or decorated with graffiti.

The door opened and Jason barged in, walking carefully as if the hallway dishevelment were contagious. "Hey, big brother. Place looks the same. Maid on vacation?"

Donnie Powers's laugh echoed in the small apartment. "Thanks for stopping by. Did you bring me anything?"

"It's just a social call. I haven't seen you in a long time. I'm on my way over to Napa."

"Imola again? I always knew one of us would end up there. I just thought it'd be me."

Jason looked for a place to sit. "If I'm a passenger on that train, you're pushing the throttle."

"All aboard." Donnie slapped his knee and faked a loud laugh.

Jason walked to the only upholstered chair in the room and snatched a copy of *National Lampoon* from the seat cushion. "I see you're into classic literature." He dropped it on a pile of newspapers, cheeseburger wrappers, and unidentifiable paper products.

Donnie clapped both hands over his heart. "Why do critics miss the brilliance of good satire? It'd be a boring world without a few out-of-round wheels. Besides, who's going to keep all the suits honest?"

"*National Lampoon* keeps people honest?" Jason flopped into the chair, and a spring jabbed his right butt cheek. He adjusted his position.

"The best way to stagnate this country is to have coast-to-coast conformity," Donnie said. "Anybody or anything that pushes an envelope contributes to societal evolution."

"What does that have to do with honesty?"

Donnie leaned against the bathroom doorway, the only interior door in the studio apartment. "Most people re-check their own ways before mounting a defense against an outlier. Except for Republicans."

Jason moved again, but he couldn't escape the pinch of the spring. "If you live long enough, you'll become a

Republican, too."

"Now, that's something to look forward to." Donnie wandered across the room and sat, cross-legged, four feet in front of the chair. "Will Dr. Leahy be at Imola?"

"How do you know about her?"

Donnie swung his arm and pointed at a large table piled high with computer equipment. "I'm an information merchant. Remember?"

"You check up on me? Your only brother?"

"Always have. You don't stop by very often."

Jason raised the middle finger of his right hand and grinned. "Maybe because you always ask for money."

"Work is sporadic. And it doesn't pay that well," Donnie said.

"With your talent for computers, you could get a real job. You could drive a Beemer."

Donnie snapped his fingers. "Oh, yeah. Me in a Beemer. Mom would have a heart attack."

Jason scowled. "Mom did have a heart attack. Two years ago. You were at the funeral. Remember? I swear. You need to lay off the weed."

"Relax, little brother. I remember. It was just a figure of speech. I like to think of her as still alive."

"Because she gave you money?"

Donnie lowered his voice to a whisper. "She was a good mom."

Jason relaxed his stern look. "Did you ever stop to

think that you might have contributed to her heart attack?" The comment was a familiar refrain, about 90 percent joke and 10 percent probability.

"What do you think the weed is for? Dad wrote me off a long time ago, both figuratively and in his will. Mom never did."

Jason turned his gaze out the adjacent window. "I know." Were the smudges on the inside or outside? Probably both. He turned his focus loose. "She always spooned out the love based on who needed it most. For the longest time I thought she liked you best. But when Eugenia dumped me, Mom was there with a ladle. Before I even told her about it. Poor woman. Maturity isn't a long suit in our family, and she had to put up with you, me, and Dad. Peter Pan cubed."

"I miss Eugenia," Donnie said. "You screwed up big time to let her get away."

"Nice sarcasm." Jason leaned forward in the chair and had to shift again to get away from the spring. "In case your mind is in some kind of drug-induced haze, she dumped me. After the wedding invitations were made out and stamped. She was seeing someone else. You do remember that, don't you? All that salad hasn't turned your brain to mush yet, has it?"

"Relax, little brother. I'm just serving you a wad of goo."

"It's all still pretty raw, asshole."

"Then I guess I shouldn't tell you she came on to me

once, about a year ago."

"Yeah, right."

"I didn't do anything. That's not something I'd do to my brother." Donnie cleared his throat. "Besides, she said she was on the rag. I'm not into earning my red wings."

Jason slumped back in the chair and covered his eyes with his open hand. "She'd rather screw a donkey. I think she used those very words to describe you once."

"Relax, Jason. More goo."

"Well, poke the open wound, why don't you? Your humor sucks."

Donnie pulled his left leg up so the knee was close to his ear. "That reminds me. I have a new favorite quote. 'You're only young once, but you can be immature forever.' I think some baseball player said it."

"That's inspirational?"

"Yeah. It is to me." Donnie picked something from his big toenail. "So, is Dr. Leahy shaping up into something for you?"

Jason leaned back farther and interlaced his fingers behind his neck. The spring didn't counterattack. It was a good question. Was she shaping up into something? He was comfortable with her. But was there more? "Not really."

"Seems to me you aren't having too much trouble getting Eugenia out of your system. You're working on collecting a harem."

"A harem?" Jason sat up straight. "What the hell is

that supposed to mean?"

"You're screwing Dr. Leahy," Donnie said. "And you can't get that killer out of your mind, either. Right? What's her name?"

Jason slumped back into the chair. "Agnes."

"Yeah. I can see that one in you. You're that transparent." Donnie slid his hands from his foot to his knee. "Falling for someone who's impossible to obtain is my gig. Are you horning in on my deficiencies?"

"I care about her, but without expectations. Nothing like that, anyway. I got really close to her during the investigation. I think she's as much a victim as the men she killed."

"I can think of several families who'll disagree with you on that."

Jason pulled his hands down to his lap and leaned forward a little. "Do you know anything about dissociative identity disorder? Multiple personalities?"

"No. And neither do I."

"I'm serious. I ran into Agnes once when Lilin was in control. She was a totally different person."

"Lilin?"

"You know the story, don't you?"

Donnie pinched the thumb and forefinger of his right hand next to his lips and inhaled an imaginary joint. He held his breath and exhaled with a shrug.

"Lilin and Agnes were twin sisters. The real Lilin

**24**

was killed by their father, Eddie, when the twins were four years old. And there was abuse before that. April thinks Agnes saw it all. And that's not all. Eddie was also Agnes and Lilin's grandfather. He molested his own daughter. She was the twins' mother."

"Who's April?"

"Dr. Leahy. I thought you were up on this, Mister Information Merchant. Anyway, Lilin is Agnes's other personality—the one who did the killings. She's a piece of work. Sexy as hell. And twice as deadly. When the murders first started, they called her the menstrual murderer. For some reason, she only killed when she was menstruating. Slit the men's throats and cut off their dongs. You remember that part, don't you? Every man in northern California thought twice before approaching a woman in a bar."

Donnie grabbed his crotch and nodded.

"They think she used the severed part for a final orgasm."

"Now that's what I call PMS."

"It's what I call a thrill kill. And Agnes is this mousy, innocent introvert. The exact opposite of Lilin."

"Lilin sounds like fun." Donnie bobbed his head up and down. "You got the hots for Agnes or for Lilin?"

"Lilin swiped a razor within inches of my neck the one time I met her. I was nearly one of her sex toys." Jason felt the chair spring and shifted on the seat again.

"And I'm not attracted to Agnes. I just want to make sure she gets better."

"Yeah. Right. Does Dr. Leahy know you're porking her just so you can stay close to Agnes?"

Jason lowered his hands onto the chair arms. He felt something sticky on his left forearm. He lifted the arm to inspect it. "I can see Agnes with or without April."

"Then why's your face so red? You know I can see through you like you're a Baggie. It's been five months now. Dr. Leahy is going to start hassling you pretty soon, if she hasn't already. You can't hump a woman more than two or three times before she starts thinking about wallpaper and children's names."

Jason lowered his arm. "You're an expert? When was the last time you were with a woman more than two times?"

"Getting laid regularly doesn't solve all the world's problems, little brother."

"It beats the alternative."

"Maybe I'm saving myself for the perfect one-night stand."

Jason looked at his watch. "I rest my case."

Donnie crossed his legs again and straightened his back. "Hypothetical, little brother. If you had to choose, who would you take? Me or Agnes?"

"Get real."

"I'm serious. Who would you take if you had to choose?"

Jason sat forward in the chair, his butt on the edge of the seat cushion. "Is this about Eugenia again? I know how you must have felt about her. I know she didn't like you. She did a pretty good job of driving a wedge between us. I was working on straightening it out with her, though."

"She wouldn't have changed," Donnie said.

"I disagree. She wasn't as bad you thought."

"You were only weeks from marrying her. That would have been the end of me in your life. And you would have gone through with it if she hadn't run out on you."

Jason felt a tightness in his belly. "You're right. I would have gone through with it. But I told you. I was working on it. It wouldn't have come between us."

"And if she came back to you now? What then?"

Jason flicked his hand like he was shooing a fly. "I'm past her. It still hurts, but she's long gone to me."

"And replaced by Agnes the killer."

"Why are you getting so weird about Agnes? I only visit her. I've slept with April Leahy."

Donnie leaned back, his arms straightened backward to support his upper body. "For some reason, I'm not worried about Dr. Shrink. But this Agnes chick gives me the willies. I just have a feeling that if it came to me or her, you'd pull a Eugenia on me."

"For the last time, that was going to change, Donnie. I was going to lay it out to her."

"Don't blow farts in my face, little brother. I was sinking fast from in-law to out-law, and you know it. Now it seems like you just come around here because you don't have anyone else."

"I come around here because you're family," Jason said. "Nothing will change that. No one will change that. If you'd given me time, I would have straightened that out with Eugenia. And as I recall, you didn't do much to help the situation. What was it you called her? Eugenics? Right to her face, no less."

"The woman had a plan. There was no limit to her arrogance. What the hell did you see in her anyway? Was she that good in the sack? She was a total yuppie, you know."

"She wasn't a yuppie. Her parents had money, but she wasn't like that."

"As blind men see the elephant." Donnie sat up straight again. "You were turning into a yuppie before my eyes. You were becoming her."

"Bullshit. I would never be that shallow."

"You can't have it both ways, little brother. You have this deep-seated hate for the yuppie lifestyle, but you drive a Volvo and wear those shirts with the little embroidered polo player." Donnie leaned over and pointed to the floor. "Looks like dog shit." He picked up an imaginary pile and brought it to his nose. "Smells like dog shit." He brought his hands to his mouth. "Tastes like dog shit." He flicked his hands toward the floor. "Eww. Glad I didn't step in it."

"A bit melodramatic, don't you think? And, I'm not a yuppie. Just look at my apartment, how I live. I drive the Volvo because it's the safest car out there, and I log a lot of miles on my job. And I have to wear nice shirts. Would you prefer I wear a coat and tie?" Jason made the sign of the cross with his two index fingers, then dropped his hands in his lap. "And I come around here because you're family, and no woman will ever change that. You're important to me. So don't worry. You're still sole beneficiary in my will."

Donnie chuckled. "In that case, drive fast and don't wear a seat belt."

Jason stood. "Before or after I go to the bank?"

Donnie jumped to his feet. "After. I love you, little brother."

# CHAPTER 5

Agnes stared at the Day Room door, then glanced at the clock on the adjacent wall. The second hand jitterbugged up the slope to twelve, then ratcheted downward, past one. It wasn't like Dr. Leahy to be late, even by seconds. Agnes leaned forward and gazed through the chicken wire-embedded safety glass panel in the door. Movement caught her eye. The familiar bounce of Dr. Leahy's walk registered before her physical features came into focus. Agnes sat back and exhaled. The clock was probably wrong.

Dr. Leahy opened the door and paused. She squinted and wrinkled her nose.

Agnes knew the sensations. The fluorescent lighting was a little too intense, as was the antibacterial smell. The odor signature wasn't like the sterile smell of a doctor's office or a hospital. It was more like an overdose of Pine-Sol.

Dr. Leahy took a deep breath, as if savoring a last gasp of hallway air, and bounced into the Day Room, her jaw working the invisible wad of gum.

Milo trudged across the room in front of her, and she had to wait to move past him. With each step, he slowly raised his foot and gave it a slight shake before carefully placing it back down. A high-pitched jingle accompanied each foot shake.

Dr. Leahy turned and watched him amble toward the hall. She pivoted and walked toward Agnes, shaking her head.

A sense of defense for her compatriots pushed Agnes from her chair. No need to play the stalling game today. "You've never shown much interest in my ward mates." She pointed. "His name's Milo. Milo McGuinn."

A smile tickled her cheeks. Normally she'd stop at that, but for some reason she didn't mind talking to Dr. Leahy. Things she usually churned in her mind tumbled out of her mouth like coins from a slot machine with triple cherries.

"He's that skinny because he doesn't eat much. He's vegetarian. He's here because he's what they call an insatiable kleptomaniac. He got aggressive about it—started grabbing things from people, hurting them when they resisted. Some seriously. That's what I heard, anyway. I find it hard to believe. He's too passive. At least in here.

No telling what medication he's on, though."

Dr. Leahy turned and looked again, just as Milo disappeared into the men's hallway.

"I got the information from Marsha Herman. She says Milo's as nutty as a pecan tree. I had to get the details from her in three different conversations: two with me, and one I overheard one day when she was talking to a coat stand. She tends to hallucinate."

Agnes walked toward the conference room but stopped and faced Dr. Leahy.

"Anyway, Milo wears bells on his shoestrings. Marsha has a theory on that, but I just asked Milo about it. He said he read about it somewhere and thought it was a great idea. He doesn't want to step on the microbes on the floor, so he gives them a warning. He probably imagines bacteria and viruses with little happy faces, complete with ears. I wonder if he realizes they're all over the plants he eats, crushed between his molars with each bite."

A young man with long, stringy hair crept up behind Dr. Leahy and paused. His hands opened wide and he raised them to chest level, but stopped and dropped them to his sides. A frown creased his brow. He looked down at her mid-thigh skirt and took a step back, bent at the waist, to his left, and tried to peek under Dr. Leahy's skirt.

"Watch out," Agnes said, more as an alert than a warning.

Dr. Leahy spun around and the man straightened up, put his hands over his crotch, and hurried toward the hall. He had to wait for Milo, who had reentered the Day Room.

"Eat some fucking meat," the man said to Milo when he could finally pass. "You'd move faster."

Dr. Leahy looked at Agnes and shrugged her shoulders.

"Stuart the Stud," Agnes said. "That's what he calls himself, anyway. His real name's Stuart Guerin. When he comes up to us like that, he reaches around and grabs our breasts and pushes himself into our backsides. He does it to all of the women. You're lucky. He must have thought you were one of the nurses."

Dr. Leahy turned to look again. "Does he take it any further?"

"No. He hurries to his room and closes the door. It's always dark in there."

*He masturbates.*

Agnes nodded her head. "He usually gets us all sometime during the week. He runs into his room like that about a dozen times a day."

Dr. Leahy turned back to Agnes. "Don't you report him?"

"No. We all talked about it. He gets really mean when he gets in trouble for it, so we just decided to take care of it ourselves. He needs help, not more trouble."

"How do you take care of it?"

*Hurt him.*

"We each have our own way. I just cover up and give him a dirty look. Marsha gives him an elbow in the ear. Tammy tries to kick him in the crotch. The only one to get him to stop is Patty. She followed him to his room one day, held the door open, and told him what a loser he was for doing what he was doing."

*Masturbating.*

"If that gets him to stop, why don't you all do it?"

"It made him cry. Then he got really mean with all of us. I guess it's easier to let him have his fun. He seems harmless."

"I don't understand. Why would they put him in a co-ed ward?"

"From what I've heard, they've had him on two or three other wards, with all men. He kept getting beat up. They say the last time he got messed up pretty bad. They probably moved him here because they're afraid of a lawsuit. Here it's our word against his. And we don't leave scars."

Dr. Leahy put her hand on Agnes's upper arm and steered her toward the conference room. "But doesn't it bother you? When he touches you?"

"You mean because of what happened when I was little?"

"Yes."

"I guess I feel sorry for him."

*Not me.*

"He's like a little boy around girls who are just developing."

Dr. Leahy put her attaché on the conference room table. They both sat. Her tongue pushed against the inside of her cheek, and her jaw went still. "What would your Aunt Gert have said about him?"

"That he's not one of the good ones." The corners of Agnes's mouth twisted upward. "Gert would've got him to stop."

*You know how.*

Dr. Leahy reached across the table and took Agnes's hands in hers. "Are you sure you're all right in here?"

"I'm fine. I've been trying to help some of the people here. They just need someone to talk to them and to listen to them. Someone who isn't judgmental."

Dr. Leahy withdrew her hands. "Am I judgmental?"

"You have to be. It's your job."

*Bitch.*

Agnes smiled. "How else can you make me better?"

"But you talk as if being judgmental is bad."

"Maybe there's a difference between helping someone and making them better."

"I don't understand."

"Spend some time in here."

Dr. Leahy chuckled. "Sometimes I don't think you belong here."

"Then get me out."

"We aren't even close to finishing your treatment. And the alternative would be prison."

"And the difference would be?"

Dr. Leahy shook her head as she picked up her pencil and steno pad. "Does everything have to be logical with you?"

"Should I strive for the illogical?" Agnes said.

"Sometimes emotion should rule over logic."

"Since when?"

"Since humans gained the capacity for abstract thought," Dr. Leahy said.

Agnes relaxed into the chair back. "I have dreams. That doesn't fall in the logical category, does it?"

Dr. Leahy posed the pencil. "It depends on how you look at them. What kind of dreams do you have?"

"Some good, some bad."

"Any that repeat?"

Agnes bobbed her head and frowned. "One."

"Is that one good or bad?"

She turned her eyes to the bare wall and deepened her frown. After a few seconds, she flicked her head back and looked Dr. Leahy in the eyes. "I don't know."

Dr. Leahy wrote. "Does it have anything to do with Lilin or your father?"

Agnes's response was immediate. "I don't know."

"It might?"

She shrugged.

Dr. Leahy leaned forward. "Can you tell me about it?"

Agnes removed her hands from the table and folded them in her lap. "I used to travel the coast highway frequently, and there's a turnout on a cliff overlooking the rocky shore—about two hundred feet below. I've seen the actual turnout a number of times. I drove by it on the way to my animal care presentations. It's just a few miles south of Mendocino. In the summer, an ice cream truck used to stop in the turnout and sell ice cream to people driving the highway. The turnout was always crowded when the vendor was there."

"Are you mixing reality with dream right now?"

"Yes. The turnout is real, and the vendor sold ice cream there in the summer. When it was warm."

"What's the dream?"

"Someone's always in the car with me. Telling me that I can stop, but I can't have any ice cream. I pull over, but the person won't let me get out of the car. Won't let me open the door."

"Do you stop?"

"Yes."

"Why don't you keep going?"

"I don't know. The view is incredible, but I don't think that's it."

"You never just keep going?"

"No, I always stop."

"Does the person hold you in the car in any way?"

"No. Just says I can't get out—that I can't have ice cream."

"Do you want some ice cream?"

"Yes. I crave it."

"Why don't you just get out?"

Agnes thought for a moment. "I don't know. I don't feel safe. I guess I don't trust the person in the car."

"Is the person a man or a woman?"

"I don't know."

"How long have you had the dream?"

"A long time."

"Weeks? Months? Years?"

"Years."

"Have our meetings affected the dream?"

"Yes."

"How?"

"It's more frequent."

# CHAPTER 6

Jason flopped onto the couch next to April Leahy and swung his arm around her head so she could nestle her forehead into his neck. The three-way bulb in the adjacent lamp seemed to be at middle click, casting a soft glow over the ubiquitous earth tones in April's great room. The television on the far wall matched the color scheme with a subtle background of flickering light and expressionless sound. April's wineglass was three-quarters empty. His was untouched.

She put her right hand on his chest. "Thank you for coming over. It's been a while."

"I had an idea. I'm surprised I didn't think of it before."

"I've got an idea, too." She dropped her hand to his lap and gently kneaded his crotch.

"Not that." He looked down at her hand but let it

continue its circular caress. "I'm not in the mood for that right now."

April kissed his neck. "Part of you says otherwise."

He pulled her hand from his pants and dropped it over her lap. "I'm serious. I don't want to."

"Since when is a man not in the mood? And don't tell me you have a headache, because even if you do, I can make it go away. Guaranteed."

He didn't have the courage to tell her the truth. That their passionate moments weren't developing the intimacy he was looking for—the incredible emotional closeness he'd felt with Eugenia. From a physical standpoint, April was an excellent lover. Excellent? Why had that word popped into his mind? Why not wonderful? Fantastic? She was technically proficient, expert, but the difference between making love and falling in love was like the difference between the proper alignment of a piston in a cylinder and the integrated function of the entire engine when perfectly tuned. The power of the former was significant, but paled in comparison to the output of the latter. And it wasn't evolving. At least for him. Then again, maybe he wasn't giving it enough of a chance. Not it. Her. Maybe he wasn't giving her enough of a chance. Was that the problem? Was he looking for an "it" instead of a "her"? Maybe he was the problem. Or was there something else?

He swiveled his body to face her on the couch, dislodging her head from his neck. "I had an idea about Agnes's case. That's why I came over. I can't believe I didn't—"

April threw her hands against his chest and pushed him back into the arm of the couch. She stood up and hovered over him, shifting her weight from her right foot to the left.

He tried to interpret her action, her expression, but his understanding of the female mind still required training wheels. So, what now? Forge ahead? Make a lame apology? He picked up the wineglass and downed over half of it in one gulp. Lame apology. "I'm really sorry, April. But you know how I am. When I get something in my head, I stay on that track until I hit the coast."

She reached for her wineglass and tightened her fist around the stem. "I need more."

More what? Wine? More from him. Crap. Should have just lain back and enjoyed it.

April stomped into the kitchen.

Jason thought he heard the sound of a cork popping from a bottle, and his mind looped back to the time he was nearly expelled from school for feeling up Diana Venturi in the middle school boys' room. His mother had frozen him with the one phrase that could uncouple time from matter and space in the theory of relativity: "Wait until your father comes home."

Now he counted three heartbeats for every swing of the pendulum in April's mantle clock. Two minutes passed. Three.

April slinked back and eased down in the overstuffed chair opposite the couch. Her eyes were dry but ringed red. A crumpled tissue was in her left hand, a full wine-glass in her right.

Jason straightened up and searched her face for a hint of what was to come. She had time to guzzle a couple glasses in the kitchen, and her drooping eyelids suggested she had.

"What about Agnes?" Her monotone seemed icy.

"We don't have to talk about her."

"Then what should we talk about?"

He fidgeted through the silence. How long before his father would come home?

April tipped the wineglass to her lips and let the liquid slide down her throat with only a few swallows. She leveled her eyes at him and then dropped her gaze to the floor.

His mind flipped back to his childhood room: His father had just barged through the front door. It hadn't taken long for the door to his room to fly open, then slam shut, the huge figure of his father charging like a bull. The memory came back in detail. His father had stopped short, glanced over his shoulder at the door, and leaned forward. His voice was a whisper instead of a bellow. "Did she let you?"

Jason remembered how thick the words had been on his tongue. "It was her idea."

His father had swatted his own thigh three times with the stick, each echoing in the room and, hopefully, down the hall. His voice remained a whisper. "This is a lesson. Girls are going to chase you until you catch them. Once you do, everything is going to be your fault. Do you understand?"

He hadn't at the time, but now his father's lesson was beginning to sink in.

April shifted in her chair, bringing his mind back. "I'm sorry, Jason, but sometimes I just don't get you. And I want to." She relaxed into the chair and tipped the glass to drain the last few drops of wine. "I know I shouldn't push you, but I just get impatient. When you come here, I want it to be about us."

"I know. I'm not very good at this. Forgive me?"

"Special dispensation. I've downed most of the bottle, and it's hitting me hard. Hell, I'm halfway to forgiving my father."

He tried to push out of the couch but failed. "I should go."

"Are you sure? You know what I like to do when I get a snoot full."

He flopped back into the couch. She was chasing. He had only one chance left. "Do you have the number of the lawyer who's handling Agnes's affairs?"

She put her glass on the coffee table and slinked over to the couch without standing up straight. She stabbed her left knee into the couch cushion next to his right thigh and swung her other knee over, straddling him.

Jason sent a silent apology to his dad.

"It's in the card box next to the phone. Get it on the way out." She fell against him and exhaled into his ear. "And don't forget to lock up."

Jason hit the button, and the driver's window of the Volvo whined down. The crisp morning air swirled around him, ruffling his hair. He needed to shed the head-bobbing fatigue brought on by a lack of sleep and the monotonous drive to Mendocino, so he channeled his mind on his objective. He was doing it for April and for Agnes. But that wasn't all. This time, his curiosity exceeded his reporter instincts. Ever since he had helped catch Agnes and send her off to Imola, he wanted to find out more about her. To help her. Why had her father molested and then killed her twin sister, Lilin? And why not Agnes? On more than one occasion, April had said that having that one piece of information would be invaluable in helping Agnes.

Jason leaned over and nodded to his image in the rearview mirror. He knew Detective Bransome had shut the investigation down as soon they found out Lilin was a construct of Agnes's traumatized mind.

Jason suspected, hoped, that Agnes's U-Store garage was left untouched. If her great-aunts had kept any information about their brother, Eddie, it wouldn't be stashed in the house. It would have been hidden away just like Eddie's identity had been hidden from Agnes until Lilin's murders started.

As far as Jason could tell, Eddie was such an embarrassment to his sisters, they had pushed him into nonexistence. And it was no wonder. He was Agnes's biological grandfather and her biological father. He had molested his own daughter, Agnes's mother, and after she died, he started molesting Lilin. April had said she was convinced that Eddie didn't molest Agnes, but she thought he made her watch everything that happened to Lilin, including her murder. Quite a satchel for a four-year-old to carry. No wonder Gert and Ella took Agnes away. No wonder they had severed all connections with Eddie. The U-Store garage would be a reasonable exile for his memorabilia, if any existed.

Getting the gate card and the keys to the U-Store garage was easy. After all, Agnes had requested that Jason take care of her things. But now he had to go in, and sliding open the door to unit E-24 brought back eerie memories of the thundering GTO clipping his foot and sending him spinning to the asphalt, the rear tire narrowly missing his head as it squealed out of the U-Store lot. Was it really Lilin driving that day, or was it Agnes?

He had agonized about that ever since it had happened, rationalized that it must have been Lilin. Agnes wouldn't have tried to run him over, would she? But the way Agnes tried to protect Lilin in the interrogation room after she was caught kept haunting him. She would have done anything for Lilin, even run him down with the GTO.

But he had dodged the four-wheeled behemoth. And his quick phone call to Detective Bransome had led to Lilin's capture. Agnes's capture. At the time, he just wanted—needed—to get away from the storage unit. Once Agnes, or Lilin, was on the run, all he thought about was her capture. Now he wanted to see what was in the garage. But the thought of sliding open the metal door brought it all back, gave him a whole-body shiver.

Jason shoved upward on the door and jumped to the side. Just in case.

The condition of the garage seemed too similar to what it had been the last time he had done his quick walk-through, as if the GTO had just peeled out of there. If Bransome's people did an inventory, either they did so without moving anything, or they were extremely diligent in returning all parcels to their original positions. Jason's memory wasn't photographic, but he did have a good sense of three-dimensional space.

With the center of the garage open to accommodate the now-missing car, Jason could breeze through the contents in a systematic way. He started by moving the furniture, all late nineteenth- or early twentieth-century vintage, into the center of the space. He not only opened drawers, but pulled them all the way out to see if anything was hidden behind or below. The combined smell of mildew and mothballs nearly overwhelmed him, and he had to make regular trips to the doorway for a lung-full of clean air.

Next, all artwork was moved onto the furniture. A quick feel of the back of each piece produced no surprises.

Last were the boxes. At least thirty of them, contents unknown. He started on the left side of the garage, nearest the door, pulling the boxes to the center of the room for examination. He replaced them, along with furniture, when he was done with them.

The entire left wall yielded twelve boxes, none of which contained a hint of Eddie Hahn. Jason saw old clothes, bedding, trinkets, and other personal effects. He slowed his search in the last two boxes when he discovered old wooden toys from an early era. The craftsmanship took his breath away. In the last box were two trains, a milk truck, a logging truck complete with logs, and a pristine set of lettered and numbered stacking blocks set in a wooden-wheeled pull wagon. No blocks were missing. He lifted the wagon from the box and gasped. Below it, a set of carved wooden figurines included at least two families: parents, children, and infants. And a dog. He picked up the dog. The piece was so finely etched that the texture of the animal's fur looked real. He carefully replaced all of the items and closed the box.

The back wall of the garage held most of the remaining boxes, so he passed them up and moved to the wall to his right and the four boxes there. The second contained memories of Agnes's life. High school yearbooks. A diploma from the University of California, Davis—BS in animal science—still in the original, opened, mailing envelope. He straightened up, holding the certificate at arm's length.

Agnes had been in Davis for at least two years if she had previously gone to a community college, and at least four otherwise. Why hadn't Lilin surfaced then? April's theory made some sense. As long as Gert was in control, her strong personality held Lilin in check. And even when Agnes was away at college, Gert maintained that tight control. Davis isn't far from Mendocino, only 160 miles, so it was close enough for Gert to drive over should Agnes need her, or for Agnes to come home. He envisioned Agnes making regular weekend trips to Mendocino, dirty laundry in hand, but really to maintain her emotional security blanket with Gert and Ella.

It was only after Ella went into the care home and Gert died that Lilin made her appearance, and the murders started. To him, that spoke volumes.

Digging through the rest of the box uncovered little else about Agnes, so Jason resealed the top and shoved it back along the wall. He turned to the back wall of the storage unit.

Among the standard-sized boxes was a large one, more than three times the size of the others. It was wedged in the corner, two double stacks of boxes on top. He pulled the smaller boxes down and went for the monster. It was heavy: a challenge to slide on the cement floor. He decided to go through it in place.

The reason for the heft appeared as soon as the aged sealing tape was sliced. Books. It was filled with books. He pulled a few from the top layer and scanned the titles. *Moby Dick. David Copperfield. The Grapes of Wrath. Leaves of Grass.*

A taste for the classics. Agnes's or Gert's? Or Ella's? Not Lilin's.

He pushed one of the box flaps closed, but something stopped him. Maybe he wanted to see some Kerouac, some Kesey. Some Tom Wolfe. He dug in. No such luck.

Everything was in hardcover. All books in pristine condition, but with stressed spines. Obviously read. By whom? He thought back. No books in the house. Strange. These were the kind of books one put on display. Especially if they were all read. They were worthy of second, third, multiple reads. Very strange.

The next reach required that he turn his head away and press his armpit into the side of the box. He moved a couple of books into a graspable stack, and his fingers hit something solid, metallic. And large. He swept his fingers toward the four sides of the box, pushing books around with his hand. The object nearly filled the box's side dimensions. He rapped on it with his fingernails. Definitely metallic. And thick walled. Very thick.

With most of the books removed, the box was light enough to pull into the center of the garage, but he didn't stop there. He pulled it nearly to the door so the harsh daylight would be an aid to identification. The box inside the box was painted battleship gray, with abrasions and scratches everywhere. He tried to lift it, but he couldn't get a grip. And it was too heavy. He'd have to cut the cardboard away; he needed his tools.

Before keying the trunk of the Volvo, he stretched his arms at the cloudless sky. He'd been going through the Hahn life-stash for nearly three hours, and the sun was finally warming the asphalt-paved driveway of the U-Store lot to short-sleeve temperatures. As he opened the trunk, its hinges complained. "Got to oil those," he said into the light breeze.

His tool kit had a small pocketknife. Not one of the fancy Swiss Army things, but a cheapie, with plastic panels of fake pearl-like finish. Of the two blades, the smaller one could possibly cut flesh, with the right angle and significant pressure. He selected the large blade— its blunted edge was missing the last quarter inch of tip. Cardboard worthy, but little else. He started in on the outer box.

It took three minutes. Much of the cardboard tore rather than cut, but the four sides of the box eventually splayed out, flat on the floor, still attached to the box bottom. The metal box wasn't tall, only ten inches or so, but it was formidable. A safe-like structure, original function unknown. It was closed with a hasp and medium-sized, rusted padlock.

Jason grabbed his lock picks. Padlocks were easy prey. But this one was old and probably as corroded inside as out.

He was right. The tumblers wouldn't budge.

A hammer. He needed a hammer. Better yet, a sledge. There was nothing like that in his trunk, but there was a tire iron. He had left the trunk open so he wouldn't have to listen to its bitchy hinges.

The lock didn't budge. Not with prying. Not with bludgeoning. Sweat bubbled on his brow despite the cool air in the garage. Probably nothing good in there, anyway. All wasted effort. But damn it. It was too late to rationalize. It was now man against man's creation. Man had to win.

He scanned the garage. Nothing there to help. He put the lock picks back into the unrolled canvas tool kit, and a bulge in the far right pocket caught his attention. He couldn't remember when he'd stashed the M-80 fire-cracker there, or why. Supposedly a tenth of a stick of dynamite, he pulled it out and admired it, remembering his teens. M-80s could blow a coffee can fifteen feet in the air if it was loosely placed over the firecracker. Farther if it was packed against it tight, if you could find the parts. Parents had cautioned about losing entire hands, not just fingers, to M-80s.

He tested the side of the metal case. It was plenty solid.

The barrel of the M-80 was close to a fit through the loop of the lock. It'd have to be forced in. Images of a spark setting off the firecracker, severing both hands and splattering fingers on the walls and floor stopped him for a moment. Fortunately, only moderate pressure was required to thread the M-80 into the lock, all the way to the side-mounted, waterproof fuse.

Jason cleared the area around the box and stepped into the alley. It was deserted. He listened. No noises from the surrounding buildings. If anyone was around, this would get their attention.

He stepped back in the garage and fumbled with the screw-cap container of waterproof matches. They were old. A strike on the bottom of the container and the first match sparked, but didn't light. Another strike and the match head broke off without a flicker. The second match did the same on the third strike.

The third match lit on the first strike, but a sudden breeze nearly extinguished it. Jason sheltered the feeble flame with his left hand and slowly moved it toward the M-80 fuse. The fuse sputtered to life.

He waited to make sure it conducted the flame, then

sprinted around the corner of the garage door. Nothing happened. He peeked around the corner. The fuse still fizzed. He leaned back.

The explosion rattled the doors on the opposite side of the alley and rang in Jason's ears. Then all went silent. Totally silent. No bird trills, no rustle of wind. No noises of day. A car alarm somewhere in the complex broke through the silence with a series of honks, squeals, and sirens, quiet at first, then louder, accompanied by the ear ringing again. The garage oozed a light film of smoke through the doorway.

He rounded the corner. The lock was intact, but the blast had separated the hasp from the box. A huge dent where the hasp formerly connected was colored with a starburst scorch mark that blended from a black center to grayish-green rays tipped in white. A slight gape separated the lid from the bottom of the box. He tiptoed to the box as if he expected a second explosion.

The box lid let out a high-pitched squeal as the rusted hinges begrudged the movement. The top swiveled all the way back to the floor. The box contained file folders and enveloped papers. This would take a while.

Old tax returns and other financial documents took up the first third of the contents. Other legal documents quickly yielded to what appeared to be more personal items: letters and other papers. At the back of the stack were three manila file folders, two of them stretched thick, the third slim. The first had "Gertrude" on the file tab. "Ella" was on the second. The third didn't have a marking. He ignored the two with labels and grabbed the thin one.

Jason felt dizzy, and his hands shook. He shifted from a kneel into a cross-legged seated position. The first sheet was a military document. Army Form 22. "Report of Separation and Record of Service in the Army." Just below that, the heading: Type of Discharge: Honorable. He scanned for the name line. Edward Albert Hahn. It was dated 15 August 1945. A stack of twenty or more pages of other military documents followed. The only other items in the file were three enveloped letters, all of standard letter size. He opened the first and unfolded the letter. The shaking of his hands increased, and the letter fell to the floor. A large cloud crossed the sun, squeezing the light out of the garage.

Jason steered the Volvo into April's complex and jerked it to a stop in the last available visitor's space. His feet hit alternate stairs up to her front door, and his knock was enthusiastic enough to trigger a curtain draw in the adjacent condo.

The peephole blinked just before the deadbolt clunked its invitation. April swung open the door with a wide smile. She stepped back to let him in.

"You're back. Two visits in two days. I think I know what we did last night, but I was pretty drunk. I'll have to try it when I'm sober if it brings you back this soon. You'll have to help me, though. I slept until noon, and I don't remember much."

Jason sniffed at the entryway to the kitchen. "Fish. But I smell strawberry, too. And what's that other smell? I can't place it."

"It's cilantro. Cilantro and strawberry. It's a fish garnish I had at a restaurant last week. It sounds gross, but it was incredible. I'm trying to duplicate it. If you're hungry, I have enough."

He turned in to the kitchen. "Sorry to barge in. I was just up in Mendocino. At Agnes's U-Store space." He waited for an objection, but it didn't come. "I found something about Eddie. It's really important."

April reached into the cupboard and pulled down an extra plate. "Go wash up. Can we eat first?"

He turned in the doorway. "I don't think so. I'll tell you while we eat."

Jason reached into his jacket pocket and pulled out a few papers before tossing the jacket onto the adjacent chair. He didn't wait for the food to be served. "It seems our Eddie was a war hero. In World War Two. He came back with a Purple Heart and a few other decorations. But it seems like the experience changed him, even before he was wounded."

April divided the slab of fish and scraped half onto Jason's plate. "What do you mean?" She loaded her plate, slid the pan onto the stove, and quickly sat down.

He unfolded one of the pages. "Evidently Gert saved a few of Eddie's letters from before and after the war. This one was written while he was stationed in France. Listen to this: 'I killed my first German today. Shot him right through the neck. The others guys in my unit took everything from his body. They even pulled some of his teeth. They get mad if we call them Germans. We're supposed to call them Gerrys or Krauts. Like they aren't human. It's all about good versus evil here. We're fighting the noble war against a band of devils. We're trying to save the world from evil. I can understand it to a degree, but I don't want to accept it. It might make killing easy.'" Jason refolded the page. "What do you think about that?"

April took a small bite and smiled. "Mmm. Got it right. Try the fish."

"What about the letter?"

"Sounds like Eddie was a very rational, sensitive person. Fertile ground for a post-trauma syndrome. Did he kill more Germans?"

"I don't know. That was the only letter in the file from before he was wounded."

April took another bite. "How was he hurt?"

"There were some military medical records, from after he returned to the U.S. He was shot in the head. He had a steel plate the size of a silver dollar, and there was significant damage to his left frontal lobe."

"So at least some of his ability to consider consequences of future events was probably blurred. Maybe obliterated."

"Whatever. But listen to this." He unfolded the next letter. "This one was written when he was in the hospital. Here in the States. 'The nurse here says I'm good when I don't bother her, but she yells at me when I have to use the bedpan or want some food. Evil doesn't only wear a German uniform. Evil is everywhere. So is good. You can't tell one from the other by looking. You have to feel it. I can feel it. I can feel the difference.' What do you think about that?"

Agnes dropped her fork on her plate. "Wow. He seems to have developed a fixation. And he did have decent memory. So far, the landscape isn't looking too good for Mr. Eddie Hahn. Fixation about good versus evil. A sense of clairvoyance about it. Memories of traumatic events, framed in terms of the noble fight. Did he receive therapy? For more than his bodily injuries?"

"I found a single record only. Evidently, he committed

himself to a VA mental hospital for a short time in 1949, but there's nothing about the reason or the treatment."

"Too bad. I wonder if I can get the records. They're pretty old."

"I like your fixation idea. I think it extended to the twins. Maybe Eddie saw them as opposites. Good and evil."

"What makes you say that?"

"Their names. I looked in one of those books of baby names. Do you know what Agnes means?"

"No. Spinster? Shy one?"

"Close. It means pure. Chaste."

"What about Lilin?"

"I didn't find it in that book. Its origin is different."

April sat up straight. "How so?"

"Are you familiar with any ancient Jewish stories on the origin of humans?"

"I'm Catholic."

"Have you heard of Lilith?"

She drummed her fingers on her thigh. "That was the name of Dr. Frasier Crane's wife on the sitcom *Cheers*. Right? And a bunch of female rockers organize concerts. They call them Lilith Fair."

"*Cheers* had great writers. And one of those rockers did her homework. Lilith was supposedly Adam's first wife, not created from his rib, but from the same soil as he was. She refused to submit to him in the standard missionary position. She thought it demeaned her. Like she wasn't his equal. She demanded equality."

"So far I like what I hear." April put her hand on Jason's arm. "And I think I remember something from last night. And it wasn't missionary."

He pulled his arm away. "Come on, April. Let me get this out. You said you wanted information to help Agnes."

"Agnes. By all means, continue."

He avoided eye contact. "Lilith abandoned Adam and became a demon. The versions go every which way from there, but there is one common thread. She preyed on unbaptized children. And on men. She was able to invade a sleeping man's dreams and seduce him. Then she'd devour him. Some versions say she ate the men. Others make the vampire tie-in and say she sucked their blood. Pretty close parallel, huh?"

"Are you going to try your fish?"

"Yeah. But there's more."

"Okay, but I'm a little lost. You just described Lilith, not Lilin."

"Oh, sorry. I forgot. Lilith had a number of off-spring who were just as bad as she was. Collectively, the offspring were called Lilin."

April pushed her chair back a few inches. "So Eddie didn't think much of his daughter, the twins' mother. Denise, right?"

"Yeah. And it'd be an easy way to rationalize what he did to her. She was evil and seduced him. The union produced two offspring. One good and one evil. He couldn't resist Denise. It was her fault."

"Or evil's fault."

"Good point."

"Anything else?"

"Just one more letter. This one really bothered me, and it seems to back up what we just talked about." His hands shook as he unfolded the note.

"Are you okay?" She put her hand back on his arm. "This one that bad?"

"It's a short letter. Eddie pleaded with Gert. I can only read a little. I get emotional. It says, 'Please take Agnes. She's one of the good ones. Not like Lilin. More seed has been spilled. Come get Agnes. Quick.'"

April was silent for a few moments. "What does he mean, 'more seed has been spilled'?"

"I had to search for that one. It goes back to the Lilith mythology. It seems her seduction of men caused them to spill their seed. In some interpretations, that means to masturbate. That seed was used to produce more of her demon progeny. The Lilin."

"So you think masturbation was part of his molestation?"

"I don't know, but maybe it has something to do with Lilin's use of the severed . . . uh."

"Penises. You can say it."

"Yeah. I hate to think of what Agnes saw."

"Saw?"

Jason refolded the letter and put the stack back in his jacket pocket. "I don't think Agnes was molested."

April's cheeks puffed with a long exhalation. She tipped her head up, eyes on the ceiling. She nodded as she tilted her head back down. "This fits with everything I've been able to get from her, and from the way she reacts. I think I told you I suspected all this. Anyway, with his fixation, I bet he did make her watch when he abused Lilin. And killed her. It was probably a lesson from him to her. Can you imagine? Her twin sister. She must have turned a blank screen during the abuse. But I bet she absorbed all the hate Lilin felt for her father. Transferred it to all men. At least when she was Lilin. This really helps. And it lines up perfectly with my therapy."

Jason slumped in his seat and looked down at his plate. The fish looked good, but his appetite was undecided.

April swigged her wine and dug her fork into the fish, emitting a whiff of strawberry. "Come on. Try the fish. It's really good."

He flaked a few segments and scooped them with a generous coating of garnish. "Whoa. This is really good."

Jason flashed on his father's words of caution. The chase was on again.

# CHAPTER 7

Agnes was the first to see him. Her favorite reading chair gave a clear view of both hallways that ran from the Day Room at forty-five-degree angles from the far wall.

Stuart the Stud closed in, but his usual stalk posture didn't fool her, nor did it fool Marsha Herman, who sat across the room.

"Red Alert," Marsha announced from the line of chairs in front of the TV. "Cover up."

Agnes swiveled in her chair. Patty was reading in a far chair, over by the high windows, apparently engrossed in a romance paperback.

Stuart picked up his pace. His right hand reached out, fingers spread wide.

"Patty. Watch out." Agnes stood.

Stuart stopped at the chair and reached his hand

around toward Patty's right breast. The spine of her book came down on the top of his wrist, knocking his hand into the metal chair arm. Stuart whimpered, then grabbed his arm and ran for the men's hallway.

Patty was up in an instant and on Stuart's heels, with Agnes just a few yards behind. Stuart turned to look at the women and nearly missed the hall. He shuffled against the wall and sprinted to his door. In a single motion, he opened it, slipped in, and slammed the door behind him.

Patty reached the door a moment later and stood panting. Agnes stopped halfway down the hall. Patty twisted the doorknob and pushed the door in. Her voice echoed in the hallway—every syllable perfectly clear in the Day Room. "You total loser. Your dick's never going to touch anything but your hand. I know you've never had a woman. You'd know something about how to treat one. Go ahead. Do your hand. It's about the ugliest hand I've ever seen." She turned in the direction of the Day Room and shouted down the hall. "He can't even get a decent-looking hand. It's *ug-ly*."

The door slammed hard on the Day Room laughter. Patty jumped. The door swung open again, and Patty dodged to her right, in a half-crouch.

Stuart stood in the doorway. Tears streamed down his face. "You're going to get it. Bitches!" The door slammed again.

Agnes hurried back to her chair. She knew Patty had needed to do what she had done, but she wished there was some other way. Stuart needed help, and this would just make him turn inward even more. And it would ratchet up his fury. She felt like he was building for an eruption. But where else could they put him? All in all, though, she was proud of Patty.

Agnes had learned that prior to her arrival, Patty Figley had been Stuart's favorite target. He liked large breasts, and Patty's were the largest in the place. But he also liked new meat, as he called it.

Patty had confided in Agnes, about how before coming to Imola, she had continually struggled with her weight, and seldom made any headway. She had the shoulders and hips of a stereotypical Midwestern farming woman, and they were padded, but not overstuffed. Just enough to make one think that she'd be a bombshell if she'd lose only twenty pounds. Those twenty pounds had turned out to be her downfall. That and her weightlifter husband, Bud.

Bud Figley pumped himself full of steroids so he could be king of the gym. As his lean muscle mass increased, his acne and quick temper battled for second place on his short list of personal attributes. And the larger he got, the more he nudged Patty to slim down. "Don't want a chub-o on my arm," he'd say. "I'm getting in shape for you. You'd better do the same, or I'll find someone who will."

And that's how it all started—her downward spiral. Bulimia made throwing up so easy she started having spontaneous episodes. Anywhere, anytime, it could come up. And if her stomach was empty, she doubled over in dry heaves that produced loud wheezes that would turn heads for tens of yards. It took a while, but she eventually realized that her stomach lurched every time she saw a model-thin woman or a ripped man. That realization gave her a chance. But she never strayed into the middle of a room, and curbside bushes were her best friends. She sought counseling and made progress, and ultimately it saved her.

She was checking her e-mail one day and accidentally called up Bud's list of internet favorites. He'd book-marked eighteen porno sites. Patty pulled up one. It was a "fat chicks" site. Another, the same. All eighteen featured grossly overweight woman doing things that slender women would decline in favor of a good headache.

It was a bad time for Bud to walk in. He went ballistic. But his fury was no match for hers. She went for his eyes and got one of them. She went for his unit, but had to settle for his shriveled scrotum. She got one of its inhabitants, too.

That's where her earlier counseling saved her. That and a great lawyer. His main point was made when a skinny woman walked into the hearing room. Patty had puked her way out of jail and into Imola.

Agnes sat back and smiled. She imagined a personal

ad in the newspaper and on the Web. Single white male, weightlifter, one eye, one shrunken nut, seeking meaningful relationship with a plus-sized woman without fingernails.

Her thoughts went to Stuart. What was brewing in that darkened room? Would he look at his hand the same after what Patty said?

Agnes didn't have to wait long. Stuart burst out of his door and shuffled into the Day Room. He scanned the room, locked his gaze on Patty, and lurched toward her. She was ready. She deflected his arms and shoved him aside. He nearly went over, bracing himself against the wall. He came at her again, and again she pushed his arms, partially spinning him, and pushed him at the wall. His shoulder hit this time.

Stuart kicked at her, and she dodged his foot. He faked another lurch, she reacted, and he slipped behind her. His left arm went around her neck, and his right hand thrust down the front of her jumpsuit. He fondled her, hard.

Patty gave him an elbow in the ribs, and his hand came out of her suit. Another elbow, higher, caught him just under the armpit. He let go of her neck. She pushed him back against the wall, and he froze.

"You bitch. I'm going to get you." He looked around the room. "I'm going to get all of you. You won't know which one first. You won't know when. But I'm going to get you all."

Agnes didn't notice right away, but Milo McGuinn was on his feet. And he was walking—fast. Faster than she had ever seen him walk. He still lifted his feet high and jiggled them at the apex of each step, and it produced a goose walk that reminded her of the Monty Python skit, "Ministry of Silly Walks." He approached Stuart.

"Keep your hands off the girls, or I'll—"

Stuart hit him square in the chest with his fist.

Milo didn't flinch. Not even an eye blink. He looked down at his chest and then at Stuart, who seemed shocked.

Milo smiled, then reached past Stuart's left shoulder and brushed off the adjacent wall with his hand. He waved it over the plaster from head-height down halfway to the floor, then stepped back and smiled at Stuart again.

This time Stuart smiled back.

Milo grabbed Stuart by the shoulders and moved him a step to the left and then slammed him into the now microbe-free wall. He pulled him back and slammed him again. Stuart's head hit hard on the second slam. His eyes gushed tears.

Milo held his left leg out straight, at a forty-five-degree angle, and shook it so hard the bell clapper couldn't keep up with the casing. He returned his foot to the floor, slightly overlapping Stuart's right leg. A shove and Stuart fell across his leg and onto the floor right under the spot where Milo had shaken his foot.

Stuart crumpled on the floor. "You're a bitch, too," he shouted between sobs. "Only fairy bitches don't eat meat."

Milo bent down close to Stuart's face. "That's right. I don't eat meat. But I'll eat a plateful on the day you go to hell."

# CHAPTER 8

April ran her fingers down Jason's bare chest, drawing a circle in the light mat of hair. The glisten of sweat gave his skin a luminescent tone, still nearly hot to the touch. His chest heaved with each breath like he was fighting the oxygen debt from their sharing. His eyes were closed but not to sleep. Contentment, she hoped.

April reached to the adjacent nightstand and removed a stick of gum from an open pack. She let the wrapper fall next to the lamp base and shoved the stick between her teeth. Her jaw worked up to speed.

She didn't want to come right out and ask it, but she didn't want the moment to pass either, just in case her intuition was on the mark. He was too easy to spook. On the other hand, it had been only a week since his last visit.

She traced another circle, and he let out a purring exhalation. She leaned up on her elbow. "Jason, why don't we ever go to your place?"

He frowned without opening his eyes. "Hmmm?"

"Why is it always here? Are you embarrassed about your apartment?"

One eye opened, accompanied by a feeble shake of his head. "What are you talking about?"

She leaned over, close to him. "Why don't you have me over?"

The other eye opened, and the furrow in his forehead wrinkled to a chasm. "I thought women were only comfortable on their own turf. You know, avoid the walk of shame thing."

She poked him in the ribs. "Maybe you just like the walk of fame."

His flinch pulled him to the edge of the bed. He rolled, facing away, and pushed her hand away from his side. "What's with the weird questions?"

"I was just wondering if you were embarrassed about your apartment."

He pulled the covers up to his chin. "No. Now tell me what you really want."

Her face went hot, so she pushed her head into the pillow and reached for his neck, caressing the hairline. "Nothing. I was just thinking." She felt his jaw tighten.

"Thinking about what?"

She ran her thumb along his jaw line. "I don't know. You. Me. Us. What we have."

She felt him smile. He turned his head and kissed her thumb.

Leaning up, she moved her hand back to his neck and gave a little squeeze. His eyes opened. "Well?"

His head jerked a little. "Well, what?"

"What do we have?"

He rolled on his back, sliding her hand to the front of his neck. "You're important to me."

"Your coffeemaker is important to you. I'd like to know if I'm more than an appliance in your life."

No movement. "Don't be silly."

She pulled his chin toward her. "Move in with me. Here." She almost said it'd be cheaper, but she caught herself.

His expression didn't change. And still no movement. She couldn't even feel his breathing, which was so forced only moments ago.

Finally, he blinked. "I don't think—"

"Shit." She fell back into her pillow and covered her face with her hands. She peeked between her fingers.

Elbowing his pillow, he balanced his head on his hand. "You wouldn't like the life of an investigative reporter. And now that I'm working for the Press Democrat and the Chronicle, I get calls at all hours. I have to pick up and run with every one of them."

"I'm sure that's it." Her voice was muffled in her palms.

"What's that supposed to mean?"

"I think you're afraid of commitment."

No response. She peeked through her fingers again. His stare seemed to penetrate her screen. It was no time to cower. She had played the hand. Now it was time to lay down the cards—see what he had. She lowered her hands. "Are you? Afraid?"

"Yes." His stare continued, but his focus seemed to change.

The gape of her mouth let a quiet gurgle escape. His response was the last she expected—so distant from her mental calculation of possible outcomes. She was speechless. In fact, to her, it was possibly a male first. The shrine on Mount Manhood had probably just lost one of its pillars.

Was he serious, or was this a clever way to derail the charging locomotive? At the least, he'd managed to pull the lever and force a track change.

He shifted over so his face was within a few inches of hers, just above and to the side. "You know I was engaged before, right?"

She exhaled.

"I was in love with her. I'm sure of it. All of the indications she gave—I was sure she was in love with me, too. We set a date. She picked out plates and silverware. I even ordered the invitations. Then I couldn't get her to complete her list of guests. She didn't change how she treated me. She just couldn't complete the list. I thought she was worried about the size of the reception. The cost." He paused.

April looked for signs of emotion on Jason's face, but it was blank, as if he were talking from another plane. She wanted to pull him to her, to comfort him, but she didn't want him back yet. She wanted to hear more. The wait was short.

"She had good reason to worry about the guest list. She'd met someone else. The only problem was that she met this someone else more than a year before, and she got around to telling me when I had half the invitations addressed and stamped." He blinked back to the bed. "I was in love. Trouble was, so was she. Once it was all out, she was gone faster than a lightning bolt finds ground, and it left me death-shocked."

All April could manage was a feeble, "I'm sorry."

His return was brief; his eyes drifted again. "Now I know the depth of vulnerability when a man gives his heart to a woman unconditionally." His eyes snapped back; they seemed almost angry. "Excuse me if I'm gun shy. I don't want to feel that vulnerable right now. Maybe never."

Her mouth jumped ahead of her brain. "So it isn't Agnes, then?"

"What?" His face crinkled like a wadded piece of paper.

April tried to shrink into the pillow. Her voice lowered

to blend with its softness. "I thought maybe you were in love with Agnes, and that's why—"

"Why are you always so worried about Agnes?"

"I'm not—"

"Physician, heal thyself."

She reached back, pulled her pillow from under her head, and swung it into the side of his.

He grabbed it and pulled so hard she collapsed against his chest, her head against his cheek. Before she could react, he wrapped his arms around her. "Don't push. Okay? I'm not a hopeless case. Just a helpless one. Can you be patient?"

"I don't know. I don't want to be . . . with you."

"Would it help if we met at my place next time?"

She smiled and slipped down to nuzzle his neck. "It's not necessary. It's enough you offered. You know, the walk-of-shame thing."

His hand slid down her back, then up again. His light touch turned into a grip on her shoulder.

She leaned her head back. "What's the matter?"

"I want to ask something, but the timing sucks. You'll take it wrong."

"If it's about Agnes, you're right."

He didn't say anything.

"Shit," she said. "You know how to spoil a moment, don't you?"

"I just want a professional opinion. That's all."

"Why now?"

"When else can I ask?"

"Come around more often," she said.

He slid toward the edge of the bed.

She grabbed him around the waist. "I'm sorry. I admit it. I'm jealous. You always bring her up. Sometimes I think—"

"List the things we have in common," he said. "No matter how long the list is, Agnes is on it, right near the top. Without her, we wouldn't have found each other."

"That's supposed to help?"

"Right now, she needs a friend more than ever. What kind of turd would you think I was if I deserted her?"

April thought about answering.

"I'll never deny that I care about her. I want her to get better. That should be another of our common points. I don't understand what's wrong with her, and I want to. I want to help, and it seems my visits do that."

April went rigid. "You want an opinion of what's wrong with her?"

"Yes."

"Professional opinion?"

"Yes."

She propped her pillow against the headboard, leaned against it, and raised the blanket just above her breasts. "How much do you know about how our minds process reality and our own identity?"

He leaned on his elbow, propping his chin with his palm. The look on his face was like that of a dog awaiting a treat. "Sounds like I'm about to get a mixture of psychology and philosophy. I know a little about both."

"Have you ever heard of the Global Phenomenal Model of Reality?"

He bobbed his head. "You know, I was just discussing it with my barber the other day."

"Was your barber real, or was he someone your mind invented?"

"He talked to me, touched me, cut my hair. My hair was shorter when I left, and some of it littered his floor."

"How do you know you didn't blank out, cut your own hair, and imagine the whole thing?"

"I just know. I've done the same thing dozens of times."

April smiled. "So, over your lifetime, you've developed a set of experiences, and all of the events from your barber visit coincided with your experiences, right?"

"You could say it that way."

"How about if I said it like this: Similarities between observations and experience make the event seem real."

His eyes didn't stray. "That sounds logical."

"Then, let's take the logic one step further," April said. "The greater the details of the observations, and the stronger their coherence with experiences, the more real the event appears. How's that?"

"I'm still with you."

"So, what happens when an event is extremely detailed, but it goes against all of your experience and your perceived order of the world?"

"Like what?"

"What if you had an experience so horrific it didn't fit any of your accumulated experiences, and it fell well outside of accepted limits of your perception of civilized society? What if your barber suddenly slashed the throat of a customer and began eating his neck flesh? Would that fit your concept of reality?"

He shook his head. "More like surreal. But if it happened in front of me, I'd justify it as an anomaly."

"But what if it kept happening every time you went to the barber? Over and over again?"

"I guess I'd have to find a way to accept it as reality and deal with it."

April shifted under the sheets. "What if it was totally unacceptable? Unacceptable, yet real?"

"I'd have to find a way to put it out of my mind. Maybe pretend it wasn't happening."

"So now, picture yourself as a little girl. You've been raised in a family situation with a father who has nurtured and protected you. But then, something happens with your father that is so unexpected and so horrible that it defies your experience-defined basis of reality. And it keeps happening over and over."

Jason shivered. "I'd find a way to adapt. How did

Agnes do it?"

"When experiences get too tough for her, she with-draws—blanks out. She calls herself 'No One.' As far as I can tell, she totally escapes. She stops observing. Her emotions succumb to the logic of survival. She doesn't have any memory of the events. But there are memories in there somewhere. That's what I'm going after."

"You think that's the solution? Get her to remember? What if that traumatizes her further?"

"If she's going to deal with her problems, she has to face them."

Jason sat up. He pulled the bedsheet above his waist. "How does Lilin fit in? Is she Agnes's way of adapting?"

"Not really. I think Lilin's more of a consequence."

"Now you're losing me."

"It has to do with how we process our own identity. You think of yourself in the first person, right?"

"Yes." He smiled. "I do."

"Right. But is a first-person perspective necessary for a conscious experience?"

"Yes?"

April snickered. "No. A dream is a conscious experience, but pain, smell, and taste aren't usually rep-resented. One can argue that a dream isn't a complete first-person experience, that we dream outside of the first person. And that's not all. Schizophrenics frequently have auditory hallucinations—voices speaking to them.

But as far as I can tell, the voices almost always speak in the second person: 'You do this. You do that.'"

"How does that fit with Agnes?"

"I'm getting there. Be patient." She leaned forward, and a breast escaped from the covers. She left it out. "There can't be a multiplication of the first-person self. More than one first person is mutually exclusive and functionally incompatible. So any additional identity occurs in the second person. And what's really interesting is that the host—that's the first-person identity—is usually amnesiac to the other, or others."

Jason lifted his eyes from April's breast. "Is this reality or just theory?"

"Mostly the latter."

"So if that's true, Agnes doesn't know what Lilin does, right? How about the other way around?"

April let the blanket slip from her other breast. "Good question. Since Lilin is a second-person, minor identity, she's aware of Agnes's world. She remains a distant observer as long as Agnes is around."

"Why is Lilin so different from Agnes?"

"Alternate identities are always exaggerated in specific dimensions, like in drastic behavioral traits. The dimensions are invented to help adapt to the trigger experiences: the horrific abuse and murder of her sister, in Agnes's case."

"So Lilin deals with violence with exaggerated violence?"

"Exactly. When things get stressful to Agnes, she blanks out; she becomes No One. That allows the alternate personality to fill in, with her exaggerated behavioral traits. And whatever happens with Lilin, Agnes doesn't remember. But Lilin doesn't go blank. She's aware of Agnes's world. When Lilin takes over, she can react to things that are happening to Agnes, or that happened to Agnes in the past."

Jason reached out and touched April's breast.

She slapped the hand away. "We're talking about Agnes here."

He shook his hand like it hurt and came back on track. "I still don't understand why Lilin didn't come out earlier in Agnes's life."

April pulled up the blanket. "I have a theory. Her great-aunts, Gert and Ella, replaced her father but without the socially inconsistent experiences. As long as they kept tight control, there were no experiences to trigger Agnes's mental lapses, letting Lilin in. When Gert died and Ella went into the home, Agnes probably searched for a substitute. That created a crack. When she found out her father was still alive, that dredged up specific anxieties and really opened the door for Lilin."

Jason tried to pull the blanket off of April, but she held it in place. "Any support for the theory?" he said.

"Plenty. Lilin talks to Agnes."

"I know."

April frowned. "Did she tell you Lilin talks in second

person—tells her to do things?"

"No," Jason said. "We didn't discuss grammatical framework."

April slumped on her pillow and pulled the covers up to her neck. "What do you think of Agnes's personality?"

"She's shy, quiet. Very conservative."

"How about emotional?" April said.

"That's not a word I'd use to describe her."

April smiled. "That's my observation, too. In fact, I think she's nearly devoid of emotion. Everything is logical to her. She cries, gets upset. But she doesn't make any decisions based on emotion. Only on logic."

Jason folded his arms over this chest. "Is that bad?"

"In her case, I think it's devastating. We all balance emotion and logic when we make decisions, and for most of us emotion is at least as powerful as logic, more so in most cases. Whenever emotion starts to creep in, Agnes heads for No One."

"And Lilin?"

April's smile widened. "My guess is that Lilin operates on emotion only, logic be damned."

Jason shook his head. "Sounds like my big brother. Tell me what you're going to do with Agnes, and maybe I can use it on Donnie."

"I have to try to get Agnes to act on emotional experiences. Set up some stressful situation where she fights back instead of backing out to No One. If she can learn to handle stress without bailing out, it'll give her confidence. It'll bring her back to a more central position. And—"

"And if she gains balance, there's no room for Lilin in her mind." He paused. "There's just one problem. If Lilin is aware of Agnes's world, won't she react to your attempts to get Agnes to handle these situations?"

"If it's a true dominant-secondary hierarchy, I don't think so, but this is an untilled field. There isn't much in the literature except speculation and anecdotal reports of therapy results. Nothing scientific."

"What if your treatment backfires and Lilin gets stronger? Are there any cases where the dominant and secondary personalities reverse?"

"It's been reported."

Jason rubbed his temples. "Shit."

# CHAPTER 9

Agnes watched the light fade through the high windows of the Day Room. Most of her colleagues were in their rooms now. Like circus animals, they followed a routine that no longer required reinforcement and didn't need a clock. Each person probably had a unique set of cues—the diminishing light, the long shadows, the accumulating fatigue of boredom—that triggered the migratory response.

It was Agnes's favorite time of day. The only time she was alone outside of her cramped, sterile sleeping cubicle. Her room was painted glossy light green, like everywhere else. Green had once been her favorite color.

She thought about why she spent the minimum amount of time in her room. It wasn't decorated like some of the others. Marsha had pictures pasted on every available inch or two of the four walls. She was about to start a third. Most were of her family and friends, although their correspondence had tailed off in the last couple of weeks, so she had started cutting photos out of magazines. She said the pictures were of her new family.

Tammy and Patty had a few photos, tastefully placed, in exactly the same locations. When Patty received a new one, Tammy went into a funk until she got something to hang in the exact same spot in her room. Patty had told Agnes about an experiment she had conducted once, moving the pictures by no more than six inches each. Tammy had duplicated the alteration with baffling exactness. The mimicry didn't frustrate Patty; she seemed flattered.

Agnes didn't know what the men's rooms looked like. They were on a different hall. One time, Patty had said that Stuart the Stud's walls were the only ones in the place that weren't green. Everyone had laughed. Except Agnes.

But why were the walls of her room so bare? A memory flashed but extinguished, and it startled her. Another flash, this time in slower motion. It was of a room, a scary room. The walls were decorated with a sparse assortment of framed photos, but that wasn't what made it so scary.

The memory pressed down on her, like weighted mist, billowing from above. And she wasn't alone. The mist clouded her eyes, reduced the framed photos to dark shadows on the light walls. She thought she heard a muffled scream. A scream for No One.

The dog. The only decoration in her room was a stuffed dog, given to her by Jason. She blinked back the memory, focused back to the Day Room and its golden tint of sunset. The dog. It was in her arms throughout the nights and assumed the place of honor—the middle of the bed—throughout the days. It was her connection to the past in Mendocino, her hope for the future. Her job in the animal shelter had been God-given. She understood animals, particularly dogs, and she felt like they understood her. They didn't have pretensions or lofty expectations. They wanted love and companionship—and what they craved, they gave back in triplicate. Even the mean ones seemed to warm to her, like she was a sanctuary. She'd loved her job.

Her future was Jason. She was sure of it. He wasn't just one of the good ones—he was *the* good one. And tomorrow was his visit day. His visits weren't as regular as Dr. Leahy's, but he usually gave a one- or two-day advance notice. On the mornings of his visit days, time crawled by like a roller coaster scaling the highest incline. It was slow, deliberate, but it didn't bother her. She knew that every inch of elevation provided energy for the belly-tickling descents, twists, and turns that paid for the wait. It was pure inertia as soon as he turned the doorknob—emotional free-fall. But she was buckled in tight. And Jason was right beside her. Their laughter merged into a single voice.

The fuzzy shadow of a wind-blown branch flickered on the wall, stealing her attention. She relaxed her smile. But she wasn't upset at the interruption. The thin wisps of movement were pretty, mostly because they were fleeting, ethereal. They were real, but they couldn't be touched.

She stood and walked to the wall. She could superimpose the shadows of her fingers on those of the branches. Mingle with them, play a game of tag. Part of her was with the branches—for the moment, the wall between them didn't exist. She held out a pinch of hair and let the shadow fall with the branches. She swore it didn't fall straight back, but caught some of the breeze that gave the branch shadows life.

An abrupt squeak startled her. She turned her head, but arms surrounded her just below the shoulders, pinning her arms to her sides. She felt a hand cup her left breast, kneading it like a lump of bread dough. She tried to twist her body, but she was forced into the wall, obliterating the branch shadows with an obscene blob.

"I told you I'd get you, bitch."

She knew what to do. Relax. Let Stuart have his feel. He'd soften his grip so she could free her arms and cover up, and he'd be off to his room in his hurried, hunched shuffle. "I'm letting you do it. Now let me go."

He didn't let go or even let up. His right hand maintained the grip on her breast while his left moved downward, across her belly. Its fingers turned inward, followed the contour of her groin. They moved against her, manipulating, probing, taking.

*Don't let him. Stop him.*

Agnes tried to spin from his grip. "Let me go, Stuart. I don't want you to get into any more trouble."

He pressed her hard against the wall so her head was wrenched to the side, her left cheek flat on the cold, green plaster. "Shut up, bitch."

"Please. I won't tell anyone."

His left hand continued to probe, harder now, and his right moved off her breast to the middle of her chest. It pulled on her jumpsuit, trying to tear it open.

*He won't stop. Make him stop.*

Agnes raised her right knee, parting her legs. His movements halted, but only for an instant. His left hand pushed farther between her legs, and he let out a low moan. His right hand stopped pulling at her garment and returned to her breast. She felt him push his pelvis against her, bracing the contact with his left hand. His moaning and movements synchronized.

*Hurt him. Hurt him.*

She raised her right leg a little higher and he responded, like a python tightening its grip with each exhalation of its prey.

*Hurt him, damn it.*

She slammed her heel down on the top of his right

foot with all the force she could muster.

A high-pitched scream rang in her ear. Stuart's grip loosened enough for her to turn and push him away.

He fell to the floor, screeching, and pulled his right foot up to his hands. He rolled on his back, his screeches turning to loud cries, then to sobs.

And, at that moment, he changed. Something in the deep recesses of her mind switched him from a harmless but misdirected boy into a dark shell of an evil man. He no longer deserved her sympathy, her help. He'd dragged her back into that foggy room of her mind. The one with the framed photos. But this time, she fought back. She fought back to the Day Room and its warm evening shadows. Back to see Stuart the Molester moaning on the floor. He wasn't misunderstood. He was pathetic.

*Kill him. Kill him.*

Agnes stepped over his straight left leg and walked toward her room.

Noises echoed from the end of the women's hallway. A door lock clunked. An excited voice grew in volume, along with the squeals of rubber-soled shoes on the linoleum. She heard the nurse's voice, but she didn't let the words register. She felt the breeze as the nurse brushed past her.

*No. Don't go. He's down. Kill him. Kill. Him.*

Agnes kept walking, into her bare-walled room. To her dog. To Jason.

# CHAPTER 10

Jason paused at the Day Room door and slid his left hand behind his back. The stuffed dog was nearly identical to the one he'd given Agnes soon after she'd arrived at Imola, but in miniature. It had the large eyes and stubby limbs of a puppy. He hoped the colors matched.

He opened the door but froze. Something wasn't right. The Day Room was nearly empty, except for Stuart Guerin, who sat in a chair under the television, his right leg propped on another chair, cushioned by a pillow. A plastic brace enclosed his foot and extended several inches above his ankle.

Jason stepped into the room and stopped again. "Where is everyone?"

Stuart twisted his head in Jason's direction. His eyes were wide, dark as onyx. "Get the fuck out of here."

Jason's arms fell to his sides. The stuffed puppy dangled.

Stuart turned in his chair and let out a grunt. He reached for a pair of crutches that leaned against the back of the chair. "Gimme that dog. Give it to me." He pulled his foot down from the other chair and cried out when it touched the floor. "Then get the fuck out of here."

Jason sidestepped to his right and nearly bumped into Nurse Dorothy, who was in a half-jog. She shuffled between the two men and thrust her right hand out to Stuart. "Stay in the chair. Or I'll put you back in your room."

Stuart froze. "Get him out of here. He came to see her." He pointed at his foot.

Nurse Dorothy kept her hand out toward Stuart. "Don't get out of that chair." She spun around to face Jason and hurried into the women's hall. "Come on."

Jason glanced at Stuart as he followed the nurse. Stuart raised his right hand, middle finger extended.

Dorothy stopped about ten feet into the hall, and Jason nearly plowed into her. "What's going on?" He studied her face. The usual smile was gone, and the calm, patient look that usually softened her eyes was replaced with a dull, hard stare.

She held her index finger against her lips. "Shhh. I just got everyone calmed down. Agnes had a problem with Stuart last night, and she stomped on his foot. Broke one of the bones. When she came out this morning, all hell broke loose. Stuart tried to hit her with a crutch, and all of the women went after him. It took four of us to break it up."

"Where's Agnes? Is she all right?"

"Everyone but Stuart is locked down. They have to stay in their rooms until after lunch. Longer if they can't behave. You'll have to come back some other time."

Jason gripped the puppy with both hands and took a step toward the nurse. He usually flirted with her, but not now. "I want to see Agnes. She's probably upset."

"She has to stay in her room until everyone calms down."

"So Stuart attacks Agnes, and Agnes gets locked up?"

"Stuart trashed his room. Maintenance is in there right now."

"And you've rewarded his behavior and punished the others. I suppose Stuart will have the run of the place from now on."

Dorothy folded her arms across her chest. "We're going to try to transfer him to another ward. I'll put in the paperwork this afternoon."

"You're going to try? What does that mean? How long will it take?"

"I don't know. It depends on the doctors. They have to evaluate the situation."

"Don't give me one of your little paper pill cups. What're the odds he'll go?"

"I don't know. It's up to the doctors."

Jason released one hand from the dog and balled it

into a fist. "Where are the doctors?"

She didn't answer. The index finger and thumb of her right hand tugged on her lapel.

"I want to see Agnes. She needs company right now."

Dorothy stiffened. "And I want a villa in Monaco."

Jason stared into her eyes and went into blink-suppression mode. She held his stare. He brought the puppy up to his chest and her eyes dipped, returned, and widened. She let out a mouthful of air and shook her head.

"A half hour," she said. "No longer. I'll knock." She walked to Agnes's room and keyed the door.

"Thank you." He smiled as he walked past her into the room. It was dark, but the light of the hall illuminated Agnes's form lying on the bed, facing away from the door.

The door slammed, followed by the sound of the key throwing the dead bolt. The room went pitch dark. Jason fumbled against the wall with his right hand, searching for the light switch. He bumped it and then flicked it upward. An overhead fluorescent fixture flooded the room. He squinted at the bed. Agnes didn't move. The faint odor of lavender enveloped him, then disappeared.

He took a step closer. "Agnes. Are you all right?"

At the sound of his voice, she turned and sat up in one motion. "You're here. They said they wouldn't let you in." She smoothed her hair with her hands.

He wrapped his left hand, and the puppy, behind his back. "They'd have a hard time keeping me away."

He smiled through the awkward silence and held out the stuffed animal. "I think your doggie needs a puppy."

Agnes laughed as she slid her legs over the side of the bed. She grabbed the puppy and hugged it tight, then reached for her stuffed dog and brought the two together. "You always know how to make me happy." Her eyes met his. "I needed this today."

Jason sat on the bed beside her. "What happened last night?"

She looked down at her dogs. "I don't want to talk about it."

"What did Stuart do to you? I'm not one of the doctors. This isn't therapy. I care about you, and I want to know what he did."

Agnes's eyes watered. "He tried to get his usual feel, but this time he wouldn't stop. He kept touching me, and he tried to get inside my clothes."

Jason leaned back and examined Agnes's face. He expected tears to fall, but instead her expression changed. Not to full anger, but it appeared to be edging in that direction.

"I had to hurt him." Her face softened, and her eyes released the tears.

Jason leaned his shoulder against hers. "I'm sorry. The nurse said they're going to transfer him. You won't be bothered by him anymore."

"I thought he was harmless, but he got so mad. I think he's evil."

Jason patted her knee. "He's not evil. He has problems, like everyone else. He just needs more help right now."

Agnes leaned into his shoulder. "And I need you right now."

The silence pressed like they were covered by a wet tarp.

Agnes jerked away. "Why do you keep coming here?"

The movement startled him, and the question threw him. Words caught in this throat. The look on her face was different again, but he couldn't place it. Her eyes were still wet, but they looked intense, like she was staring straight into his brain. "To see you."

"I know, but why?"

"I care about you. I want you to get better."

"And all you talk about is how I'm doing. You know all about me, but I don't know anything about you." She pressed her shoulder into his again. "And I want to."

He broke eye contact and looked down at his hands gripping each other on his lap. "Like what?"

"I know you're a reporter, but that's it. Do you have family? Brothers? Sisters?"

"I have a brother."

"Older or younger?"

"Older. His name is Donnie."

"I've never heard you mention him before. Are you close to him?"

"Yeah. We get along okay."

"How about when you were young? Talk to me.

**94**

Don't just answer questions."

He shifted his eyes and peeked at her. She was still looking right at his face. It wasn't like the Agnes he knew. She rarely held eye contact that long. "We were the typical American family. Donnie and I had fun, but we fought a lot, too. He'd tease me, punch me in the arm—until I hit high school. I passed him up in height in my sophomore year and in weight that summer. He stopped hitting when I started hitting back. But, yeah. We were close. Still are."

"What does he do? Is he a reporter, too?"

"It's hard to describe what Donnie does. Mooches off of me, mostly. He's into computers. Really good at it. His hobby is hacking. Not individuals—corporations, governments. He just plays with them. Puts jokes into their programs. Nothing to bring down the systems."

"He doesn't have a job?"

Jason turned his body and looked straight at Agnes's face. The intensity was still in her eyes. "He makes a little money here and there. Under the table. Nothing Uncle Sam knows about, anyway."

A frown creased Agnes's forehead. "He's dishonest? Does he break the law?"

"Petty stuff, mostly. Every August and September he pulls in a bundle making fake IDs for college kids. I guess that's his specialty."

Agnes turned her head and looked straight ahead,

at the door. "I don't know much about that. Is it a serious crime?"

"He can get in a lot of trouble, but he has a clean record, aside from parking tickets. He does something else that could earn him time, though. He manufactures identities."

"What does that mean?"

"It means he supplies the paperwork to make a person become another person in the government's eyes. I guess he's pretty good at it. He gets quite a few requests."

"Haven't you tried to stop him? Get him to look for a regular job?"

"Nobody gets Donnie to do anything." Jason chuckled. "He has to want to do it on his own. I've beat my head against that wall too many times. Someday maybe he'll grow up, but that's something I can't help him with."

"I don't believe that." Her head swung around to face him again. "You're helping me."

"That's different. You want my help."

"I thought you said he mooches off you. He must want your help."

"He wants my money."

"And you give it to him? Why?"

Jason looked down at his lap again and shrugged.

"Because you love him," she said. "Because he's family. Right?"

"I guess you can say that."

"What about your mother? How does she feel about Donnie?"

"She died a few years back. But she doted on him to the end. A mother's love is unconditional. She only saw the good in him. And in me."

"Your father?"

"He's in Georgia. Recently remarried. He gave up on Donnie a long time ago. I think he's given up on me now, too. He has another life and we're adults. He remembers our birthdays. That's about all."

He felt an increase in the pressure of her shoulder against his.

"So it's just you and Donnie."

"Yup. He's my family. I guess that's why I look after him."

Out of the corner of his eye, he noticed her head bob. "Family is important to you."

"Yes."

"Me, too."

"I know about you and Lilin. I'm—"

"Can I meet him?"

Jason recoiled, pulling his shoulder from hers. "Who? Donnie?"

"Yeah. Can you bring him here?"

"I don't think he'd do too well in Imola. He's got a sarcastic streak. And no tact. He'd probably start a riot."

"I don't care. I'd like to meet him."

He relaxed and let his shoulder fall against hers again. "Why?"

"I don't have any family left. I'd like to meet yours."

Agnes rested her head on the edge of his shoulder and reached across and touched his hand.

He folded his hand around it and interlaced his fingers with hers. He looked down and flinched, but maintained his grip, tightened it. He leaned his shoulder back, and she slid her head into the crook of his neck. This time, he didn't flinch.

"You know, I'm a virgin. I've waited for the right man."

His mind went blank, as if it'd been jolted with twenty thousand volts. The intensity of her eyes, the sudden boldness—it all tossed his mind like he was in a rowboat in the middle of an angry ocean. When his mind cleared, all he saw were images of the murder scenes—what Lilin had done to those men. How she had seduced them. Then he flashed forward to what Lilin had suggested he do with her on their one and only meeting. She had wanted him to take her right there on his patio. When he refused, she went after him with her razor. That wasn't the behavior of a virgin. Far from it.

Agnes reappeared in his mind. The baggy clothes she used to wear. Her shy, introverted demeanor. The way she had seldom made full eye contact. He could believe Agnes was still a virgin, no matter what Lilin had done.

He felt his grip tighten and hers respond. Deflowering was removed long ago from his to-do list, and right now his thoughts weren't anywhere near sex. But he suspected hers weren't either. If he was right, Agnes was talking about something that went way beyond the physical. She was offering to share herself, but more than her body, with him.

With that thought, he felt the stirring. A stirring he hadn't felt since Eugenia. The sensation he couldn't quite reach with April Leahy. A warm rush ascended his neck and face. He caught her scent and inhaled it. Confusion followed the pleasurable tingle. It was Agnes speaking—wasn't it? Or was this Lilin elbowing in on Agnes's world again? He wanted it to be pure Agnes.

A door-rattling knock startled them both. The deadbolt clunked, and the door swung open. Nurse Dorothy stepped in. "You're going to have to leave now."

Agnes leaned upright as Jason stiffened.

"I thought you said I had a half hour," said Jason.

"The doctor's coming in. Sorry, but you have to leave. Now."

Jason stood and pulled Agnes up into a hug. "I'll be back next week. We'll have more time then." He leaned back and looked at her face. "The thing with Stuart the Stud. It'll all work out."

Agnes turned her head upward and kissed his cheek. "Thank you for the puppy." She released him and cradled her dogs to her chest.

Jason walked past the nurse and flinched when he heard the door lock clunk again. He hurried into the Day Room.

Stuart sat in the same chair, one crutch flat on the floor, just out of his reach. He turned his head when he saw Jason. "I thought I told you to get the fuck out of here."

Jason stomped over to the chair and grabbed Stuart's chin. He squeezed hard. "You listen to me, you little asshole. If you bother Agnes or the other girls again, I'll rip your throat out with my bare hands." He shook Stuart's head. "Do you understand me?"

Stuart whimpered.

Jason raised his voice. "Do you understand me, you little piss ant?"

Dorothy rounded the corner and went into a sprint. "Let him go." She grabbed Jason's arm and yanked it back. "You need to leave. Now! Let us take care of this."

Jason stepped back and nodded at the nurse. He looked back at Stuart, who was crying, his hands covering his face. "You remember what I said."

Stuart pulled his hands away and forced a smile. The middle finger of his right hand stabbed the air.

# CHAPTER 11

Jason varied his squint through the dark lenses of his sunglasses as April Leahy's BMW clung to the twisting secondary road outside of Santa Rosa. Their general direction was west, but the road waggled up to forty-five degrees to either side of the primary vector. The sun was past overhead, but not yet to a visor-worthy angle, and the intermittent trees strobed the light to tease his eyes.

"What's the mission?" he said. "I'm not good with surprises."

April kept her eyes on the road. "Wine tasting. Today, it's Russian River Valley Pinot Noir. This year's bottling is supposed to be incredible. You game?"

He had never acquired a tongue for the subtleties of the different varietals, probably due to a lack of effort. When it came to alcoholic beverages, a cork couldn't compete with a bottle cap, but he enjoyed a good wine with dinner on occasion. His sorting was done by color.

"I thought women liked white wines." He looked over to catch her reaction.

April's eyes didn't leave the road. Her voice was steady. "I drink whites when the company is more important than the wine. When the wine is the goal, I go for the reds." A slight upturn twitched the corner of her mouth.

"It's nice to know where I fit on your priority list."

She glanced over at him and accelerated into a turn. "Don't get sensitive on me. You know you're more than company."

He turned until he felt slight pressure from the shoulder belt. "So how would you like to be stranded on a desert island? With me or with a top shelf Pinot Noir?"

Her right hand grappled air, then found his left knee. "Don't ever give a single woman an either-or choice. You might not like the answer." She exaggerated a grin with raised eyebrows, and brought her hand back to the wheel.

"Will they have Zinfandel? I like that one." He leaned back into the car seat. "Donnie's the one with the mouth for wine. If I want to perk him up, I just bring a bottle of Sebastiani Barbera. He says he prefers the Chianti types. I go for the whatever-they're-serving types."

"Do you want some lessons? They come with an overnight stay and some personalized attention."

"I'll have to make a drugstore run on the way home. I'm out of wetsuits."

The car decelerated more than necessary for the slight bend in the road.

Jason noticed her knuckles go white on the steering wheel. "Anything wrong?"

April stared at the road. "You don't need condoms." Her eyes watered.

Her body language told him to just say okay, but the reporter in him kicked in. "You can't have kids?"

Emotion drained from her face. "No. I can't."

"Sorry. You want to talk about it?"

"No."

The next few minutes of silence ended with a noticeable acceleration of the BMW.

April leaned forward in her seat. "We're around Forestville. Keep an eye out for the Blanchard Family Winery. It's first on my list." She glanced at a computer-generated map on the dash. "It should be right around here."

They both said, "There," at the same time as the billboard-sized sign came into view.

April turned onto the tree- and shrub-lined driveway and buzzed her window down. With a quick turn of her head, she launched a wad of gum from her mouth with a loud *ptoo*. She raised the window like nothing had happened.

"You chew a lot of gum."

"Halitosis phobia. I'm afraid it's untreatable.

Probably a dopamine receptor problem." She laughed alone.

Jason looked up at the rough-wood beams that criss-crossed the tasting room. Although he lived minutes from the wine country, this was his first tasting room experience. And his impression was mixed. Below the ceiling, the place looked like a fancy bar, clean to the point of sterility. But not really his kind of place. The dark plank paneling and crystal chandeliers dripped arrogance and artificial aristocracy, while the open beams and high-pitched roof countered with a sense of landed gentry. Perhaps the difference, heredity, came from the vines themselves. Either way, he felt the all-too-familiar modern reach for the yuppie checkbook.

Even though those around him swirled, swished, and spat, he gulped his wine in the hopes that April would speed through her sampling routine. No such luck. She was as meticulous as an obsessive-compulsive orb weaver spider, running through a series of facial expressions that would make Marcel Marceau envious. Twenty-five minutes seemed ten times that long, ticked monotonously by a grotesquely ornamented grandfather clock in the corner. The only thing he really liked was the smell, the scent of musky oak casks and in-progress fermentation.

The scent brought back a memory. He'd experimented

with fermentation in his late teens, squeezing some of his mother's backyard Concord grapes into mason jars and throwing in a little baker's yeast. The initial smell permeated his bedroom closet, his fabric cologne for a few months of his senior year in high school. He managed to get a little alcohol out of the must, but it was barely palatable, even under the alcohol-any-way-you-could-get-it circumstances. Unfortunately, it had produced little more than a nasty headache.

Now, well past the magic of the twenty-first year, not much had changed for him. Wine still hadn't climbed out of the lowest reaches of his alcohol list, and it still gave him a hellacious headache if he drank too much of it. He looked over at April but failed to get her attention. He wished he had some aspirin for a little preventive medication.

The box wasn't full, so he didn't have any trouble carrying it out to the BMW. "So how was it?"

April tapped the side of the box. "I don't have a large collection, so you can tell by how much I buy. It has to be really good for me to buy any. The most I've ever bought is ten bottles. But usually, I don't take more than five, like here. With this vintage, I'm prepared to get five from all of the wineries I visit, but I'm hoping for a ten or two before the day is out."

With the spoils in the trunk, the BMW hummed into motion with April at the wheel.

"Their Zinfandel was good. Was that a good vintage?"

April shrugged. "According to my source, it was so-so. You won't find the best Zins in the Russian River Valley, although some wineries contract with vineyards from other regions." She chuckled. "Some fans claim that northern California Zins are like sex: the worst they'd ever had was wonderful. I think the nutty flavor forgives a lot."

"How come they didn't have White Zinfandel?"

Her look lowered the temperature in the car. "White Zinfandel was marketing genius and enological heresy: fast, mass production of a marginal wine that became trendy with the yuppie crowd. It's barely aged. Might as well drink flavored malts."

The temperature stabilized from the heat radiating from his face. "Where next?"

"Tedesco Vineyards. If we can find it. Then it's off to Graton. There's one winery there I want to taste. Then we loop around to Sebastopol and hit three or four places. That should do it for this afternoon."

"That's a lot of wine sipping. You worried about driving? I can be the designated driver."

"No problem. I spit most of what I taste. Only swallow a little bit."

He jabbed her in the ribs and laughed. "Pity."

She veered so the right wheels left the pavement, bouncing the car. "Your mind goes in the gutter, so does the car."

"Better go all the way off-road," he said. "Wine hits me fast and hard."

She glanced at his lap, yanked the wheels back onto the road, and pushed on the accelerator, lurching the car. "Let's get to the next glass."

About a quarter mile and the car slowed. April's eyes were glued to the road but open wide, moist again. "Jason?"

His body shifted toward her. "Yes?"

Her mouth opened, but nothing came out.

He reached over and patted her right thigh.

A forced smile moved her lips. "I'm sorry. I wasn't truthful before. I am capable of having children. I just choose not to. I'm on the pill. I've lied about it so much it just comes out, like it's real."

"Who would you have to lie to about being able to have kids?"

No words came through her moving lips.

Jason sat back in the seat. "If it's none of my business, don't worry about it. I'm not ready to have kids yet, either. Maybe I'll mature enough by the time I hit forty."

The sign for Tedesco Vineyards seemed to rescue her, although the relief was brief for Jason. Suddenly, he wanted to sample a few more wines—this time more for the side effects than for the tastes.

The afternoon dragged on, made more tolerable by April's curious admission. A half-drunk reporter was still a reporter. And Jason's skills were still sharp. Only his tact was blunted.

April grunted as she carried the box toward the back of the BMW.

"Why don't you let me carry that for you?"

"It took five stops to find my ten-bottle Pinot. And you're not very steady on your feet. For what I paid, I don't want them dropped."

Jason leaned close. "I'm feeling pretty good right now. And I noticed you stopped spitting two wineries ago. This time you asked for a second glass."

"I was told that the best would be around Sebastopol, so I made the loop so we'd be here last. The information was accurate. One more stop to go, and I'm told this one is the best of the lot. No spitting that kind of quality."

Jason leaned against the passenger door as April re-arranged the boxes in the trunk. "I'll sit the next one out. I'm beyond the point of taste discrimination. You could give me 7-Up and I'd have trouble telling it from champagne."

She opened the door and slid into the driver's seat. His second try caught the door handle, and he flopped into the seat.

She helped him click his seat belt. "Don't go to sleep on me, party boy. I'll want to celebrate my acquisitions."

"Some things are beyond mortal control."

"Fast and hard, huh?"

She reached over and cupped his crotch, lightly massaging. "This help?"

"Heart rate's up." He straightened in his seat.

Her hand returned to the wheel. "Good. One more stop. I have to loop around the town. Shouldn't take too long."

The BMW sped out of the parking lot. His eyes closed two miles down the road.

"It was my father." The words were loud.

Jason jumped. "What? What was your father?" He fisted his eyes.

"The person I've been lying to."

It took a minute to play back the previous conversation and regain a mental focus. "Did he pressure you about grandkids?"

"It wasn't that."

The reporter resurfaced. "You just don't want kids?"

Tears welled, this time cresting the levee. "Part of me does."

"But part doesn't. Why not?"

April pulled the BMW off the road onto a tamped dirt turnout and circled under a large oak tree. She lowered her window and cut the engine. It looked like she was fighting a lip quiver. Her head turned fast, startling him. "I'm afraid."

"All women are a little afraid of pregnancy and childbirth. It's normal."

"That's not my fear." Her middle fingertips blotted the corners of her eyes. "I had a little brother."

Had. A shiver penetrated his torso. "What happened to him?"

"He was born with a problem." She looked him in the eyes. "Have you ever heard of microcephaly?"

He scanned his memory files. "No, but it must have something to do with a small head."

"It's a developmental problem. The head and brain don't develop properly and, yes, they are undersized. In his case, there were severe mental and physical deficiencies."

"Did he have a name?"

April's hands shot to her face. "Oh, God." Sobs accelerated to a bawl.

Jason unbuckled his seat belt and moved so his arms could surround her. She leaned her head onto his shoulder.

"I'm so sorry," he said. "You don't have to talk about it if it bothers you." He hoped she'd go on.

Her head pulled away. "His name was Harry. Harold. Saying his name brings it all out of the abstract for me. It was so sad. He died when he was only four."

He took a chance. "You seem to carry some guilt."

"I was young. I didn't deserve so much responsibility for him. Sometimes he was so cute, but most of the time he fought me. He had seizures and an uncontrollable temper. I guess I was glad when he died."

"How old were you when he passed away?"

A heavy exhalation heaved her shoulders forward. She seemed to relax. "Seven."

A green light for him. "Why did you have to take care of him?"

"My father left us. Mother had to work nights so I could go to school. I didn't sleep much his last year."

A large truck whizzed past and sent a shock wave through April's open window. A puff of dust followed. She reached to turn the ignition.

Jason stopped her hand. "Sorry, but I don't understand. Why would you not want kids? Are you afraid there might be a hereditary problem? Genetic counselors can sort that out."

She flopped back in her seat. "That's part of it." She reached for the key again.

Jason flinched but didn't stop her hand.

The BMW fired and lurched onto the road.

Two deep breaths seemed to cleanse April's mood. "I don't want to ruin the day any more than I have already. I'm excited about this last winery."

"I'll still sit it out," Jason said. "Any more wine and I'll go from sleepy to obnoxious."

The headrest cupped his head, but his mind spun too fast to let go. He closed his eyes and hoped the warmth of the late afternoon would do its job.

A strong jolt shook the car. Jason's legs shot out, and his toes struck the floorboard. The haze gradually cleared to give him his bearings. He turned in the seat and caught sight of a young man closing the trunk. April slipped the man a bill and skipped toward the driver's side door.

She threw open the door and slid into the seat. "You're awake."

"I thought we were having an earthquake."

A turn of the key and the BMW matched April's enthusiasm. "That was the best Pinot I've ever had. That thump was a full box, a dozen bottles." A slight slur stained her speech.

He squinted at the brightness that emanated from both outside and inside the car. "A new record."

"It's incredible. I'm going to have to hoard some of it. This one's for special occasions only."

Jason tapped the fingertips of his left hand with his right index finger. A frown doubled his squint.

"What's the matter?" she said.

"I thought you said you didn't have a large wine

collection."

"I don't."

"By my calculations, you bought forty-two bottles of Pinot Noir today. To me, a small collection is around ten bottles."

"A small collection is under two hundred. I'm closer to one hundred."

"After today?"

"Yes. My collection isn't diverse. I concentrate on a few favorites."

"Where do you keep them? A second floor condo usually doesn't come with a cellar."

April laughed. "You really don't know anything about wine, do you?" Her right hand patted his thigh. "There are several storage lockers around town. Temperature controlled. I rent a small room in one not far from home."

Jason bobbed his head. "I keep my beer supply in the refrigerated section of Belletini's Liquor Store. I'd call mine a large collection." He waited for another laugh, which didn't come. "What do you do with all that wine? I know you have some with dinner, but it seems a bit much for personal use."

"I entertain sometimes."

"I can't remember a single time since I've been around."

She gave him a long stare, then returned her eyes to

the road. "You don't come around very often, so how would you know?"

"You threw parties and didn't invite me?" He tried to make the hurt sound sincere.

She shrugged. "Don't take it personally. I don't think you'd have much fun around some of my colleagues."

"Ashamed of me?"

"Not at all. I work with a lot of pompous asses. You're too honest to be in a room with them for any length of time, particularly if alcohol is served. These people don't do well in mixed company. They either talk business all night or they try too hard to be the life of the party. Either way, you'd escape at the first opportunity."

"You're ashamed of them?"

"Not that, either. I enjoy their company because of our common interests."

"So, you're kind of like your wine collection."

Her chuckle was truncated by a frown.

He settled into the seat and opened his window enough to put a hitch in his inhalations. The day was winding down around him.

"What kind of reporter are you?"

Her vacillating mood seemed to take a new form—a matter-of-fact, detached air. Jason pulled his head from the headrest.

"There's more to the story," she said. "Don't you want to hear it?"

"Do you want to tell it?"

"I do this for a living. This time I need to be the patient. If it helps others, it should help me, too."

"My fee is a six-pack an hour. And it'll require multiple sessions."

"Deal." She backed off the accelerator but remained serious. "My father was a religious man. Very devout. My mother wasn't. She believed in God, but she didn't have much time for organized religion."

"That's not so unusual. You're describing my family now, but with the genders reversed."

"But my father was LDS. You know. Mormon. He wanted a large family—at least five children."

"Are you religious?"

"Let me get this out. Ask me later." The car lurched. "My mother was raised Catholic. And she liked to drink wine in the evenings. Not a lot—two or three glasses. Sometimes four. It drove my father nuts. He wanted her to adopt the LDS attitude about alcohol. He wanted her to convert. She wouldn't."

"An age-old conundrum."

"When my brother was born—"

"Harry."

She glanced over. "Yes, Harry. When Harry was born, my father blamed my mother. He wouldn't get off her case. He said the wine did it—created Harry's problems. She started drinking more and more. That's when the fights started to get really bad. My father wouldn't have anything to do with Harry. He said it was her problem. She caused it. It wasn't his seed but her drinking that did it."

"Jerk. Is that when he left?"

"No. He stayed for almost a year after that. He tried to get her to stop the wine. He wanted more children. But not as long as she was drinking. We had a lot of visits from people from the church. But as soon as they left, she headed for the wine again. My father would get furious. Eventually, he said he'd had enough. I think he divorced her, but she never talked about it."

"Is your mother still alive?"

"No. She lived long enough to see me get into medical school. She worked so hard to make sure I could get there, and she didn't make it long enough for me to pay her back. I think she died a lonely woman. It broke my heart."

"I have a feeling she was happy in the end . . . seeing you get into medical school."

The tires let out a muffled squeal as the BMW turned into the driveway of her condo complex and lined up with her garage. She stopped short of the door, which remained closed. "You coming in? I have a party in mind right now, and you're invited."

"Can I take a rain check? Wine always gives me a doozy of a headache, and this one's just getting started. I think two aspirin and my pillow are the company I need right now. Unless you're in need of unconscious company.

Are you all right?"

"I'm fine. I should get the wine over to the locker right away. I'll have to get into some of the good stuff tonight. It'll be your loss." She forced her lower lip out into a toddler pout.

He pulled the door handle, but froze. "So, are you? Religious?"

A slight smile escaped from her bowed head. "I believe in a supreme being."

"But you're not religious?"

"Religions were invented by man to give hope for a sometimes hopeless existence. They were formed to give a moral framework to human societies. Most modern religions have pushed those tenets to the back of their priority lists. Look at most of the wars throughout history. See if religions were involved. I choose faith over religion."

"Did Harry's problems alter your beliefs?"

She looked over, scowling. "Do you think microcephaly was punishment from God for my mother's drinking?"

The rapidity of her response, and its forcefulness, surprised him. He watched her eyes, but they didn't say a word. "No. If there is a supreme being, he or she probably doesn't intervene in our daily lives. It'd be too big of a job. I think we're judged on a lifelong balance of actions. I don't think a deathbed repentance can erase a lifetime of sinning or a single behavioral trait can damn us."

Her look intensified. "But, from a medical standpoint,

alcohol can cause problems during embryonic development."

"I wouldn't dwell on that. There are too many things that can go wrong: genetics, developmental mistakes."

"And it could be hereditary."

"There's always a chance. Is that why you don't want to have kids?"

"Please, go. I have to get this wine to the locker."

Jason slid out of the seat and leaned back into the car. His head throbbed with his change in posture. "There's always a chance. For everyone. But the odds are incredibly small." Her watering eyes shook him.

Her words flew at him. "The one thing in this life a man can't handle is the thought that he produced a defective offspring. I don't want to watch another man slam the front door for good. I don't want to die lonely like my mother. Now, let me go."

Jason turned and walked to his car like he was balancing a stack of books on his head. Despite the headache, he decided to take the longer, scenic route home—his thinking route.

April's words kept him driving. Psychiatrists were like everyone else. They had their own personal baggage to carry through life. And April's interest in wine seemed intertwined with that baggage. Did she enjoy a few glasses of wine each evening because it validated the side-step of her biological urges?

The afternoon was eye-opening for him; it gave him

a window that looked deep inside her. And it drew him to her. But it still wasn't like the feeling he had with his ex-fiancée, Eugenia. That whole mess had changed him and his views on women. But, recently, something else had changed in him as well. And that's where he felt a common ground with April. Despite their different interests, they both seemed to take the same approach to life. Their age? Was that it?

He passed his turnoff and headed for Belletini's. It had to be age. Once the twenties passed from windshield to rearview mirror, romantic adventures seemed to take on a different tone. One with more immediacy. And he wrestled with it. He still believed in a certain kind of love despite the innate tendency to compromise. He knew both he and April no longer toed up to the fountain of youth and flipped in pennies. They chucked quarters from a distance. But the goal was still the same. At least it was for him.

And where did Agnes fit into all this? Why did she pop into his mind every time he thought about his relationship with April, every time he was with her? There was no way anything could happen between him and Agnes. It was impossible. Then why did the thought of her keep forcing its way in? Why was she able to make him forget about Eugenia, when April couldn't? Maybe this was his subconscious way of holding back from anything serious with April. Maybe it didn't have anything to do with

Agnes. Maybe this was just another one of Eugenia's long tentacles.

He parked the car and stood leaning on the open door. The fluorescent lights of Belletini's were already on, competing with the sun as it dipped into a layer of molasses that coated the horizon.

His feelings for April were comfortable. But were they enough to take away his scars? Or to take away April's scars?

# CHAPTER 12

The quiet of the Imola Day Room no longer soothed Agnes's desire for solitude. The silence was a threat. Instead of staring at the shadows of the outside world, cast on the wall opposite the windows, she sat with the wall to her back, where she could see the entire room. Relaxing and being on guard were on opposite extremes of her behavioral continuum, and it distressed her because she wanted to do both.

It felt like her life in Imola was degenerating, falling apart. And it was all Stuart's fault. He'd cracked her globe of security. Without it intact, serenity no longer existed.

Stuart hadn't been transferred as everyone had said he would. He still lived down the men's hall. Still came into the Day Room. But he didn't bother any of the girls anymore. No more fondling, anyway. No more hunched shuffles to his room. He still spent time in his room, but he half stomped, half limped down the hall in his walking cast. Each trip, his door slam reverberated throughout the wing. It shook the television on the overhead wall bracket.

In the Day Room, he stared. He sat and stared all day, his eyes nearly closed to slits. They flicked like the eyes of a nervous ferret, from one girl to the next.

Agnes shuddered. Mostly, Stuart's eyes found her. If she moved, flinched, breathed deeper than a sigh, his stare pierced her. And his middle finger would go up. It was seldom still, jabbing the air at anyone or anything that moved. He wouldn't say a word. He'd just thrust the finger in the air and sneer.

Agnes stayed in the Day Room as long as she could. But the comfort she craved didn't show. The room had never felt drafty before. Now there was a constant chill. The kind a sweater couldn't tame.

She stood and stretched. The nervousness of the night had triggered a series of eye-closing yawns, each making her lightheaded for an agonizing instant. She backed up against the wall and looked around the Day Room. The sun touched the horizon, stretching the branch shadows across the ceiling. Giving them a pink tint.

Something didn't seem right.

A noise from the men's hall startled her. She leaned back against the wall, spreading her fingers out on the

cold, smooth plaster. She had to cross the hallway entrance
to get to the women's hallway. A door creaked. She
couldn't tell where. The outside light ratcheted down
with an abrupt flicker and turned orange. The branch
shadows seemed to pulsate.

A shoe squeaked on tile. This time, she caught
the direction. The men's hall. She had a choice: circle
around the entire Day Room or dash across the opening
of the men's hall. She froze.

*Go across.*

A shuffling sound echoed in the hallway. Distant?
All went quiet.

Agnes sidestepped to the edge of the hall, her back
pressed against the wall. She leaned, then straightened.
The quick glimpse was useless. The hall was dark.

*You hurt him before. You can hurt him again.*

She slid her hand around the edge of the right-angled
wall joint. She peeked again as her eyes adjusted to the
failing light. The hall didn't seem so dark: she could see
down half of its length. It was empty. She slid one foot
into the opening. Her leg, her hip.

*You're ready. Hurt him.*

Agnes pivoted into the hall opening, facing the long
dark corridor. She crouched, hands held out, fingers
ready to jab and gouge. There was nothing there. No
movement.

She slithered to the other side of the hall opening

and stopped. Another squeak. A hinge? A door closed. No attempt to silence it. She sprinted for the women's hall but skidded to a stop at the hall entrance. The light was better on this side. She peeked around the corner. Nothing was visible well past her room, but the end of the hall was obscured by the shadows of distance. She swung her head back toward the other hall. No movement.

*Don't go. Wait for him. Set a trap. Hurt him.*

Agnes hesitated. Peeked again. The hall was clear. She turned the corner and pranced on the balls of her feet. Past three closed doors. Her doorknob slipped in her hand, and she banged her shoulder into the wood. Was there a noise behind her?

She fumbled with the knob, and it turned with a clunk. The door gave. She slipped in and slammed it behind her.

The room was dark, and her breathing seemed to fill that darkness, pulsing against her. She smelled something strange. The smell of a person.

She hit the wall, searching for the light switch, and found it on the third whack. The sterile light flooded her eyes. She squinted.

The room was empty. She could still smell him. She looked at the bed, the narrow space between the box springs and the floor. "Get out!" She backed against the door.

*He's ours. We can take him out. We have cause.*

Agnes bent down. She could see halfway under the bed. Nothing. She bent farther, put her hands flat on the floor, and leaned until her cheek felt the cold of the tile. Nothing there. No one in the room. But the smell . . .

She stood and rubbed her face with her palms. Her hands were cold against her moist forehead. Someone had been in her room. But why?

She sat hard on the bed and bounced once. Her dog fell against her hip. She pulled it into a hug. Swiveling her feet onto the bed, she leaned back against the pillow and snuggled the dog into her neck.

Her scream hit full pitch before she reached a sitting position. The puppy. Where was the puppy?

# CHAPTER 13

Agnes peered out of the conference room window. Stuart stared in. He thrust his middle finger in the air.

April Leahy wrote in the tablet that balanced on her knee. "Did they find your puppy?"

Agnes turned her head back to Dr. Leahy. "No. They tore Stuart's room apart, but they didn't find it. They searched Milo's room, too. There's no trace of it."

"I'm sorry. Does Jason know?"

"I don't think so. Please don't tell him. He might go after Stuart. That'll make everything worse."

April took a deep breath. "You could confront Stuart. You need to stand up for yourself."

*Listen to the bitch.*

"What good would it do? I already hurt him once. It just made him meaner."

"Sometimes you have to act, or continue to act. Even if it doesn't seem logical."

Agnes looked back at Stuart. He raised his finger again. "What do you suggest I do?"

April glanced out the window. "Right now, raise your finger back at him."

"What good would that do?"

"It would show him you can play his game. He's trying to intimidate you. Show him you won't be intimidated."

*He can be intimidated. It's easy.*

Agnes looked down at her hands. She tried to raise the middle finger on her right hand, but it pulled the adjacent fingers with it. She forced the other two down with her other hand, but the middle one curled down with them. She looked up at April.

"Like this." April made a claw with her fingers, and then curled them all down tight. She slowly raised the middle finger, wrapping her thumb over the others to keep them curled.

Agnes repeated the moves. Her middle finger straightened. She looked up at April, who smiled. Holding her hand in position, she looked out the conference door window. Stuart raised his middle finger and sneered.

*Do it.*

"Do it," April said.

Agnes raised her hand.

Stuart sat upright. He held both middle fingers up,

reaching them toward the window, then bolted from his seat and hobbled off toward the men's hall.

Agnes lowered her hand and turned to April. "What do I do now?"

*Hurt him.*

April wrote in her tablet, then looked up at Agnes. "Remember what you did today. If you get in a situation that makes you nervous, confront it, like you just did with Stuart."

"But what if it makes him meaner?"

"Then you do the same. Get mad. Let your emotions loose. Confront your fears."

*Yeah. Hurt him.*

Agnes leaned back in her chair. "Is it all right to hurt someone on purpose?"

*Oh, yeah.*

"You don't have to hurt anyone. You can confront without getting physical. But it's all right to defend yourself against anyone who tries to hurt you. You need to keep control of the situation. It isn't all right to hurt someone for no reason. Or for fun."

*Bullshit. It's all right to hurt men. Men hurt women.*

"I don't know."

April put her pencil down. "Didn't it just work with Stuart? People like him who try to intimidate are easily intimidated themselves. It takes a little inner strength, but you have it. You have a lot of good in you. Stand up for that good."

Agnes smiled. "I have a confession. I didn't feel bad after I hurt Stuart's foot. It made me feel kind of good."

*Good girl.*

April picked up her pencil and wrote.

"And I had a new dream that night," Agnes said.

April stopped writing. "What kind of dream?"

"Seagulls were flying around the cliffs over the ocean. They didn't beat their wings. They just rode the air currents, dipping and gliding. They circled and dipped, like they were on a roller coaster. And I was with them. Flying. Floating. Dipping and looping. I was smiling, and they smiled back."

"How did it make you feel?"

"I felt good. Peaceful."

"Have you had the dream more than once?"

Agnes's eyes drifted upward, toward the ceiling. "No. Just once. But it was so vivid. I remember every second of it. It makes me feel good to remember it. It was so . . . relaxing."

April wrote. "Why did it feel relaxing?"

"I don't know."

"Was it a feeling of relief?"

"Maybe, but it felt like something else."

April put her pencil down again. "Freedom? Was it a feeling of freedom?"

Agnes frowned at the ceiling. "Freedom. That may

be it. But not from this place. From something else."

April put both hands on the table and leaned forward. "Freedom from Lilin?"

*Freedom from Stuart the Stud.*

"I don't know. Maybe."

April reached for her attaché and slid the tablet and pencil inside. She pushed her chair back and smiled. "Agnes, I think you're in the process of a major breakthrough. You're starting to realize that you can handle stressful situations. You're starting to show some real emotion. And your dream underlines it all. Freedom is the key. Freedom from your past. Freedom for your future. I'm so proud of you." She stood. "I can't wait for next week's session."

Agnes remained seated. Her smile pushed at her ears. "Thank you, Dr. Leahy. I feel better today than I have in a long time."

April tip-tapped out of the conference room and across the Day Room. The door closed slowly behind her.

Agnes stood and walked to the conference room door. She walked out and closed it behind her. In the window, she saw her reflection and she liked what she saw. Her eyes were bright, her mouth turned upward at the corners. She didn't see the scared look of the past several days. She didn't see the nearly constant quivering of her lower lip. She didn't see Stuart coming.

She barely turned her head before a hand pushed on

it, crashing it into the window. The glass shattered, but the safety film kept if from showering the floor. Stuart pulled her head back and shoved it into the glass again. The window bowed inward, and a few shards fell into the conference room. A warm trickle heated Agnes's forehead. Stuart raised his knee and thrust it into her lower back. She half collapsed and grabbed the doorknob to stop the fall.

Her head spun as the room light spiraled down. She heard screams. Someone pulled Stuart away, and she collapsed against the door. She turned the knob and crawled in, pushing the door closed behind her. Shutting out the commotion. Shutting out the hurt.

The room lights ramped up to an unbearable glare. And then the pain came.

*Pick it up. Put it in your pocket.*

She was No One.

# CHAPTER 14

April opened the refrigerator and grabbed the half-full bottle of Pinot Noir by the neck. She yanked the cork from the bottle, and the pop echoed in the quiet condo. This Pinot was one of her prizes, or was it? Just what did she have in her refrigerated storage locker across town? A collection of favorite wines or a collection of carefully selected excuses? She tipped the neck of the bottle toward the goblet but stopped.

Circular behavior. She'd used that very phrase with a patient the previous afternoon.

She cocked her arm, the bottle still grasped by the neck, and turned toward the breakfast nook. She wanted to throw it, to smash it against the off-white walls and earth-tone ceramic tiles. Make them bleed red. The religious tie between blood and wine came to her, and she chuckled.

Maybe that was what she needed: a good old-fashioned bloodletting.

She turned back, lowered the bottle mouth to the goblet, and glugged it full. The bottle clinked on the marble countertop. The cork remained on the counter.

She pulled the goblet to her mouth so fast the wine nearly spilled. A large mouthful rimmed her upper lip and filled her mouth, but she didn't swallow. The wine swished through her gritted teeth, bulging one cheek, then the other. She spat it in the sink.

She tipped the goblet forward and let loose the stem. The goblet fell into the sink, and a large, smile-shaped piece broke free, setting off a treble beep from the security system glass-break detector. Good thing the system wasn't armed. On the other hand, maybe that would have been appropriate. The injured goblet bled the sink red.

A shove, and the bottle followed the goblet into the sink. It didn't shatter on the porcelain, but it finished off the goblet with another treble beep.

April jogged down the hall to the powder room and simultaneously hit the light and fan switches. The bright glare, desirable for doctoring a morning face, always hassled a morning-after face with a bad case of the realities. Today the glare made her look ugly. And the drone of the fan seemed more like a fighter jet coming in for a strafing run. Even the vanilla-tinged potpourri seemed a bit too strong.

A pull on the glass door of the medicine cabinet,

and it rebounded against its hinges. She pulled the small, circular packet from the middle shelf just before the door slammed shut. She threw the plastic case on the floor and stared at it. The wine, the pills, the excuses—they towered over her emotions, wagging a finger of reproach, of warning, giving her the easy way out. She didn't have to trust anyone with that kind of intimacy, with that kind of future. But why hadn't she opted for a more permanent solution? In case someone came along and broke through her fears, let biology reign over psychology? Someone like Jason?

She kicked the pill case to the middle of the floor and stomped. The plastic shattered. Stomped again, and small shards danced on the tile. Another stomp, and another, another, a two-footed dance, and the powdered remains of the birth control pills puffed across the floor.

Dr. April Leahy ran into the bedroom and launched herself onto the bed. She buried her face into the stack of pillows and sobbed.

# CHAPTER 15

Agnes swung her legs over the edge of her bed, raised her hands, and tugged at the lapels of her jumpsuit. She was swamped with a feeling of clarity, driven by a nervous energy she hadn't felt since the weeks after her great-aunt Gert had passed away.

*You know what you have to do. The doctor agrees. Take charge. Deal with the problem.*

She pushed on her door and squeezed through the narrow gap, tiptoeing into the dark, cold corridor. The silence of the medicated nighttime pressed around her, made her realize the power of the pills her ward-mates were forced to take after dinner. Her lips moved in a silent thank-you to Dr. Leahy.

She rounded the curve of the Day Room and slipped down the men's hall, hugging the right side wall. It was just as cold and dark as the women's hall. She counted doors. One. Two. Three. She stopped.

*It's unlocked. Try it.*

Agnes gripped the doorknob and turned it slowly. She held her breath. The knob passed the lock stop—it turned until she felt the latch release. Her breath escaped slowly but drew back in fast, her mouth wide open. She pushed on the knob. The door moved.

*You know what to do. You can do it. This is where you take charge.*

Agnes wiggled around the door and pushed it until it hit the doorframe. She let the knob slowly return to its original position. The latch ticked into the strike plate and caught.

The room was dark, but her eyes had already adjusted, giving her a gray-tone view of her target. Besides, she knew the layout. The bed was four paces forward, the headboard to her left, against the wall. He always slept facing away from the door. She'd done her research.

*Good girl. Go for it.*

She inched forward until her knee brushed the bedspread. She measured the distance from the wall by reaching out her hand. Her position was perfect.

Her right hand slipped into the pocket of her jumpsuit and carefully fondled it—the four-inch shard of glass she had picked up from the conference room floor when Stuart had attacked her. Freshly broken glass—one of the sharpest edges known. She folded her hand around the fat end. It was wrapped in tape.

*Not now.*

She released the shard and withdrew her hand from the pocket.

Leaning over the bed, she could smell him. Hear his breathing. Feel his heartbeat against the mattress. Her own heartbeat doubled his. It pounded in her temples, sounded in her ears, and gave her fingers a rhythmic twitch.

*You know what to do. Do it now.*

Agnes lurched, sending a knee into his side, pinning him down. Her right hand covered his mouth while the left gripped his neck, her fingernails digging into the flesh around his Adam's apple. Her left leg extended for balance.

The struggle was brief. After an initial reaction, he lay still. His nose exhalations were quick, forceful. And wet.

*That's not the way.*

Agnes bent her head close to the side of his head, her voice a whisper. "Where's your stash?"

*That's not the way. Here's how.*

She removed her hand from Milo's neck and reached for his right hand. She pulled it up and placed it on her left breast. She moved the hand to the zipper of the jumpsuit and helped him pull it down, then thrust his hand in so it cupped her bare right breast.

Milo relaxed.

She pulled him over on his back and straddled him,

leaning forward. Her breath caressed his ear. "Tell me where your stash is, and I'll give you more." She exhaled a tickling stream of air. "Much more."

Milo shook his left hand free from the covers and pointed at the far wall, toward the sink, below it. "In the wall. The tiles come loose."

Agnes helped his hand knead her breast, and pulled it from her jumpsuit. "I'll be right back. Just stay right here."

She rolled off the bed and flipped the light switch on. Milo didn't move, except for a slowly spreading grin that dimpled his sunken cheeks.

Under the sink, the tiles were tight, but with a fingernail grip, the first one came free. The rest peeled away easily. The hole in the wall extended from one stud to the next, from the floor to the bottom of the sink. It was packed tight. She rummaged through the booty, amazed at how much was wedged into the space. From the pile on the floor, she pulled aside a white lab coat, three ID badges, and door-lock pass card.

She stuffed the other items back into the hole, ignoring the original organization, so she had to press hard to make it all stay within the confines of the hollow. She looked back toward the bed.

Milo hadn't moved. She slipped off her jumpsuit, rolled it tight, and pushed it into the top of the cache. The tiles lined up perfectly, giving no indication of the hiding place for anyone who didn't know to look closely.

Naked in the harsh fluorescent light, she moved across the room and crawled onto the bed on all fours.

*See how easy this is? Watch me and learn. Maybe you'll even enjoy it.*

She pulled down the covers and straddled Milo once again.

# CHAPTER 16

The knock on the door was so quiet Jason wasn't sure he'd really heard it. It could have been one of those creaky sounds sturdy buildings make for no reason other than to alert all inside to the impermanence of all things manmade. But the second series of sounds came with the same cadence, louder this time, and definitely from the front door.

Who would be knocking at this time of night? April's confidence in their relationship had grown to the point where she would have knuckled the door with purpose. Donnie would simply pick the lock. The only person he could think of who would give such gentle taps was Agnes, and she was locked away in Imola. He debated if he should wait for a third report or just open the door. He opted for the peephole.

# IMOLA

The fish-eye image triggered his quick withdrawal from the door and an immediate thumping in his chest. It looked like her, but in a sorry caricature sort of way. He leaned forward and peeked again. It was her . . . Eugenia.

He unlatched the deadbolt and listened for movement, waiting for the sound of foot strikes hurrying away across the parking lot, re-creating his nightmare. He waited for the laughter. But there were no sounds. He looked in the peephole again and pulled back. It looked like she hadn't moved a muscle. His hand found the doorknob before he even thought about opening it, and then the hinges squealed. He paid no attention to the warning. In full view, she brought a wash of memories that nearly buckled his knees. But he caught himself.

Her silent stance brought an immediate comparison. The Eugenia who stood before him was thinner than before. More like skinny. Her blouse hung limply on her shoulders as if from a coat hanger. And her eyes. They were still the pale blue that had mesmerized him before, but they were deep set, sunken into hollows that seemed ringed in soot. The cheekbones that framed her beauty now jutted out as skeletal ridges.

Still, she didn't move or make a sound. A slight curl at the corners of her mouth gave a hint of animation, but it caught on the apparent impossibility of a smile.

He was sure he was reflecting her inactivity, so he stepped back and pushed the door fully open. "Do you want to come in?" He slid along the door to open a path through the entrance hall.

Eugenia still didn't move. She just stared with a vacancy that suggested her focus was somewhere in the distance.

"Please. Come in. Are you all right?"

A downward head bob and she looked back up. "I need you, Jason." She tiptoed past him and into the front room. Jason pushed the door shut and followed her, keeping more than an arm's length between them.

"Please. Sit down. Do you need anything? Water? Something to eat?" His cringe punctuated the last query, but she didn't react. She just lowered herself onto the couch in a slow-motion squat that barely dimpled the cushion.

Jason moved to the recliner chair directly opposite her, but her eyes didn't follow his path. They seemed to once again focus off in the distance. He sat down.

"Why are you here?" Again, he cringed, but he wanted to break her trance, to get her to return to a human countenance.

Quick blinks and the corners of her mouth twitched again. Her hands moved to her lap, and her fingers interlaced. "I need your help."

"Why? What happened?" From the inside he thought his tone came out impatient, but it was also tinged with a little aggravation. He tried to soften it.

"What happened to your boyfriend, the writer?" He wanted to ask her why she had cheated, left him right before the wedding, but he already knew. And now she had the gall to ask for his help. The temptation to make her pay for that help surfaced. "Talk to me."

"I need help."

"You already said that. Tell me what's going on. Why did you come here?"

Her voice was barely audible. "I didn't have anywhere else to go."

A burning sensation traced his neck. He couldn't believe she thought those words would make him feel generous. His jaw clinched, and his words filtered through his teeth. "Why should I give a shit about what you want? Or what you need?"

Her eyes glazed, and her face contorted into a crying expression, but tears didn't release. It seemed as if there was no fluid in the depths of her tear ducts. "I need help, and I don't have anyone else. I have nowhere else to go."

"You already said all that." Again, the burn. "Tell me what's going on, or get the hell out."

Her face relaxed, as if all sensation had drained from it. Her gaze went distant again. "Ferrell kicked me out. He blew through his grandmother's inheritance, and his parents threatened to take away his condo. He blamed it all on me."

Ferrell. Back when it all happened, Jason had used

his connections to check out the little rich boy. He'd been kicked out of Dennison University, just south of San Francisco, three times. The first two, his parents had bailed him out by threatening to withhold their high six-figure donations. Evidently, three was the charm, and they put him up in a new condo in Sausalito. Last Jason heard Ferret, or Ferrell, was writing the next great American novel. "Blamed all what on you?"

"At first everything was great. We had fun. Lots of parties—"

"Are you forgetting who you're talking to? You left me holding a full book of wedding plans for that fun, for those parties."

The venom in his voice didn't seem to trigger any emotion in her.

"I couldn't live a lie," she said.

"But now you have nowhere else to go, so you're willing to come back to this lie? Maybe you should leave now before I remind you of that note you left for me."

A slight crease appeared on her forehead. "I really am sorry, Jason. I just couldn't do it."

"You did it for a year before you finally walked out." He scooted forward in the chair and tried to control his temper. "I need a beer to continue this discussion. You want one?"

"No. What I need isn't a beer."

What did she mean by that? He stood and walked

into the kitchen. When he came back, she was still frozen in place. A long swig and he suppressed a burp. "How about if you tell me what you need."

Finally, her posture shifted: her shoulders slumped, and her chin dipped nearly to her chest. "I think I need to go into rehab."

"For what?" He couldn't suppress it. "Stupidity? Self-centeredness?"

"Cocaine." Point-blank, no emotion. "He got me hooked, and when I told him I needed help he accused me of going through all his money, and then he threw me out. He said his parents threatened to cut him off if he didn't get rid of me. I don't have anything. No place to go."

"And you immediately thought of me? What about your family, or did you screw them over, too?"

No response, just the blank stare. "I'm tired of it all. I just need help. To get clean. Then . . . maybe we could start over—"

"Start what over? I don't give a shit about your boy-friend. I don't give a shit about your drug problem. I don't give a shit about you. Why should I?" He remembered how she had poisoned everything: his interactions with other women, his job. How he couldn't look at another woman without seeing her. Every woman except one, and she was locked up in Imola. But this woman on the couch didn't look like the image that haunted him. She was a shell, a rind. She was Eugenia in name only. "I really don't give a shit about you."

"You don't have any feelings left for me at all? You're all I have." She inched closer. "I'm not the same anymore."

Jason moved took a step back. He still saw little flickers of the old Eugenia.

"I know I can get back to my old self," she said. "I just need some help."

"Rehab? Just go. Why do you need me for that?"

"I don't have any money. It costs, you know."

Did he detect a hint of irritation in her voice? "Wait. You came here to try to get money out of me? To pay for your rehab?" The absurdity fought with flashbacks of the old Eugenia. He almost asked how much, when Donnie's words came back to him—how Donnie felt Eugenia would come between the two brothers. How Donnie needed his monthly checks. But the flickers wouldn't let up. "I don't have any money for you."

"Jason, I need you. Please. I can't do this by myself."

Who was more pathetic? Eugenia, or that soft spot that was expanding within him? He jumped to his feet. "I can't help you, Eugenia. And you have to go before I do something I'll regret." In more than one way. If she didn't leave soon, he would either weaken or go far in the other direction. "Please leave."

"But I don't have anywhere to go."

"You stopped being my concern when you walked out on me. If you need help, you'll have to find it somewhere else." Now guilt was piling up. But he had to do it. It really was down to Eugenia or Donnie right now. And Donnie was family. "Please leave."

She stood, wobbled, and caught herself with a hand on the couch arm.

Drama?

"I'll get myself right, Jason. I'll find a way. And when I do, I'll show you it can be like before. I've learned a lesson. I'll show you."

But no apology. No explanation. Again, he wanted to ask why. What about him had pushed her to someone else's bed? What had he done besides give her his heart? He resisted the temptation. "I do hope you can get clean. I care about that. But that's where my caring stops."

She stopped partway to the door. "Then care enough to help me. I need the money."

Another slap. He passed her and opened the door. "You never gave me the chance to say this to you before. Goodbye, Eugenia."

The report of the phone sounded distant, but with each ring came closer, louder. Jason stirred. He didn't want another assignment this early in the morning. He'd been up most of the night writing up two others. The red numerals of the clock radio glared 7:33. Normal people were up by now. Normal people.

The ringing continued. He had a habit of switching off the answering machine when he was in the apartment to force himself to answer the phone. It would have been a good time to make an exception, but it was too late now. He caught the receiver midway through the next ring.

"April? What's . . . Whoa. April. Calm down, you're talking too fast. What's wrong? Holy shit . . . No . . . I'll be right over."

Jason turned the knob and pushed, but the door didn't give. He banged on it with his fist and waited. There was no sound from inside, no blink of darkness through the peephole. He swung his fist again just as the door flew open, and his fist nearly hit April in the chest.

She was in a white bathrobe, belt tied tightly around her waist. Her eyes were ringed red, and her hair was a mess.

He walked past her, stopped, and went back for a hug. A kick of his foot and the door slammed closed. Grabbing her hand, he pulled her to the couch and forced her to sit. He plopped next to her. "Tell me what you know."

April's upper lip quivered, and she had to clear her throat twice to get the words out. "Agnes escaped from Imola last night. She killed Stuart Guerin. Cut his throat. Cut off his . . . you know. Just like all of the other murders." She burst into tears.

Jason surrounded her with his arms, but his mind launched from zero to way past sixty in three seconds. "How do you know it wasn't Lilin?"

April bent her head up from his neck. "Does it matter?" Her voice was a near scream. "The way I feel, I'm not so sure there is a Lilin. Maybe Agnes is an incredible con artist and she's sucked us both in."

"You don't really believe that."

"I don't know what to believe. But it really doesn't matter now."

"It does matter. Agnes and Lilin will do different things."

April buried her head in his neck again and sobbed. "I thought we made a breakthrough. She was getting better. I was sure of it." A rapid series of sobs took her breath. She inhaled deeply. "Why now?"

Jason thought about a previous conversation about the possibility of Lilin reacting to the therapy along with Agnes. About Stuart and his accelerating attacks. Pushing Agnes. Opening the door for Lilin. Jason whispered a curse and pounded his forehead with his fist. "I should have seen it coming."

His mind flew through various scenarios. If Agnes was in control, her actions would be predictable. She'd probably head back to Mendocino. She'd be caught. If Lilin was running the show, she'd probably know how to disappear. To stay invisible. She'd be able to get whatever she needed, but there'd be a trail of male corpses, one for each need. And a few just for fun. He shuddered.

April looked up. "What's wrong?"

"Just thinking. How did she get out?"

April wiped wet tear tracks from her cheeks. "The security cameras show her in a long, white doctor's coat, swiping a card in the locks. It looked like she wasn't wearing any pants."

"How'd she get all that?"

"I don't know. One of the patients is supposedly a violent kleptomaniac, but I don't know how he'd get such sensitive items."

"Which one are you talking about?"

"Milo. Milo McGuinn."

"No way. The hippie vegetarian? Bells on his shoes?"

"That's him."

"Violent? Sorry, but I can't see it."

April put her right hand to her left forearm and pushed an imaginary syringe plunger. "Almost all of the patients are medicated in there."

Jason's eyes widened. "Was Agnes?"

"Not all the time. Just when she got depressed."

He shook his head. "So, this Milo character. Does he know anything?"

"I don't know. When I talked to the people there, they said he wouldn't answer any questions. He just sat there and smiled. And get this. They said he ate nothing but bacon for breakfast." She bobbed her head. "He had to be in on it."

Jason stood up and walked to the window. The morning light was too bright, but it raised a dawning clarity in his mind. "No. He wasn't."

"How do you know that?"

He turned to face her. "It was Lilin."

April stood in front of the couch. "How do you get that?"

"What would it take to get pilfered goods from a kleptomaniac?"

She shrugged. "Either a serious threat or some persuasive individual with something to trade."

"From what you described of his behavior, does it seem like Milo's received a serious threat?"

"No. But what would Agnes have to trade?"

Jason spun back around to face the window. He squinted into the distance. "Nothing. But Lilin would."

# CHAPTER 17

Agnes blinked several times, each time forcing her eyes closed. She rubbed her eyes with her fists. The scene came back the same. No green walls, no Day Room, no grassy grounds with oak trees. No Imola. Instead, she stood next to a two-lane highway. Across the road was a marsh-like expanse with thigh-high weeds. A water-filled channel cut a serpentine path through the marsh and opened to a large body of water in the distance. On her side of the road, rectangular flooded fields, bounded by earthen levees, were partially full. On the banks where the water had receded, a white precipitate covered the dirt. It looked like sugar. No. Salt. She scanned her memory banks. Could it be the northern reaches of San Francisco Bay?

A car whizzed past and blew the tails of the white

coat that hung loosely from her shoulders. She looked down. Baggy pants, several sizes too big, were cinched to her waist with a belt that was punched through well beyond the original buckle holes. The tail of the belt dangled to mid-thigh. The white coat, like the ones the doctors wore, covered the pants down to her knees.

She pulled out on the coat lapels and gazed downward. She didn't have anything on underneath. No shirt. No bra. She released the lapels like they were hot. A badge caught her attention, pinned just above the left breast pocket. She pulled it out and twisted it. "Dr. Wilhelmina Smetzer." She'd heard the name. She looked around again as a car blew past on the opposite side of the road.

How had she escaped from Imola, and how had she ended up here, so far from anything resembling civilization? And whose pants was she wearing? The gaps in her memory triggered a painful thought. Where was Lilin, and what had she done?

She looked back. A car appeared in the distance, getting larger.

*Put out your thumb.*

Agnes jumped. She'd never hitchhiked. Even during her college years.

*Put it out. Now.*

Her arm rose. Her thumb was limp, barely projecting from her fist.

The car slowed and went past. The brake lights flared against the low morning sun, and the car swiveled onto the shoulder, raising a cloud of dust. White lights went on next to the red ones, and the car shot backward toward her. It skidded to a stop just short of where she stood. She watched the driver lean over, the passenger door open.

*Hurry. Get in.*

Agnes walked up to the open door and bent over to peek in. She remembered she was braless as her coat fell away from her chest, and she pulled her arms up to press the fabric against her chest. The driver was young, maybe ten years her junior.

"Where you going?" he said.

"Santa Rosa," she said without hesitation. She didn't know why it had come out, but it had. There was no deliberation.

*Good girl.*

The man patted the seat. "I'm going to Cotati. I go to school at Sonoma State. I can take you that far."

Agnes swiveled into the seat and clicked the seat belt. The driver's jackrabbit take-off flung the door closed.

"Name's Roger." He held out a hand.

Agnes shook it. "Agnes."

*Don't use your real name.*

He pointed at the name tag. "Agnes?"

She looked down, and her next inhalation caught

in her throat.  She felt like she was going to cry.  The next breath came easier, and she held it.  And exhaled. "Would you go by Wilhelmina?"

Roger laughed.  "Are you a doctor?"

She looked down again.

*Ph.D.*

"Not really.  I'm a psychologist."

"A hitchhiking psychologist.  That's a good one. Out in the middle of Sears Point Road?"

*Your car broke down.*

"My car broke down."

"Where?  I didn't see a car."

"A ways back.  I pulled if off the road a bit.  I've been walking for almost an hour."

"It would have been closer to go back the other way."

*Change the subject.*

Agnes shifted in the seat.  "What's your major?"

He looked over and smiled.  "I'm in the honors program.  I get to design my own program of study.  It's called interdisciplinary studies.  I'm combining biology with philosophy and ethics.  With the new genetics and molecular techniques, legal and ethical problems are popping up by the bushel.  I'll probably go to graduate school after I finish.  The University of Chicago has a great program.  Either that or law school."

Agnes didn't want him to stop talking.  She wanted time to speed up, the miles to fly by.  She wanted out of the car. A trickle of sweat bubbled on her forehead. She felt dizzy, like she was going to throw up. She swallowed hard.

*Not now. Get control.*

Roger looked over. "Are you all right?"

"I'm not feeling too good."

He pushed a button, and her window whirred down. "Maybe some air will help. Do you want me to pull over?"

The breeze caught her breath, and the nausea receded. "No. Thank you."

"Let me know if you do. I just got the car." He patted the steering wheel. It was one of the new Volkswagen Bugs, metallic silver. An artificial flower stuck up from the dashboard, nodding with each bump like a bobble-head doll.

Agnes smiled. "I'm all right now." She pushed her window button and stopped it when the window was an inch from the top.

They skirted the northern reaches of San Pablo Bay, crossed a small bridge, and lost sight of the water. Roger turned on a small, paved road and headed inland. "I use the back roads from here. It cuts about fifteen miles off the trip." The road wandered between shacks, undeveloped hills, and a few scattered ranches. They picked up a slough for a short time and then left the water for good. Oak trees appeared again, with dense stands of eucalyptus. The smell of freshly cut grass came and went.

The road narrowed a little, and signs of habitation

thinned. Roger guided the VW on the curvy road like he'd designed it.

*Say you're going to be sick. Now.*

Agnes looked at Roger, then at the road. She swallowed hard.

*Do it. Now. Have him pull off the road.*

Agnes rolled down her window.

*Hurry.*

She mopped her forehead. "I'm sorry, but I think I'm getting ill. Could you pull over? I don't want to mess up your new car."

Roger accelerated. "There's a small dirt road just ahead. Can you hold it?"

Agnes nodded and put her hand to her mouth.

He hit the brakes hard and nearly slid into a ditch that guarded the double-rutted road. He was ten yards off the main road before he pumped the VW to a stop.

Agnes unclipped her seat belt and threw open the door. She staggered from the car.

*Farther away.*

She walked into the thigh-high brush and crested a small rise.

*Farther.*

She walked a few steps and hunched over. The Volkswagen was no longer in view. She crouched. And waited.

*Take off the coat.*

Agnes hesitated. She didn't have anything on underneath.

*Take it off and kneel on it. Bend over like you're sick.*

Agnes slipped the coat off and spread it on the dry, grasslike weeds, pressing them to the ground. She put her knees on the coat and turned to look in the direction of the Volkswagen. No movement.

A voice startled her. "Are you all right?"

*Say no.*

She tried to speak, but nothing came out. She was feeling sick, for real this time.

"Agnes?"

*Ask for help.*

She suppressed a retch and burped. If she opened her mouth, she wasn't sure what would come out.

*Say it.*

She took in a deep breath. "Can you help me?"

*Now, bend over. Hands and knees.*

Agnes fell forward, onto her hands. A light breeze gave her a chill.

She heard Roger's footsteps crest the rise, then stop. "Are you all . . ."

Agnes held her position. Her breasts dangled in full view. "I need help."

Roger walked over. His steps were slow.

Cautious?

"I have a blanket in the car."

*No.*

"No. I'm feeling better now. Can you help me get up?"

Roger didn't move.

Agnes peeked at him. "I'm sorry. This must look really strange. I'm really feeling weak."

*The right coat pocket. Get it.*

Roger stepped forward.

Agnes's hand slipped into a pocket of the splayed coat. It was empty.

*The other one.*

She fumbled with the fabric. Where was the other pocket?

*Find it.*

Roger's foot crunched a twig, close by.

Agnes jumped as her hand found the other pocket.

*Grab it.*

She reached inside.

Roger leaned over, his voice close. "Here. Take my hand."

She felt a knife—a folded pocketknife, larger than a Swiss Army knife. A single blade bulged from the handle.

*Open it.*

"Agnes?"

*Agnes? No. Not now. Don't go away on me.*

Roger touched her shoulder. "Here. Take my hand."

*Don't go away. We can do it together. I'll help. You'll learn. We need to do it.*

She turned and grabbed his hand. When he pulled, she rose in one quick motion and threw her arms around his shoulders, pressing her breasts into his chest. Her hands met behind him and pulled on the knife blade.

His hands wrapped around her hips. He held the hug.

*Take off his shirt.*

Agnes shifted the knife to her right hand and grabbed the edge of his sweatshirt with her left and lifted. He leaned back and crossed his arms, grabbing the lower edges of the sweatshirt. He pulled it over his head and peeled it from his arms in a quick motion. Agnes kept the knife hand behind his back.

She grabbed the sweatshirt, tossed it to the ground, and pressed back into the hug. She felt his warmth against her breasts.

*Agnes. We can do it. We'll do it fast. You'll like it. A quick slash. We have to go deep. In the neck.*

She tightened her hug, and he responded by dropping his right hand around the curve of her left buttock.

*It's okay. We can do it together. Just stay with me. I want you to see it this time. How easy it is. You'll love the feeling. The power.*

She brought her left hand to his right cheek and stroked his jaw. He dropped his left hand onto her butt and pulled her abdomen tight against his.

She grabbed a handful of his hair and pulled his head to the side. Hard. She hesitated. Her mind flashed on the doctor shows. The initial incision.

*It's okay. I'll do it.*

The knife blade flashed in the sun as it dug into Roger's neck.

# CHAPTER 18

Agnes turned her head right, then left. It was happening again—the time jumps, the immediate changes in scenery, like she was transported in some small-scale time machine. The missing memories weren't the disturbing part. It was the unsettled feeling that something bad had just happened, a hollow sensation of missing time, like with her missing years. And there it was: the connection with the past, the common denominator. It all centered on Lilin.

Agnes looked down, past the steering wheel. She still wore the baggy pants and cinched belt, but on top she had a Sonoma State University sweatshirt. Roger's sweatshirt. She remembered getting him to pull his car over. This car. She remembered pulling close to him, hugging him. And then there was Lilin.

Her eyes jumped to the road. It was familiar. She was on the way to Mendocino. In Roger's car. In his sweatshirt. The road went blurry as the first tears fell on her cheeks. Roger seemed like a nice young man. His future was bright. Was? Was there any chance he was still alive, walking that country road, the back way to Cotati and his university?

*He was a man. He proved it. He got what he deserved.*

Agnes tried to shake the voice from her head, but it just made more tears fall. There was no way around it. She'd participated in the trap. Now she was driving a stolen car. Of a dead man. He was dead, wasn't he?

*Oh yeah. He's dead. Look at your shoe.*

Agnes bent her head over and looked around the steering wheel. On the toe of her right shoe was a starburst spatter of blood, halfway from crimson to brown. She stiffened in the seat and tried to stifle the hitches of sobs.

*We did it. Together. We make a great team.*

Agnes wiped her cheeks, but the tears didn't let up. The familiarity of the road and the comfort of the destination—home—didn't soothe as it should have. And home wasn't even home anymore. Her house had been rented soon after she'd gone into Imola. Jason was taking care of it.

Jason. She wanted to see him. She needed him, now more than ever. He must be looking for her. Would he go to Mendocino?

She wanted to turn around and go back to Santa Rosa—to find him. He could straighten this all out. He had connections.

*No. We go to Mendocino. We need money. The college boy only had twelve dollars. And the other man had forty.*

The other man? What other man?

*Your pants. Where did you think you got the pants? He was the right height, but way overweight. And he only had forty dollars.*

The tires chattered on the shoulder of the highway, and Agnes had to wrestle the steering wheel to correct the car's course back to the center of the lane. The pants. The sweatshirt. The car. All from dead men. How many lay behind them? How many ahead?

*Three. And it depends. Now keep driving. We know where Gert and Ella hid their money. We have to get it.*

Someone lives in the house. And the police are probably watching it.

*We need money. Keep driving.*

The afternoon sun was setting the Pacific ablaze with reflective ripples when the Volkswagen turned away from the ocean and onto Reese Drive. Long shadows of the car drifted along the sidewalk as it inched past the old Victorian house. Lights were not yet on, no cars in the driveway. And there were no cars anywhere along the street that would signal a stakeout.

*Up ahead. Pull onto that road. Go up about a hundred yards and stop. We can watch from the vacant lot.*

Agnes turned and parked. The tears started again, and she had trouble lifting her legs out of the driver's seat. It felt like she wore ankle weights. She stumbled and nearly went over on the uneven ground.

Just short of the side fence, she went into a crouch, then to hands and knees. At the front corner of the house several large shrubs gave good shelter with a clear view of the street and driveway. She crawled under a huge hydrangea and pulled off a few low branches to hollow out an observation post.

*There he goes.*

Agnes craned her neck around the house corner and pulled a branch below her visual field. A white Ford cruised past. The familiar features of Officer Steven Wilson brought back memories of the days leading up to her arrest. She didn't have a watch, but she could estimate the time by the angle of the sun. It was off the horizon by no more than the height of the trees across the road.

The Ford pulled over and stopped. A blue Nissan came up the street and slowed as it turned in to the driveway. Agnes counted two people in the car. The driver waved in the direction of the white Ford. The Nissan continued on the driveway and disappeared. After a minute or two, lights went on inside the house.

*A couple. No kids. Kids are problems. We can't hurt kids.*

Agnes flinched at the shred of morality from some-one who took both emotional and physical pleasure in killing then mutilating men. But the more she thought about it, the more it made sense. Kids wouldn't hurt kids. Not like that anyway.

The sun made its last call when the Ford came by again, its headlights gaining boldness in the sinking light. The car slowed but didn't pull over. By Agnes's estimation, it was about an hour and a half between checks.

*Plenty of time. We know where the money is. We can be in and out in fifteen minutes. Maybe ten.*

Not tonight, Agnes thought. Not while the couple was home. She was tired. She needed sleep. She needed to stop crying. And she didn't want to leave two more corpses.

She waited, ready to argue her case, but the voice was silent. In her world, silence was as good as agreement. She felt around the base of the plant and smoothed out the leaf litter that was mounded against the stem of the hydrangea. She pulled it into a C-shaped pile and curled around the stem, settling into the crunchy mattress. She shivered against the cold and pulled her torso into a tighter arc. The chill was bearable for now.

Agnes shivered awake, but not due to the air temperature. It seemed as if it had warmed overnight. It was the
dream that sent her muscles into spasm. She'd hoped it
would have been the one about the gliding seagulls. That
it somehow had been a premonition, now a confirma-
tion, of her escape from Imola—her return to freedom.
Instead, she got the highway turnout and ice cream vendor
dream again. What did that foretell? Her shivers intensified.

She forced the dream out of her mind just in time to
see the Ford cruise past.

A muted glow from behind the house reminded her
of how the sun always brought the overhead black to a
hopeful shade of indigo, nowhere near the sky-blue of
daylight, but with a distant promise of another clear day.
But the sun's light preceded its warmth, and she noticed
that she had shifted during the night, her body no longer
wrapped around the hydrangea stem. A tight fetal ball—
her knees pulled up into the honor student's sweatshirt,
her hands pulled well inside the sleeve openings.

She stretched her legs and leaned on an elbow to
watch the Ford drive down the street. It flipped around
and came back again, this time faster, then disappeared.

*It's time we got ready. They'll probably leave soon.*

Agnes had heard that the coldest time of the morning

was when the sun made its first showing and heated the air next to the ground, which rose, replaced by more dense, cold air. Pinned under the shrub, she felt the lesson's substance. The chill combined with nervousness produced an uncontrollable shake. The shake brought another sensation: she had to pee. And she hadn't eaten since . . . when?

She duck-walked to an adjacent bush, an azalea, and unfastened the belt, letting the pants fall from her hips. She squatted expertly, and steam rose from the wetted leaves.

She couldn't refasten the belt. The new, makeshift hole was small and tight, and the shake of her hands couldn't bring the movement of buckle and belt into synchrony. She was about to give up when she heard a familiar noise: the whir of the automatic garage door opener. In her distraction, the blade of the buckle found the hole. She jumped to her feet, in a crouch, and crept to the corner of the house.

The blue Nissan backed down the long driveway and bounced when the rear wheels fell down the curb. The car accelerated backward on the street, rocked to a stop, and shot forward, leaving a cloud of mist to gradually settle on the cold pavement. Were there two people in the car? It looked like there might be.

*There were two. Let's go. To the back door.*

Agnes moved to the back corner of the house and continued along the backyard fence, pushing on each slat as she went. One-third of the way to the back, two adjacent panels gave, each hinged near the top with a single, half-in nail. She pushed them aside and climbed through. How did she know about them?

*We know, don't we?*

The backyard looked like it always had. The tenants had kept all of the plants trimmed, neat. The grass was short and even.

She tiptoed across the wet grass and jumped the last three feet, landing on the bottom step of the back porch. She skipped the second step. Presumably, it still had its high-pitched squeak. The third was solid and led to the landing and the cover of the porch half-walls. To her right, the flowerpot still stood. Bowers of the rosemary still cascaded down both sides of the wall. She lifted the pot from its saucer-like base. The key was still there. But had the tenants changed the locks?

She gripped the doorknob with the palm and fingers of her left hand, resting her right hand on the wrist to stabilize the half-chilled, half-frightened shake. Once the grip was secure, she brought the key up to the lock. It quivered and missed its mark, missed again, then found the slot. It pushed in without resistance. She turned the key, and the doorknob moved. An exhalation bathed the doorknob in a stream of mist.

With little effort, she pushed the door open. The rhythmic chime hit its second, then third beep before she focused on the sticker pasted just above the doorknob: "Alarm Monitored by ADT." She froze.

*We can still do it. We just have to be quick. No time to check the place first.*

The beeping wasn't loud, but it was irritating. It seemed to speed up, gain volume, as she moved through the kitchen. She thought about smashing the keypad, but that wouldn't stop the alarm, only the beeping.

*We'd better grab a knife. Do it.*

Agnes went to the place on the counter where she had kept the knives, but a coffeemaker occupied the space. She twisted her head around, spinning her body in place. The beeping timed her movements, making fun of them.

No knives were on the counter. She started opening drawers—near the stove first, then near the sink. Now the beeps sounded like numbers to her, in a final countdown. Nine . . . eight . . . seven . . .

She yanked a drawer near the far wall, and it nearly slid out beyond the worn stop. Several knives nearly jumped from the drawer. Five . . . four . . . three . . .

*Take the big one. With the fat blade.*

She grabbed the knife and sprinted through the swinging door that separated the kitchen from the dining room. On the far wall, the stained wood of the small, square door, of the dumbwaiter contrasted with the off-white walls. No. Yellow. They must have painted.

She stubbed her toe on a chair—not where it used to be—and the knife fell from her hand. It hit the floor at the same moment the alarm horn went off—loud, obnoxious, sending her into a curled hunch. Making her feel like she was shrinking.

*Get up. We have to get it.*

She left the knife and ran for the dumbwaiter.

*No. Go back and get the knife first.*

Everything was happening too fast. Everything was confusing. The alarm hurt her ears. The light coming through the windows seemed too bright for this time of day. The door to the dumbwaiter stuck. She yanked it open.

Her hands shook again. She wanted to put them over her ears so she could concentrate. Was it to the right or the left? The noise wouldn't let her concentrate.

*The left. Pull up on the rope. Get the tray out of the way.*

She grabbed the rope and pulled. The tray slid up, past the top of the door. She reached for the wood panel to the left.

The phone rang. That would probably be the alarm company. If no one answered, the police would be called. She heard three, maybe four rings. She grabbed at the knobs at the top of the panel, but it didn't move. She strained. It held fast.

The phone stopped ringing, but the alarm continued to blare.

Agnes pulled her hands to her ears and hunched over.

Tears fell from her eyes. She wanted to scream for quiet.

*Get control. We can do this. Pull up and out. We can do it.*

Agnes reached into the shaft again and gripped the knobs. She lunged forward, shoving her hands upward as she pulled. She felt it give. The panel hinged down and came loose. She let it go and reached into the dark. Nothing. She reached in farther. Where was it? The police were on the way. Where was it?

Her hand brushed a solid object. A small metal box. That was it. Gert and Ella's money box. She pulled it to the edge of the hole and slipped her other hand under it. But it wasn't heavy.

She thought she heard the roar of an engine over the alarm horn, so she tucked the box under her arm and ran for the kitchen door.

*No. Get the knife. We need the knife. It's too late to run.*

Agnes stopped. She couldn't think. Should she run? Should she pick up the knife? Where was it?

*By the chair. Get it. Hurry.*

Agnes leaped to the chair and bent down. There it was. She reached, and the box slipped from her arm. It hit the hardwood, but didn't open. She scooped it up along with the knife, and straightened. Someone knocked on the front door. The doorknob rattled above the alarm horn. The door shook and then went quiet.

*Go to the back door. Behind it.*

She pushed through the swinging door and toe-walked across the kitchen. Just inside the back door, the wall indented for the small eating alcove. She placed the box on the adjacent counter and squeezed around the corner. The doorknob turned and gave. The door pushed inward. Slowly. The high-pitched squeak of the hinges argued with the horn in a cacophonous scream.

Too many things were happening at once. The noise. The swinging door. The voice—a man's voice.

"Police. Anyone in there? I'm coming in. I have a gun."

Tears blurred Agnes's eyes. Her fingernails dug into the knife handle. She wanted to drop it. To surrender. But her fist held firm.

*Stay together. We can do this.*

Agnes's eyes dropped to the level of the doorknob. She saw movement. The barrel of a gun. Fingers wrapped around the handle. An overlapping thumb.

*Get ready.*

She could see the forearm. The elbow.

*Not yet.*

The short sleeve of the blue uniform moved into view and stopped.

"Police. Come out with your hands up. I have a gun."

*Not yet.*

The arm moved inward again. She saw a shoulder, his chest. He moved slowly. His head rounded the door. Agnes leaned back.

*Let him get inside.*

He moved in and turned toward the alcove. The gun swung around with him.

*Ready.*

He shuffled forward another step.

*Now. Go for the wrist.*

The knife came down just behind the gun. She heard a scream and a clunk on the floor.

*Now the neck. Slice across. Feel it. Feel. It.*

The knife flew through the air without resistance. The initial incision. Sharp steel through clean flesh. It was just surgery. Just like on television.

# CHAPTER 19

Jason ran up the steps to Donnie's apartment, skipping every other one. The fifth step was missing the overhanging lip, and he'd nearly lost his balance on it a month ago.

He'd never heard his big brother sound so scared. No, panicked. Donnie was flaky, but he wasn't a wimp.

The door opened before he could knock. Donnie turned and paced to the far wall, then back. He couldn't hold still. "It was her." He held out the front page of the San Francisco Chronicle. An old edition. Agnes's picture was near the bottom. "I just found this. I thought she looked familiar."

Jason stood just inside the door and kicked it shut. A step farther and he would be in Donnie's taxiway. "What did she want?"

"A new identity."

"Did she try anything?"

Donnie pivoted and kept walking. "I'll tell you one thing—she's as ballsy as a crocus. She was coming on to me until I asked for a reference. She seemed confused, but then she said your name. I had to think of something fast, to get her out of here. I told her I had to hock some of my equipment so I couldn't do the job. I referred her to a colleague in San Francisco in the Tenderloin District. She seemed to like that."

Jason stepped into Donnie's path. "Do you know how lucky you are?"

Donnie stopped and looked down at his crotch. "Yeah. I almost lost Captain America."

"And about 90 percent of your blood volume."

Donnie chuckled nervously. "It isn't that big."

"From a slit throat, jerk-off." Jason shifted his weight to his right leg. "How long ago?"

"I don't know. I smoked three straight and then called you. It must have been around an hour, but time is going sideways for me right now."

"She's in the city by now. It's easy to disappear in the Tenderloin."

Another nervous chuckle. "Yeah. I'm thinking of moving there."

Jason stopped his older brother when he walked past. Donnie reeked of pot. "How do you do it?"

Donnie pushed past him. "Do what?"

"Give someone an identity."

"There are as many ways as there are people doing it."

Jason raised his voice. "How do *you* do it?"

Donnie stopped. "Don't ask a magician to give away his secrets." He started pacing again on a new path.

"How about a hypothetical?"

"Okay. For a woman, I might start with a credit report. I'd get it from someone with a low to moderate income. Maybe a teacher. And from someone far from here. So I'd find . . . say . . . a teacher from Bowling Green, Ohio. Teachers are good because they tend to be conscientious. They also have to rely heavily on credit. Probably even missed a payment here or there. I don't want a spotless record."

"You steal an identity?"

"No. I lift the credit report for a cut-and-paste job. And it gives the client a previous home: Bowling Green, in this case.

Jason lowered himself into the chair and dodged the wayward spring. "What's next?"

"A social security number."

"How do you do that?"

"Never mind how. But I like to go with the ten-year plan."

"The what?"

Donnie stopped again. His hands picked up the motion

for his now-still legs. "Ten-year plan. I find a little girl around five years old—in this case, from Ohio—and lift her number. Chances are she won't do anything with the number until she's at least fifteen. So I tell the client she'll have to redo the whole thing in about ten years."

"Is that how other people do it?"

Donnie started walking again. "Probably not. That's one of my approaches. One guy took names off of milk cartons. I cut all ties with that bastard. That's fucked up. As bad as during the Vietnam War. I hear some pervert used the numbers of MIAs. They used to stamp their names and social security numbers on those copper bracelets the hippies wore. That guy got stomped."

"Honor among thieves?"

Donnie grabbed his chest. "Ouch, little brother. We provide a service. If the people use it to do something bad, that's on them."

"Guns don't kill—people kill. Right?"

"Did you major in psychology or clichés?"

Jason shook his head. "So you referred Agnes to a colleague. Do you know what technique he uses?"

"He's really good, so he probably uses several. I know he uses foreigners sometimes."

"Illegals or visitors?"

"Foreign-born naturalized citizens."

"He isn't worried about language problems?"

"Lots of people from other countries speak good

English. They have to take it in school."

Jason rubbed his forehead. "Right. I did a story on it once. Other countries are way ahead of Americans on that. In my mind, two things explain why so few Americans are bilingual: laziness and arrogance."

*"Pablo esta bien, pero Louisa tiene catarro."*

"What? Paul is fine, but Louise . . ."

Donnie giggled. "Has a cold."

"Where did that come from?"

"I took one semester of Spanish at the community college. That's all I remember, except for the dirty words."

"Congratulations. You're bilingual." It was Jason's turn to chuckle. "That means two-tongued. The girls would love that."

Donnie's eyes drifted toward the ceiling. "The teacher was really pretty. Blonde, but not a real one. Roots. Dark eyebrows. I sat in front. Every day she nearly tripped on my feet. She'd always say the same thing: *grandes pies.* Damn. I wonder if she was making a connection. Maybe she was telling me something. She was a former stewardess, you know."

"They don't call themselves that anymore."

"Sorry. She was a former air mattress."

"Flight attendant, jerk-off."

He blinked and made eye contact. "Don't go all PC on me, little brother. I'll have to disown you." His eyes drifted again. "Maybe I should have put a move on the little air mattress. But her left hand had a diamond the size of a Chiclet. Probably from a pilot." He formed a circle with the fingers and thumb of his right hand and moved it up and down in front of his crotch. "I know who I'll be with tonight. It'll bring back old fantasies."

Jason nodded at the hand. "If the two of you can hold off, I have another question."

Donnie kissed his hand. "Later, darling." He looked up. "What do you want?"

"Where can I find this person you referred Agnes to?"

"You can't."

"Why not?"

"You can't find him unless he wants to be found. And he never wants to be found when he's doing a job. He only does one at a time."

"Shit."

Donnie spun around and took a step toward Jason. "What about me now? Am I in on her slice list?"

"I don't know. My guess is she's done with you. But can you disappear for awhile?"

"Not without some money."

"How much do you need?"

"Five hundred."

Jason shook his head. "I'll give you three hundred."

Donnie's laugh echoed in the small apartment. "Two would've done me, but thanks for the three."

# CHAPTER 20

Agnes looked around the small, scruffy room. Despite the brightness of day, a flickering light caught her attention in the late afternoon shadows just outside the single, square window. A vertical sign at the corner of the building was missing two middle letters, so it read, "Ho l." Below it, a fluorescent "no" winked on and off to tease the following solid glow of "vacancy."

She wasn't one for elaborate interior furnishings, but she did insist on a functional setting. This place wasn't functional. It was barely habitable: a combination of modern flophouse and early fracture. It was the kind of room in which the lonely were never alone. The gauzy walls and herds of insects saw to it. In some places, scratches in the plaster showed multiple layers of peeling paint that she imagined would reveal the age of the hotel like the rings of a tree trunk. Was this the price of listening to Lilin?

Listening? That was a joke. Lilin was getting more and more pushy. And she was the one who didn't listen.

Agnes flopped on the bed and nearly bounced off the other side. She settled in to think. Since she'd escaped from Imola, she wasn't sure what was real and what wasn't. The last few days were peppered with nightmares so real she remembered every minute of them: her initial arrest for the murders up in Mendocino, Jason and his attempts to find the killer, the devastating realization that it was Lilin, and the emotional search for her twin sister. She felt the pain as Dr. Leahy's words came back to her, telling her over and over that Lilin wasn't real. And she sensed she was losing control of her life. She had more control inside Imola.

But right now, in this dump of a place, everything was quiet. She loved quiet times—craved them. Her thoughts were her own when it was quiet. When nothing was happening other than the movement of time. She could do what she wanted to do. And she wanted to do something right now.

She rolled off the bed and stood for a few seconds. No objections, no orders. She walked to the door and grabbed the knob. Nothing. The door squeaked to her pull. She stepped outside, down the stairway with more peeling paint, more deep cuts in the plaster. Finally outside.

It was nice to go out. The air was cool, foggy. A light

breeze brought the smell of the ocean through the maze of unkempt Victorian buildings. The street was busy, but most people walked like they didn't have a destination in mind. Some were lying in doorways; others slumped against the corners of buildings. No one seemed to look up. There was no eye contact. No greetings. Was it all a trap? Of her mind?

Someone bumped her shoulder. Without looking, the person growled and kept walking, faster. He called over his shoulder, "Watch where you're going, bitch."

Agnes wanted to just walk, too, but she had something to do first. Down the block, she saw what she needed.

She scurried across the parking lot of a convenience store and pulled open the door. A bell on the door announced her entry. On a shelf in the corner, she found a writing tablet, a pen, and a box of envelopes. Near the counter, she saw a stack of newspapers. Grabbed one. She stepped to the counter, then stopped and turned around. She hurried two aisles over and stood, staring. Which should she choose? There were so many. Why did decisions like this have to be so hard?

The green one. Her favorite color had always been green. That was before Imola and all of its shiny, green walls. But she wasn't in there any more. Green could be her favorite color again. She grabbed the bar of Ghirardelli Mint Chocolate and pranced to the counter.

Her hand pushed in her pocket, and she froze. It

was full. Of bills. She worked the wad so she could pull out a single bill without exposing the lot, and the crinkled face of Andrew Jackson came out. A twenty. How many more were in there? She tried to remember where she'd gotten them, and the memories that came back scared her. Gert and Ella's stash from her house in Mendocino had come at a steep price, paid in Lilin's currency, with the swipe of a knife.

The clerk handed her the change. Her hand stopped at the edge of her pocket. "Do you have a stamp?"

"For a dollar," the clerk said.

She peeled a bill from the change and folded the others over the stamp before shoving the wad into her pocket. She hurried out of the store.

A block down, an oasis caught her eye. A patch of green in a quilt of drabs: asphalt, cement, and the long-faded paints of the building façades. As she walked closer, the bright, primary colors of a children's playground played on her senses, teased her with the imaginary sounds and smells of a county fair. The fog seemed to lift over the park. The sound of laughing children wafted on the ocean breeze.

She aimed for a bench inside the nearest gate, but a small, Asian woman pulled her arm. "Where's your kid?" The woman pointed to a sign next to the entrance.

Its bold letters proclaimed, "Sgt. John Macauley Park. All adults must be accompanied by a child."

Agnes scanned farther down. The park was named after a police officer who was shot during a traffic stop. She swept her gaze across the field of happiness. Sgt. Macauley would be proud.

Agnes waited until the nearest person was at least twenty steps away, and then she slipped through the gate and hustled to the nearest bench. The writing tablet and pen were free of the bag and on her lap in an instant. In another, the pen flew across the paper.

A squat man, fortyish, stomped in her direction. She turned her head toward a group of children on the locomotive of the play train and gave a petite finger wave. The man reversed direction and disappeared.

Agnes pulled an envelope from the box and balanced it on her knee. She wrote the first two lines of the address without directing her fingers: Mr. Jason Powers, c/o San Francisco Chronicle. She pulled the newspaper from the bag, opened the front page, and copied the address on the envelope. She returned the paper to the bag, scribbled the return address as a single word. Agnes.

Her hands shook as she bent the letter into a trifold and slipped it into the envelope. The stamp wasn't the licking kind, so she peeled off the backing and pressed it on the envelope. She hoped Jason would get the letter. She had to tell him. Herself. He'd understand. He'd help. He'd be there for her. He was one of the good ones.

Agnes swept her head back and forth, scanning the

area around the park. Mailboxes only showed themselves when one wasn't needed. Otherwise, they hid in the shadows, behind buses, or under low-growing trees. She stood at the corner of the park and let her mind free-fall. She wanted to see the beach. The ocean. But the fog obscured all navigation cues except for the fresh-smelling breeze. She walked into it. A mailbox would appear eventually.

It took only five blocks. And the box was in the open, in plain view. She pushed the envelope through the swivel door and opened it again to make sure the letter had dropped. A foul odor surrounded her. She turned and jumped. A dirty man stood close, nearly against her. His stringy hair hit his shoulders and mingled with his beard. Both were streaked with gray.

"Give me some money." The man's breath smelled of day-old alcohol and filth, blending with a background tinge of sweat and urine.

Agnes tried to step back, but the mailbox blocked her path. The man matched her first sidestep, then her second.

"Gimme money." His hand patted her pocket—the empty one. He reached for the other side.

Her right hand flew to the man's neck and clamped down on either side of his Adam's apple. The fingernails dug into his flesh.

The man made a gurgling sound and tried to step back.

She tightened her grip and started to work her fingernails

into his skin. Red bubbled on both sides of his neck and slid to his collar in small rivulets. She ripped her hand away, twisting it as she pulled, and a patch of skin came away in her fingers. She shook it to the ground.

The man's eyes were wide, like those of an unbeliever. His hands gripped his throat. He gurgled again and stumbled away in a lopsided, galloping trot.

Agnes felt her eyes open wide, pulling back the brightness from the long shadows.

You could have killed him.

*He's lucky I didn't have a knife.*

He wanted the money.

*Why am I out here?*

You don't know?

*No. How did I get here?*

What do you remember?

*I was in the hotel room. What's going on?*

You don't know!

# CHAPTER 21

Jason jumped and the groan of the old recliner chair brought him upward, from a vague feeling of apprehension to full-sensory alertness. Light leaking under the drapes at the far end of the room told him it was morning. He scanned the surroundings, noting the panorama of familiarity. He'd slept in the chair again.

The sound again, the doorbell. He didn't move. The drapes hung still. He hadn't opened them since Lilin's visit to his brother's apartment, right here in Santa Rosa. Since he'd installed the extra lock on his sliding glass door. The landlord would be pissed. Drilling into the doorframe voided the warranty on the double-pane glass.

Another chime. Jason flipped the lever, and the chair ejected him. He slinked into the entryway in a timid, sideways crab walk. As his hand reached out and touched the door, the memory came back, intact, every detail in agonizing slow motion. How he had half jumped, half fallen over the patio wall just as Lilin's razor had swiped within inches of his neck. He remembered the animal growl that had come from her throat as he'd run into the darkness of the golf course fairway.

Even after Agnes's capture, the feeling of violation, of insecurity, had permeated his apartment in a knee-deep swirl of anxiety. And that was when Agnes was safely locked away in Imola. Now Lilin was back, and she was on the loose again, leaving another trail of corpses.

Knuckles rapped on the metal security door. Jason pulled his hand away. The door wasn't his doing: it was a bonus.

He stood to his full height so he could look downward through the peephole. He saw a massive chest in a navy blue jacket. His knees flexed so he could see the face. Thank God.

The heavy door flew open, startling the visitor. Jason thrust a hand through the opening and was surprised when the man dodged it. "Detective Bransome. It's good to see you."

A different set of memories flew through Jason's mind, covering the two times his job had run him headfirst into Bransome. The first was three years back, during his exposé on the problems with the DNA lab. A clear mental picture brought back Bransome's fury when the article triggered the release of three felons. Then Jason flashed on the more recent, latent antagonism when he reappeared in Mendocino to report on the original Agnes Hahn case. It took a second, but his mind hovered on how they eventually settled into a mutual tolerance that evolved into efficiency, almost friendship. How they had worked together to capture Agnes and expose Lilin for what she was.

"You scared the doo-doo out of me." Bransome said. "You always open the door like that?"

Jason felt his face go hot. "I thought it was somebody else." He realized how stupid that sounded. "Come in. The place is a mess."

Bransome walked through to the living room, lifting his feet like he was afraid of stepping in something. "More like a funeral home. I knew reporters were bloodsuckers. You adopting the lifestyle?"

"Lilin's on the loose. I may be on her list."

Bransome shook his massive head. "It's Agnes, not Lilin. Remember?"

Jason started to say something but gave it up. "What brings you to Santa Rosa?"

Bransome fell into the couch and adjusted his weight. "She's at it again. This time in Frisco."

"San Francisco. You know how much they hate it when anyone calls it Frisco."

Bransome smiled. "Another poor stiff with his throat slit and his penis on his chest. I'm heading there to talk with the investigators."

"Did it happen in the Tenderloin?"

"Why? Do you know something?"

Jason considered telling him about Lilin's visit to Donnie's apartment, her request for a new identity. "No. Just guessing."

"You obviously know the city. It was in the Castro District."

"You seem to know it, too."

"I got my start there. Quit when my partner got shot making a traffic stop. Crazy place back then."

Jason couldn't sit down. "Any idea who the stiff is?" He hoped Donnie hadn't been stupid enough to go into the city.

Bransome pulled a spiral notebook from his jacket pocket and flipped a few pages. "Male. Obviously." He looked up and chuckled. "Five nine. One sixty."

Too small. "Caucasian?"

Bransome looked at the notebook. "Hispanic."

Jason's exhalation echoed.

"This one was unique, though. The place was ransacked. A computer is missing, and a whole file cabinet was dumped. They said the guy was obviously into making documents."

"Creating an identity?" It just came out.

"You sure you don't know something about this?"

Once again he thought about telling Bransome what he knew, but he had to protect Donnie. "No, but it makes sense. She's trying to disappear."

"She?"

"Lilin. Agnes."

"Then coming here was the right move."

Jason sat on the arm of the recliner. He frowned.

Bransome closed his notebook and slid it into his jacket pocket. "Agnes may try to contact you. It seems you two had a connection. And I know you visited her in the hospital."

Same thorough Bransome. "If she's trying to disappear, I'd be the last one she'd try to contact."

"That shrink you're screwing said the Agnes part of her would try." He blushed. "Sorry about the way I said that."

"Right now, Agnes is the last person I want to see." He looked down at his crotch. "I'd like to be able to keep screwing shrinks." His laugh triggered Bransome's.

The detective squirmed against the soft cushions. "We need a favor."

This was a reversal. Jason's requests for favors had so angered Bransome in the early part of the Agnes Hahn case. Jason used a singsong voice to mimic Bransome's favorite line. "I knew that was coming."

"If she contacts you, I want you to set up a meeting. We'll make sure you're safe."

Jason rolled his eyes. "Oh, great. A decoy. A friend hunts ducks. Do you know how many of his decoys have holes shot in them?"

"We need to get her off the street. Besides, don't you smell a hell of a story in it? After the fact, of course."

Now the reversal in roles was total. But Bransome had a point. A great point. "Any ideas how I should do it?"

"I'll leave it to you, but make sure it's in a public place. Daytime, please."

"And if she won't go for either?"

"Then do the best you can to make sure we have a chance of nabbing her. You've been around the business for a while. You know what we need."

"Can you give me a chance to talk her into giving herself up first?"

"Talk all you want. Before the meeting. If we see her, we're coming full force. We have to get her off the street."

"I still don't think she'll get in touch."

Bransome struggled but got to his feet. He held out a card. "In case you don't still have one. My cell phone is always on. I've got to get down there. To Frisco."

"Don't think much of the place, do you?"

"Not anymore. I used to love it. Before the yuppie invasion. And all the queers."

Jason thought about Donnie's challenge to political correctness. He and Bransome would get along quite well. Donnie. Jason hoped he'd gone into hiding. She could still get him. He was a loose end.

The door slammed. Jason didn't move to lock it. He had to get out of there. He had to find Donnie.

# CHAPTER 22

Jason rushed up the stairs and waited to catch his breath outside of Donnie's apartment. He hoped no one would be home. Noises leaked through the door. Laughter. And music.

He ground his teeth and didn't bother to knock. The knob turned easily, the door flung open with his shove.

Donnie sat at the table, his shirt off. Opposite him, a young woman perched on the edge of her chair, naked except for thong panties. In the sitting position, the thong strap bowed out, exposing her butt crack. They each held a hand of playing cards.

The girl jumped, but Donnie acted as if nothing had happened. "Bad timing, little brother. I'm about to call her drawers and raise her a blow job."

The girl's giggle bounced her breasts.

Jason scanned the table. A vial of white powder sat next to the girl's left hand. A nearly full Baggie of weed was next to Donnie's right. Three rolled joints were lined up next to the Baggie, and two joints were in a kitty in the center of the table.

He took a step forward. The girl didn't cover up. "Is this where my money went?"

Donnie grinned at his partner. "Easy come, easy go." He faked a toothy grin. "And then, easy come."

The girl let out another annoying giggle.

"Not so easy come anymore, asshole."

Donnie feigned hurt. "Asshole? What happened to jerk-off? Don't you want me to be happy?"

"I want you to be alive. You need to get out of here. Don't you remember your last female visitor?"

The girl turned her head toward Jason and then to Donnie. She tilted it like a curious puppy, her pigtails dangling like puppy ears.

Donnie winked at her. "Give me a little while. I need to collect my winnings first."

Another giggle, more throaty this time.

"Jesus Christ." Jason turned for the door.

"You couldn't spot me a little more, could you, little brother?"

Jason slammed the door so hard it nearly left the hinges. But he hesitated at the top of the stairs. Maybe he should go back in and knock some sense into his brother. Donnie was older but not a physical match. Yet trouble seemed to roll off Donnie, rarely sticking long enough to bring him bodily harm. Jason knew that first-hand. Long before he outgrew his older brother, his way of dealing with the constant teasing and abuse—the normal order of sibling business in their house—was to tattle to their father about events that would surely bring swats from their father's "stick of discipline." Some events were real, some totally fabricated. And yet, Donnie rarely felt the sting of that stick on his backside. And it puzzled Jason to this day.

A high-pitched giggle leaked from Donnie's door, and Jason stomped down the steps. At the bottom, he let out his own little laugh. He remembered the time when he was in the just-learned-to-write grade in school. He had written, in indelible marker, "Donnie did this" on two inside walls, a door, and an outside wall of the house. He'd even etched it into the wood of the coffee table. That's when he discovered his parents were clairvoyant. Despite the clarity of the message, they somehow knew it was he, not Donnie, who had desecrated the family home.

On the sidewalk, he turned and looked up at the windows of Donnie's apartment. "In case you didn't know, big brother, it was me. And I'm not sorry."

# CHAPTER 23

A wasted day nagged Jason and promised another night of worry. Fast food was just fine with him, even though most of his colleagues refused to admit they sometimes strapped on that feedbag. But two double cheeseburgers sandwiched around a cold beer, in the pyrite dusk of his patio, kept calling his name—in all capital letters—until reality caught up to him. No patio until Lilin was caught. He'd have to eat in the artificial light of his apartment, all drapes and blinds closed tightly.

The restaurant was only a few blocks away. It was too far for a walk, particularly this close to dusk, but hardly far enough to get the car manifold up to full temperature. The mealtime crowd in the drive-through lane solved the temperature problem but not his worry. Could Donnie be that stupid? Well, yes. Obviously.

But his carelessness was at an all-time high.

He pulled away from the restaurant, and a small compact car fishtailed in behind him, so close he couldn't see its headlights in his rearview mirror. He accelerated a little, and the car kept pace. Rather than turn in on the golf course road that led to his apartment, Jason accelerated even more and drove straight past his turn. The small car kept pace.

An illegal turn at the next intersection produced two sets of tire squeals, and the little car bobbed into the opposite lane and corrected, nearly ramming the rear fender of Jason's Volvo. A quarter mile up ahead was a freeway entrance. He could kick it into turbo and lose the little four-banger.

A thought pulled his foot from the accelerator. What if it was Agnes? He leaned close to the rearview mirror, but between the gathering dark and the reflected glare of the car's headlights on the rear of his Volvo, Jason couldn't make out any features of the driver. Not even a silhouette.

He stepped on the accelerator again, but the little car shot out from behind him, into the oncoming traffic lane. It jerked alongside and swerved toward the Volvo. Jason reacted, trying to stay on the road without hitting the curb. He looked over. The driver was definitely a man. A smallish man with his hair pulled tight into one of those stubby, high-placed ponytails.

The little car lurched forward, even with the Volvo's front fender, and swerved again. Jason hit his brakes and so did the other driver, pinching the Volvo to the right. Jason swerved into the driveway of a strip mall, and the little car matched the move, now in full broadside again. It continued to inch at the Volvo, forcing Jason to pull to a stop, diagonal to the painted stripes, and against the planter border of the parking lot. The little car screeched to a stop, partly blocking a backward retreat.

Jason wasn't sure what to do. If the creep had a knife, the car was the safest place. If he had a gun, it was the worst place. It was better to run for it. He caught sight of the man in his outside mirror, walking in his direction.

The man's arms hung at his sides, each hand empty. And he appeared to be at least a few inches shorter than Jason, and of very slight build.

Jason shoved the door open and stood to his full height as quickly as he could. "What the fuck are you doing, asshat?"

The man stomped toward Jason and stopped just out of arm's reach. "Where's Eugenia?"

"What?"

"You heard me. Where's Eugenia? Bitch stole my money and ran off with my car. Where is she?"

"You . . . you're . . ." What was his name? "The writer?" Ferret. "Ferrell, right?"

"Just tell me where she is. I know she came back to

you. I want my money. And my car."

Jason straightened his arm and leaned against the Volvo. The prick had a load of shit coming to him. "You have a car, and a mighty nice one."

"It's a fucking rental. It's all I could afford. That bitch maxed out all of my credit cards. I had to go begging to my parents, God damn it."

Jason lowered his arm. He pulled in a deep breath and let it out as if he were trying to blow the little man over. "Eugenia did stop by." He wanted to tell a burning lie to get even with the little jerk, but just thinking of saying that he and Eugenia had hot, sloppy sex nauseated him. He opted for the truth. "She said she was hooked on drugs, no thanks to you. She wanted money to go to rehab."

Ferrell's knees seemed to buckle. "She was playing you, too?" He put his hand to his forehead like he was shadowing his eyes. "I'm getting help. I offered it to her, too. I would have paid for it. But she just kept using more and more. Then she split. With my stuff."

Jason suppressed the twinge of sympathy. "So the monster you created turned around and bit you. If you want a Band-Aid, go somewhere else."

"I don't care what you think about me. I just want to know where she went."

Now for the uppercut. "She probably ran off with some other guy with full pockets and a handy pharmacy. In fact, she probably hooked up with him months ago.

Sound familiar?"

Ferrell's voice seemed to be missing some of its original bluster. "She has more than my car and my money. She's pregnant. I need to find her."

A new wave of nausea cinched Jason's stomach. "And she's still using drugs?" No matter how much her behavior had changed, he couldn't see her using through a pregnancy. She had always wanted a family. Not a child, but children. At least that was what she'd said. "Maybe she was faking it."

"We did the urine tests, then had an ultrasound."

Another twinge of sympathy. "Sorry, man. But the best thing that could happen to you right now is if the baby isn't yours. You'd better hope she did to you what she did to me. Otherwise, you can kiss your trust fund goodbye."

"I'll ask one more time. Do you know where she went?" He shoved his hand into his pocket and brought out what looked like a toy derringer. He pointed it at Jason's chest. "I'm desperate. And when I get desperate, I do desperate things. Right now, I'm out of options. I'm down to using this. So answer me."

Jason backed up as much as his car would allow and raised his hands in front of him. "I told her to get out. She left. That's all I know."

Ferrell stood in place, the gun still raised. Jason could almost see his mind turning through the options. With a head shake, Ferrell lowered the gun and slipped it back in his pocket. "If you're lying, I'll find out."

Jason wanted to push back, to tell him he'd be ready for him next time, but he didn't want to push the twerp into the meltdown he may have just sidestepped. Again, he opted for the truth. "I don't ever want to see her again. Same with you."

Without another word, Ferrell turned and walked back to his car. He climbed in, started it up, and hit the accelerator hard.

Jason read the license plate number and repeated it as the car sped away. He repeated it again, then leaned into his car and brought out a notebook with a pen shoved through the spiral wire binding. He jotted down the plate number and flipped open his cell phone. He'd report the gun incident to the police and press charges. He didn't want to deal with either Eugenia or Ferrell ever again, and now he could get one away from him. He didn't need this nightmare. He had his hands full with Agnes. And Lilin.

He closed the phone without making the call. The desperation in Ferrell's shaking hand when he'd pulled out the derringer told Jason to just steer clear. Once Ferrell found Eugenia, he wouldn't come around again. And Eugenia would likely occupy Ferrell well into the coming months, dodging him, enraging him, or reconciling with him when all other sources of money proved difficult. It was a do-nothing situation, and Jason imagined he was done with both of them for some time.

# CHAPTER 24

Lilin drove the Volkswagen across the Golden Gate Bridge and turned off on the last marked Sausalito exit. She wound through the narrow streets, nearly to the water, and turned left. The road ended with a wooden roadblock, but a double-rutted dirt path took off to the side and headed up a small hill. She'd scouted the road before.

At the crest of the hill, the makeshift road split. To the left, it led to a series of sharp rises that were used for four-wheeler and dirt bike hill climbing. To the right, it opened into a turnout that overlooked the water. Probably a make-out site.

She turned right and pulled the Volkswagen to the edge of the short cliff, facing the water. Before getting out, she searched the car for belongings of importance. Sitting on the passenger seat, an old copy of the Chronicle had a front-page article about a North Bay honor student whose body had just been found. He was the latest victim of the escaped serial killer.

"Not the latest."

Lilin walked to the edge of the cliff and looked over. It was only a fifteen-foot drop and not straight down. The eroded dirt formed a steep ramp, the kind a four-wheeler would like. Except this one went right into the water. By her calculations, the shore dropped at the same angle as the cliff, although she could be mistaken. At the least, the car would be covered with water at high tide, which was an hour away. At low tide, who cared?

She opened the driver's door and swiveled in, pushed the clutch, and shifted into neutral. She got back out, reached in, and released the parking brake. The car rocked and then crept toward the edge. She slammed the door, ran behind the car, and pushed.

*How will you get back?*

Shut up. I don't need you yet.

The VW picked up speed. The front tires dropped over the lip of the cliff; then the rear tires. The car accelerated until it hit water. The front end bounced when it hit the water, and the momentum launched the car like a boat. It didn't go down right away.

Lilin let out a loud laugh. "I'll be damned. They do float. For a while."

She watched the car slowly move outward and down

into the dark water. She didn't wait for it to disappear: the tilt of the front end told her the water was deep enough.

*What are you going to do now? You don't have a car.*

I told you to shut up. You know I don't need you.

Lilin walked back to the paved road, then to where the highway was in view. In this direction, the road didn't continue beyond the two on-ramps. She stayed back from the highway so any passing highway patrol officers wouldn't see her. She waited, her thumb ready.

It didn't take long. A powder blue BMW pulled to a stop, and the electric window whined down. A young blonde gave a white-toothed smile. "You going into the city?"

Lilin nodded and circled to the passenger door. The inside of the car reeked of one of the trendy perfumes. Be Delicious, or something like that.

Lilin settled into the soft, beige leather and turned to look at the driver, who stared back.

"You have to buckle your seat belt. If my Dad sees anyone without a buckle, he'll take my keys for a week. I just got the car. Do you like it?"

Lilin forced a smile. She wanted to ride in silence, not hear testimonials from a Chatty Cathy.

"I'm not kidding. I'm going to sit here until you buckle up."

Lilin snapped the metal buckle and slipped her hand into her purse. Her fingers fondled the folded razor.

"Thank you. I just couldn't bear it if he took the car

away. Besides, I have an appointment." The acceleration squealed the tires. "Where in the city?"

"What?" Lilin wanted to cut her, but she didn't do women, or a girl in this case. Maybe a Glasgow Smile would serve a higher purpose here, kind of like that chick from Ella's home. The one who stole from Ella and a few other old ladies. Lilin smiled at the memory of her first woman kill. At least there was a man there as well. A two-for-one.

"Where do you want me to let you off, silly." The girl's head bob brought the perfume level back to overpowering.

"Anywhere on Van Ness. Is that okay?"

"Right on my way. Isn't this great? I can take you right where you want to go." She pushed on the accelerator, and the car shot up the on-ramp. She merged without looking over her shoulder. "It's nice to have company."

Lilin's fingers twitched on the razor.

The young woman remained silent all the way across the Golden Gate Bridge, until she pulled into the toll plaza. She pushed the window button, and as it whirred down, Lilin felt the cool air, replacing the perfume with the smell of the ocean. She took a deep breath as the scent swirled around her. Wherever she went next, she'd have to stay close to an ocean. She needed this smell.

"It's okay," the girl said as she pulled to a stop. "I got it." She reached into her Prada bag and pulled out a handful of change. "I like to make them count it." She chuckled.

As they entered San Francisco, Lilin pulled her hand from her purse. She wanted to close her eyes and rest, but she couldn't let Agnes back in. No telling what she'd say to the girl. And for some reason, Lilin felt no awareness, no memory whenever Agnes was around. It wasn't like before Imola, when Agnes was in charge. She had been aware of every one of Agnes's actions back then, even her thoughts.

"So, don't you want to know?" The girl punched the accelerator again.

"What?" Lilin squinted the girl into focus.

"Back there." She hooked her thumb back over her shoulder. "I said I have an appointment. Don't you want to know what for?"

"It's not really any of my business."

The girl chuckled again. "That's okay. I don't mind talking about it. It just so cool." She looked over at Lilin and let out another irritating laugh.

*Please let her just shut up.* Lilin envisioned the girl's crimson blood cascading down the beige leather upholstery of the car. Or would it come out blue, the color of the car?

"Okay. I'll tell. It's my present from my mom. The Beemer is from my dad. For my graduation. And for getting accepted at St. Mary's. I don't really want to go to college yet, but I kinda have to." She looked over at Lilin, but swung her head around when the car swerved toward the next lane. "So don't you want to know what my mom got me?"

Effervescence was supposed to bubble off with time, wasn't it?

*Maybe if she spilled her information, she'd shut up for five minutes.*

Lilin flinched. She looked at the girl. "What's the appointment for?"

The girl giggled again, this time with ascending staccato notes. She took a deep breath as if she were about to go under water. "It's for a consultation." The last word came out loud, pronounced with a halting emphasis on each syllable. She blew out the remaining air and took another huge gulp. "I'm gonna get a boob job. That's Mom's present. Isn't she just the greatest? Of course, she's not my real mom. She's my stepmom."

BMW from Daddy, boob job from Stepmommy— all for high school graduation. Lilin gritted her teeth. Her hand slid back toward her purse.

*You don't do girls. Remember?*

I want to make an exception. The world will be better off. I promise.

No response.

Hit a common note, didn't I?

*She's pretty busty. She doesn't need bigger breasts.*

Lilin nodded in agreement. But the girl lived in Sausalito, where extraordinary wasn't quite good enough. She tried to think of a word that went a step beyond extraordinary. Maybe D-cup.

Lilin looked down at her own cleavage. Women who didn't know how to use what they were born with had no business thinking artificial enhancement would make their lives any better. They were amateurs in a game that led in only one direction—to unhappiness—for all but the professionals. Shiny tools were no match for the dull, hardened steel of functionality, and functionality came from a self-confidence that was earned the hard way, not purchased from some outpatient surgery center.

The girl started talking again, but to Lilin the words trailed off to a dull hum. The girl was obviously nervous about the procedure, although the end point would surely dull the apprehension. Lilin wondered if the girl's step-mom was one of those cosmetic surgery addicts. One who felt the fountain of youth sprung from the sharp blade of a scalpel. It was a puzzle piece that didn't have to be forced into place.

Lilin's request to be let off anywhere on Van Ness put her only a few blocks from the Tenderloin and within a mile of her destination. She leaned into the car before closing the door. "Good luck with your titties."

The girl gave one of her patented giggles. "Thank you. Aren't my parents just way cool?"

Lilin slammed the car door before she was tempted to extend the girl's ride to forever.

*You want to go the other way.*

Shut up. I'm not going back to that mangy hotel. Not now anyway.

Later, she'd make a brief stop back there to pick up her belongings. It was moving day. And moving day meant it was probably a day for something else. A little business and a little fun.

*What are you going to do?*

Shut up.

A block from the destination, she saw it. It was in the front line but to the side. The owner of the small used car lot wanted to lure customers in with the lower-priced cars. The GTO was visible, but its price tag wasn't. It wasn't displayed at all. An interested party would have to ask. Lilin intended to ask.

It was a 1970 two-door. Bright red. She'd seen only a couple flaws when she'd checked it out earlier. The biggest in the lot, it had an automatic transmission. That's probably why it was still on the lot. That and the price, whatever it was. She laughed. The price didn't bother her.

Lilin unfastened the top two buttons of her blouse and pushed her breasts upward so they bulged from the top of her already uplifting bra. She undid the bottom two buttons and tied the shirttails into a knot high enough to expose her tummy. Who needed implants? She smoothed her hair with her hands.

A stout man, presumably the owner of the lot, met her at the door of the small shack-like office. He oozed salesman stereotype, and he made no attempt to raise his eyes from her cleavage.

She wanted to slap the grin from his face. "I want the GTO."

"Would you like a test drive? It drives like a honey. Has the big engine. You'll need rear tires every ten thousand miles if you aren't careful."

He had a tittering laugh. It pissed her off. "No. I want to buy it."

"Well, I can let you have it for—"

"Don't bullshit me. Here's what I'll do. I'll give you middle Blue Book because it's an automatic, and it's been in a wreck. The frame needs some straightening, and you don't have the equipment for it. And the odometer has probably been rolled back. I'll take it as is. Cash okay?"

"It's worth more than—"

"Here's my one-time offer." She stepped close. "Middle Blue Book. Cash. If you say yes right now, I'll take you in the office and let you fuck me in lieu of a handshake. You have ten seconds to decide. Ten . . . nine . . . eight . . ."

The man pirouetted on his right heel. "Deal." His jacket was off before he reached the door. He kicked his shoes off in the three steps it took to navigate around the front desk, and his pants hit the floor two steps later, in the doorway of the rear office. By the time Lilin cleared the door, he was in his boxers, the infuriating grin expanded to show coffee-stained teeth. They were alone in the shack.

*Don't do this.*

Lilin's grin matched his as she slipped off the blouse and released the bra. She reached in her purse. "You'll have to wear protection."

"Everything here comes with a warranty." He blurted his tittering laugh, apparently pleased with his attempt at humor.

She stepped close.

He reached for her breasts, but before the first touch, the stun gun made contact with his side. He fell on the floor, jerking. The rise in his boxers deflated like a punctured tire.

*Take the keys. You don't have to do this.*

Lilin admired the stun gun. It was her first time. She'd used a taser before, but she was tired of the expensive reloads and replacements. This one could be recharged and used over and over.

*Just take the keys.*

Shut up. This one is for you. You're going to stay with me through the whole thing this time. You're going to see how good it feels. Your first orgasm. You and me. We're going to do it together.

*Please. Just take the keys.*

Lilin pulled the straight razor from her purse and

looked around. She went back to the doorway, pulled the man's pants into the office, and closed the door.

Watch and learn.

*No. You do it yourself.*

Not this time. Here's the best way. You have to have something ready so the blood doesn't squirt all over. She poised the razor, with the pants in the other hand, right behind it.

Come on. Your hand is on it, too. We're doing it together.

The razor swiped.

Now, you just hold the cloth here for a few minutes.

The man twitched and went still.

Wasn't that easy? Now for the good part.

*You don't have to.*

This is the best part.

She lowered his boxers to his ankles and lifted his flaccid member.

This is the male's weapon. He uses it to hurt. We are at war. We have to disarm our foe.

*Don't.*

Her breathing was quick, panting, like a dog. A wrist flick and she let out a whimper. Her knees shook. She stood up and wiped the razor on the man's shirt, which dangled from the edge of a desk. She folded the blade and put the razor back in her purse.

Now for the best part. In case you didn't notice, we

just had a little one.  Now we get the big one—one you'll never forget.

*I am No One.*

Don't pull that crap on me.  You're right here, right now.  You see everything I see.  You feel everything I feel.  Your hands were on the razor right with mine.  Now, enjoy the spoils with me.

She pushed her pants and panties to her ankles and lowered the foe's disarmed weapon for the victory dance.

# CHAPTER 25

Detective Art Bransome hurried down the disinfectant-scented hallway of the Mendocino Police Station and burst into the detective's workroom. Agnes Hahn was on the loose, his most experienced officer was dead, and the replacement officer the state had sent was a wet-behind-the-ears rookie from Sonoma County, barely three months out of the academy.

Within minutes, Officer Andy Pfeffer pushed through the door and quietly walked toward Bransome. "My assignment, sir?"

Under different circumstances, Bransome would have welcomed the rookie into the investigation, even taken on the role of mentor as well as boss. But Agnes's escape, and the subsequent murders, represented such a dose of lip-puckering bitterness that playing teacher was beyond his current patience threshold.

He had lived and breathed Agnes Hahn for way too long to have this happen all over again. How the hell could they let her get out? Before, the way they caught her was a fluke. Jason had stumbled upon the storage garage behind Agnes's house on a blind hunch, a long shot to gain further information. He had no idea Agnes, or Lilin, or whoever, was hiding in there. And now she was loose again, in San Francisco, and seeking a new identity. If it took a fluke to find her before, what would it take this time? What was less probable than a fluke? Maybe divine intervention?

Bransome thumbed through Pfeffer's personnel file, but he didn't read a word. If Agnes-Lilin was smart, she'd simply disappear. The only hope of catching her was if Lilin would take charge and continue the killing. He slammed the file shut. How horrible was that? He kicked an empty wastebasket across the room. To hope for more homicides.

Pfeffer jumped and dodged the can before it crashed into the far wall. His eyes were wide, like he was face-to-face with a demon.

"You're on traffic for now." Bransome said. "Go see motor pool for a car. It's out back."

Pfeffer took a step, then stopped. His voice was timid. "I thought I was transferred here to help with the Agnes Hahn case."

Bransome stared. "Do you believe in human spontaneous combustion?"

"Huh?"

Bransome took a step closer. "Did I just give you an assignment?"

Pfeffer retreated a step. "Yes."

"And you're still standing here because . . ."

Pfeffer inched farther backward. "I was sent here to help with the Hahn case. I've been familiarizing myself with the file."

"Have you? How many people has Agnes Hahn murdered?"

Pfeffer looked at the floor. "I'm not sure of the exact count. At least five. I think."

"You think?"

"Detective Bransome, I excelled in the crime scene investigation part of my training. I bring fresh eyes to the investigation."

Bransome took a quick breath. "Who is the lead investigator on the Agnes Hahn case?"

"You are."

"And who is the lead detective in the Mendocino Police Department?"

"You."

"And who makes the assignments for the Mendocino Police Department?"

"You?"

"So who's going to get his ass out to motor pool, check out a vehicle, and get to work on traffic detail before his superior puts him to work cleaning out the latrines in the holding cells with a toothbrush?"

Pfeffer pivoted and stomped down the hall.

Bransome paced the room. He spoke to the walls. "She's already killing again. Maybe I can put Pfeffer undercover. His pecker seems to be expendable."

# CHAPTER 26

The GTO checked out of San Francisco via the Golden Gate Bridge and followed Highway 101 for a short distance beyond Sausalito to the Muir Beach exit. After a twisting drive, Lilin turned the car onto Highway 1, the famous and scenic Shoreline Highway, and growled past Stinson Beach.

The car was perfect. It was pure, raw power. The one thing she craved. If only she'd had some of that power when she'd been a little girl.

Lilin leaned over and opened the glove box. A manila envelope nearly fell out. She grabbed it and laid it on the seat next to her. The fool at the car lot kept all of his inventory records in hard copy. Not a single computer in the place. Everything of importance was in this one folder. Records of purchases were mixed with records of sales. And all license paperwork was in there, too. She'd burn it when she had a chance. It'd be difficult to trace the GTO, difficult for the authorities to know if a car was missing from the lot. She'd already switched the license plate with one from a mid-70s Pontiac Bonneville she'd found parked near the panhandle of Golden Gate Park.

She leaned forward from the seat back. A smirk dimpled her cheeks.

You there? Or are you still in a glow over your first big O?

*You didn't have to kill him.*

I did it for you.

*You did it for you.*

But admit it. You felt it right with me. Didn't you?

*You had an orgasm. With a dead man's penis.*

Is there a better kind? Of orgasm and of man? Lilin leaned back and chuckled. Come on. You know it was the most intense experience you've ever had.

*You had it.*

Okay. I'll play your game. But you're no longer pure and chaste. You've had a taste, and a taste leads to a meal, and then to a banquet. I'll go out on a limb here—with a wager. I bet you'll never have a sexual experience that intense as long as you're around.

She chuckled again.

But you better hurry if you want to take the bet.

This time, Lilin belly laughed.

No comment, huh? Just as well. I'm getting tired of showing you the ropes. I'm getting tired of you. From now on, everything is for me.

Near Woodville and the Point Reyes National Seashore, the GTO cut off Highway 1, and after a short jog, picked up Sir Francis Drake Boulevard. The southern reaches of Tomales Bay came into view. The car hugged the road along the western bank of the bay.

Lilin perked up when she passed the mileage sign: Inverness, 5 miles. Her arousal was a mixture of excitement and anger, like most things in her existence. Inverness was the site of her greatest triumph, the ultimate payback for her father. But it carried the memories of her worst experiences as well. She turned from the main road.

And it all happened right there. The cabin—former residence of Mr. Edward Hahn, father of twins Agnes and Lilin—was vacant. Two remnants of yellow police tape flapped from the porch posts like streamers. After a brief glance, she kept her gaze straight ahead. She didn't want to look at it any more. She wished it would be demolished, or burn to the ground. Her eyebrows rose. Fire could be arranged.

Almost a mile past the cabin, she slowed down and turned left on an unmarked road that was nearly overgrown by car-high scrubs. They scratched at the car as if they were trying to get to her. As if they didn't want her to get through. As if they knew what she had done. She pushed the accelerator, and the tires kicked up gravel and tree litter. The branch arms shook angry fists in her wake.

Bushes pulled at the doors of the car for what seemed like an eternity but abruptly thinned to a small open space. The road bent to the right, then in a left-hand arc that circled tall shrubs fronting a dense screen of trees. Behind the trees, a military green trailer came into view. It was a single wide, with an add-on extension that jutted out of its middle as if it were pregnant.

It had taken her a while to discover the place. To find out that Eddie Hahn owned this whole plot of land, from the cabin to this trailer, and that he had purchased the trailer years earlier at a military surplus sale. He must have known that someone would come after him someday.

This was where he'd hidden when the murders started. His abandoned cabin out on the road was the perfect misdirection. Who knew that his disappearance involved a short move to the far end of his property, where he was sequestered in a well-hidden government-issue trailer? That he was so close all along?

But she had found him, surprised him in his sleep, and brought him back to the cabin for her ultimate revenge. And now, as a final piece of irony, she could use his hidey-hole for the first stage of her own disappearance.

If anyone suspected she'd come to these parts, they'd check the cabin and close the report. Quite a gift from father to daughter. From such a hateful relationship.

The trailer door was unlocked, just as she'd left it on that night. She'd only been in the trailer that one time: on that final night. When she'd pulled the pathetic old man from his bed and literally dragged him down to the cabin. Back then, the trailer had electricity and water. Now it was dark and cold. But it was only a base of operation. A place to hunker down. To catch her breath. She had business in Santa Rosa. Just a few days and everything would be tied into a tidy bundle and sealed forever. Then she could leave the Bay Area, maybe leave California. She had a new name. New documents. She could move on. Start over. Whatever that meant.

The pregnant room was the living room, and it had a thick but worn carpet. She went into the back, to the bedroom, and pulled two blankets from the bed. On the carpet, the blankets would keep her warm. There was no way she could get in his bed. It was still early in the afternoon, and she'd be gone later in the night—when the cold would have a fanged bite.

She curled up on the rug and drifted off.

Agnes threw off the covers and crawled over to the

two bags that were dropped just inside the trailer door. She thrust her hand into the first, then the second. Near the bottom, she found the pen, but she couldn't find the writing tablet or the envelopes. Did Lilin find them? She pushed her hand around in the bag and found a dollar bill-sized receipt. She didn't care about the printed side.

She scribbled a quick note on the back of the receipt and folded it in half. Gripping the paper, she opened the door and stepped out into the warm afternoon sunshine.

There was a store a few miles back on the main road, and the physical activity in the fresh air would do her good. She could get an envelope and a stamp there. She could get writing paper, too, but she was in a hurry. She could just slip the receipt in the envelope, folded to show the writing, and drop it in the mailbox. The GTO would get her there faster, but she didn't want to alert Lilin, and she didn't want to have anything to do with that car.

She wound along the side road, but the bushes didn't bother her. They didn't grab at her as they had Lilin. Maybe they could tell the difference.

At the paved road, Agnes picked up her pace. The roads were clear in Inverness, but when it got dark, it was pure black. On this side of Tomales Bay, lights of civilization were few and far between, and the trees and shrubs shielded the moonlight as if it were toxic.

The cabin came into view, and Agnes noticed a sluggishness in her legs. Her muscles felt tight, as if she were carrying a heavy load. Memories flooded her consciousness. Lilin. Her Father. The Bad Room.

Her left calf went into a painful spasm, and she had to stop to stretch it. In her peripheral vision, she noticed the yellow tape streamers on the cabin porch. They curled at their tips, like fingers motioning to her, inviting her into the cabin for a visit.

She didn't remember much from the cabin that night. It was Lilin who had killed their father. But she'd seen the photos after her arrest. Now she didn't want to walk past the place. A feeling of panic boiled from her stomach and pinched her throat, constricting her breathing. In her mind, the door was opening. The door to Lilin.

She turned around and speed-walked back up the road. Despite the increase in activity, her breathing eased and her muscles loosened.

Then another wave of panic tightened her stomach. The note. How could she get it to Jason? She folded it into a tiny square and pushed it into the small change pocket of the Levi's she wore. Something would come to her. She'd find a way. She looked down at the jeans and cringed. They were all Lilin.

Agnes hated Levi's, particularly when they were this tight. But she didn't have a choice. Not anymore. Now she'd have to look for another opportunity. In the skin-tight Levi's. But her chances were dwindling. Lilin had said it. She had business in Santa Rosa. Agnes could think of only one thing that could be.

She turned up the bush-lined road and headed back to the trailer. She had to find a way to get word to Jason. There was time to think about it, but she'd have to be ready in an instant. Her opportunities were fading. Lilin was getting stronger. She patted the change pocket.

Be ready.

"Jason. Please. Be careful."

# CHAPTER 27

Lilin stirred at the first shiver of evening and bolted upright on the floor. She strained to see out the front room windows. The last light stained the western horizon a deep royal blue, but it blended to black within the height of a tree in the foreground. How long had she been asleep? It was midafternoon when she settled on the floor, but she didn't feel the relief of those hours. Something told her it was a restless time. But it wasn't worth worrying about that now. It was time to get moving.

The GTO was a willing partner, firing to a growl on the first turn of the ignition. It lurched on the road, eager to run the gauntlet of bushes and settle into a throaty purr on the paved roads. If the used car merchant really had turned back the odometer, the car must have been pampered, because the engine was as smooth as a broken-in youngster. There was no slip in the automatic transmission.

Lilin wanted to travel in silence, to savor the expectation of the upcoming adventure. She liked to let the anticipation and tension build slowly. Only at the end would it get intense. Her anger was channeled into sexual energy, so any slowly building event, sexual or not, could trigger a sensual explosion if the intensity of the anger ramped at the end. She had her father to thank for that.

*Why don't you just take off? You have what you need to disappear.*

Her foot pushed on the gas pedal and the GTO lurched. She tried to remain calm. It was too soon to get agitated.

*Please don't do this.*

She had to back off. The speedometer needle pointed past eighty. She brought the car down slowly, along with her breathing. If she concentrated on her respiration, she could get Agnes out of her mind.

*You can't.*

Then you'll come for the ride in a front row seat again. You know what we're going for, and there's nothing you can do about it.

*You don't have to do it this way.*

What do you suggest? Solve it with logic? Dealing with threats that way just doesn't work. Threats are neutralized by greater threats. Violence by greater violence.

*You're not doing this because of any threat.*

How would you know? You back away at the slightest difficulty, threat or not. Doing it your way, you'd have me caught by now. I'm still free, and I intend to stay that way. That's because I deal with threats; I don't sidestep them. All of your threats are still hanging around. None have gone away. I make mine go away.

*Was the student a threat to you? How about the car salesman?*

The GTO lurched again.

I needed the cars. I was threatened if I didn't have them.

*You know that's not why you killed them.*

What do you know about it?

*You know you didn't have to kill them to get the cars.*

Lilin spoke aloud, in a shout. "You want to know why I do what I do? When we were young, you just stood and watched. You didn't do anything to help me. You let yourself go away. I couldn't go away. I had to be there. And this is what I got for it." The speedometer swept passed ninety. She backed off the pedal and breathed deeply.

*You know the truth about that, too.*

There's nothing I can do about it now. All I know is that I have to deal with everything I see as a threat.

*Why are you going out of your way looking for one tonight?*

You know why. This person is dangerous.

*You only think so.*

I know so. I've got news for you. What I deal with

tonight is only secondary to my major threat. But this is the only way to deal with that primary threat right now. Sometimes a challenge can't be dealt with directly.

*You're still dodging the truth. You do it for the thrill. The threat is your way of rationalizing it. You do it because it makes you feel good, emotionally and physically. Nothing else.*

I don't see a problem in mixing business with pleasure. And you're right about that one thing. You know how good it feels to finally yank a wood splinter from your finger. It's almost worth the pain and irritation of the original injury. To me, it's more than worth it. The pain is just an expense. Overhead. No, not overhead. More like an investment. The payoff is everything—and the more it festers, the greater the payoff. Do you know how long my festering has been going on?

*You react that way because you're weak.*

Lilin's fist crashed down on the steering wheel, and the GTO swerved. She corrected and hit the accelerator, pushing her back into the seat. Her voice filled the car. "That's why I'm going to Santa Rosa tonight. I have to deal with the person who makes you feel this way. Because you are the threat to me. It's you I have to defeat." She let off the accelerator.

"That's why you're going to have your hand on the razor along with me tonight. You're going to watch it all. Experience it all. Do it all. Feel it all. Especially the final pleasure. An important part of you will die tonight, at your own hands. And that territory will be mine. I'm taking you apart piece by piece, and there's nothing you can do about it."

Lilin turned off Highway 101 and pulled into the parking lot of a twenty-four-hour supermarket. In the back, a flower display had large, mixed bouquets for $7.95 plus tax. She grabbed one and hurried to the checkout counter, thrusting a ten-dollar bill in the cashier's hand. By the time the change rolled down the automatic dispenser and into the tray, she was already gone.

Lilin weaved the car along the surface streets of Santa Rosa. She knew the way. She'd followed Jason around before Agnes's arrest.

The GTO pulled into the complex, and she slipped it into a parking space between two generic SUVs. It was late—most people would be in for the night. No foot traffic.

The walk to the front door started slowly, but she picked up the pace as she neared the welcome mat. Her pulse raced, but nowhere near her red line. That would come later.

Holding the flowers high, in front of her face, she pushed the doorbell button. She expected caution, a telltale blink of light from the peephole viewer. But the door opened without the squeak of hesitation. She pushed the flowers forward a little, still in front of her face, and took a small step. The threshold was only inches from her toes.

"Yes? Can I help you?"

Lilin lowered the flowers in a quick swipe and pushed her way into the entryway, knocking April Leahy backward.

The element of surprise has a strange effect on the surprised.

April's eyes bulged and her mouth gaped, but she made no sound. Lilin kicked the door shut and continued pushing April into the living room. The flowers fell to the floor.

"Sit down and shut up, and nothing will happen to you."

*You lie.*

April sat. Her mouth moved, but no words came out.

Lilin sat on the coffee table, directly in front of April. Her knees forced April's legs apart slightly. "You need to do me a favor tonight."

April found her voice, but it was tentative. "Agnes?"

Lilin slapped her knees into April's inner thighs. "No! Not Agnes. Guess again."

"Agnes, what's going on? You need to turn yourself in. You've messed up all the progress we made."

A cackle-like laugh accompanied Lilin's second knee slap. If Dr. Leahy was trying to sound professional, she'd failed. She sounded scared. "If you made so much progress, then why am I here instead of in Imola? And why is it me instead of Agnes?"

April's lips moved again, but again no sound came out. Her eyes watered.

*She can help you.*

Lilin leaned forward. "Do you want to know about your progress? The latest killings—Agnes did them with me. She was there. She helped. And she enjoyed herself. With me."

April's hands shook in her lap. "Agnes? Why are you saying this? Why are you pretending to be Lilin? Lilin is dead. She died when you were four years old."

"I didn't die. I'm here. Right now. Agnes is the one who's gone."

Tears released onto April's cheeks. "What do you want from me? You need to turn yourself in. I can help you."

Lilin rested her hands on April's knees. "I want you to admit that you failed. I was there the whole time you talked to Agnes. You kept talking about breakthroughs, but your breakthroughs were with me. And you didn't even know it." She squeezed April's knees. "Tell me you failed. Tell Agnes you failed. You didn't make Agnes stronger. You made me stronger. Tell her that. Tell her."

April took a deep breath. "Agnes? Remember what you did to Stuart the Stud? He tried to intimidate you. You gave it back to him. That's what you need to do now—"

The slap knocked April over onto the couch cushions.

She rose slowly. "Agnes. Don't be intimidated."

Lilin reached in her purse.

*No. You're not going to do that.*

Lilin hesitated, but her hand stayed in the purse.

April's eyes fell to the purse. "You can do it, Agnes."

*Take your hand out of the purse.*

Lilin's hand eased back but stayed close.

April rubbed her jaw and grimaced. "People who intimidate are weak. You're strong, Agnes."

Lilin looked into April's eyes. "Tell her that you failed."

*She didn't fail. It's you who will fail. You're the weak one.*

Lilin brought her hand back up to April's knee. She spoke, but not to April. "Weak? Where have you been the past few days? What did you see? Was that weakness, what happened to those men? The predator doesn't survive if it's weaker than the prey."

April sat still. Her eyes stayed on Lilin's hands.

*You're not a predator. You're just a run-of-the-mill, cowardly murderer. You seduce. You surprise. But you're just a coward.*

"I'll show you who's a coward." Lilin reached for the purse again.

April flinched backward.

*No. I won't let you. Not this time.*

"You can't stop me."

*Yes. I can.*

Lilin rummaged in the purse.

*I'm in charge now. Take your hand out of the purse.*

April inched back and pulled one leg up on the couch cushion, hugging it to her chest.

Lilin pulled her hand up and slid it behind her knee. "You can't stop me."

*I just did. Let her get up. She didn't fail. You did. You underestimated her. You underestimated me. It's over now. Let her get up.*

Lilin leaned back a little. She nodded at April. "You can get up."

April moved slowly. She lifted her leg across Lilin's knees and pushed herself from the seat back. She scooted over and stood.

Lilin didn't move, but her eyes locked onto April's eyes. *Now let her walk away.*

Lilin nodded for April to move away.

April took a step and turned to face Lilin. "Thank you, Agnes. You're much stronger than Lilin."

A snarl puckered Lilin's upper lip, and she lunged. The stun gun she held behind her knee dug into April's rib cage and three hundred thousand volts surged into April's body. She went rigid and collapsed on the rug. Lilin fell to her knees and leaned over her convulsing victim.

*No. Don't.*

Too late. She's mine now. No. Ours.

*I won't let you.*

Okay. Then you'll have to do it.

Lilin's hand went to her purse again and came out with the razor. She unfolded it.

*You can't. I won't let you.*

You're right. You're the strong one.

*Put the razor down.*

Lilin put the razor on the coffee table.

*Move back away from her.*

Lilin stood and moved back a step. April still twitched.

*Now we're going to make a phone call.*

Lilin laughed. She reached down and picked up the razor.

*You're not going to kill her. I'm in charge now.*

You're right. I won't kill her.

*Then put the razor down.*

Lilin held the razor out at arm's length.

You're going to do it.

*You can't make me do that.*

Lilin's lips tightened into a narrow grin.

Yes. I can. Who do you think she's been seeing since you went into Imola? Who do you think she's been fucking? Right here in this apartment. Your precious Jason.

*I won't.*

You feel it, don't you? That's anger. It's not much now, but it can build. It can make you do things you didn't think you could do. You feel it.

*No.*

Lilin sat down on the arm of the couch.

I'll bet she fucked him right here on this couch. Her head was probably right here on this arm. Moaning. She probably told him how much she loved him.

*No.*

And right over there, in front of the fireplace. She fucked him right there, too.

*No!*

Now you feel it. You can feel the power. It's getting stronger. It's making you strong.

Lilin unbuttoned her blouse with her free hand and slipped it from her shoulders. Here's the razor, and here's the shirt you can hold over the incision. Just like I showed you. You're going to do it. Because she's fucking the man you love.

*You can't . . . make . . . me.*

Lilin held out the razor.

She pulled the razor across April's neck and pushed the shirt behind it. April's twitching stopped, and her breathing went shallow.

Good girl. You did it. You were in charge through it all.

Silence.

Nothing to say? You're not done yet. You still have the best part to go. I'll just watch.

She lowered her Levi's and panties to her ankles.

Not a man, you say? Then you'll break new ground. I'll leave it to you. You can find a way, but be quick. While your pulse is still up.

She bent and pulled on April's right index finger. She pushed the razor to the bone and then worked it through the joint. She held the digit up in front of her face.

You know what to do now. Don't worry. You don't have to say anything. That's right. You know what to do.

The intensity of the experience left her sprawled on the couch, incapacitated. For how long? She glanced at the clock on the far wall. Good. Probably only five minutes. She stood and raised her panties but stepped out of the Levi's and walked down the hall to the bedroom. The closet was filled with clothes, all close enough in size. She picked out a pair of casual pants and slipped them on. Same with a matching blouse. She pulled three more outfits from hangers—nothing too businesslike. She spotted a pair of jeans and yanked them down as well. Not Levi's, but they'd do.

The GTO backed up with a low growl and upped the volume as it pulled out of the parking lot.

Say something.

*You're not as strong as you think you are.*

You're right. I couldn't kill her. But I was strong

enough to get you to do it. You killed her. You let your anger take charge. For once, you did something that went against logic. It was pure emotion. And because of that, you killed the one person who could have helped you. How does that make you feel?

Silence.

No comment? You must be tired. I won't drive back to Inverness tonight. There's a motel just around the corner. I want you to stay in town tonight. Close to where you took charge. Close to where you murdered Dr. April Leahy.

She laughed.

# CHAPTER 28

Agnes rose up on the bed and threw open the covers. She wore a blouse and panties, nothing else. Crumpled pants lay on the floor, next to a pair of shoes. She slipped them all on and crept to the motel room door. It opened with a clunk. Fortunately, the hinges were silent.

A light fog confused her senses and her internal compass, so she picked a direction at random and started walking. A convenience store or gas station couldn't be too far away.

A small mom-and-pop store appeared after seven blocks, an invigorating stroll in the misty night air. Her pace picked up when she spotted the desired oddity at the far end of the parking lot: a phone booth. In this area, like others, the proliferation of cellular phone usage had shoved public phones onto the endangered list, but the usual cries for preservation hadn't followed. If any-thing, the condition of the few remaining booths seemed to have deteriorated exponentially.

Hopefully, the phone was functional, and a reasonable remnant of the phone book still hung on the hinged clip. She was lucky on both counts.

The page with the listing for the Santa Rosa Press Democrat was torn halfway down, but the main switch-board number was there. She pressed in the coins and punched in the sequence of numbers.

The receptionist was polite for the late hour. Agnes visualized her with a television tuned to cable's twenty-four-hour soap opera station.

"I can't give you his number. It's policy."

Agnes leaned against the glass. "It's really important."

"I can't give it to you. But I can connect you." She paused. "Do you want me to do that?"

Three rude returns chugged through Agnes's mind before she sighed and settled for civil. "Yes, please."

A series of clicks preceded a painful pause. Finally, the earpiece gave a loud whine, a click, and a ring. Two, three, four rings. Five. She had the rhythm, so she grimaced for the sixth when another click interrupted.

"Hello?"

"Jason. It's Agnes."

Silence.

"Jason, it's me. Please. I need your help."

"Is this some kind of trick?"

"No. I need you."

A pause. "Okay. What did I give you on my last visit to Imola?"

"A stuffed puppy. It was the same color as the dog you gave me before."

"Agnes. Where are you?"

"I'm in a phone booth. Can you come?"

"Where? In San Francisco?"

"No. In Santa Rosa."

The silence confused her. Why wasn't he saying anything? "Jason?"

"Sorry. I'm just crossing the Golden Gate. This is my cell phone. I have to be at the Chronicle in fifteen minutes. They've got a story that's going to go well into tomorrow, and I have to take it."

"Please. You don't understand. It's all happening again. I need you."

Silence again.

"Jason?"

"I'm here. I want to come. I really do. But this is an inside tip job. The TV people don't know about it yet. If I don't get there fast, I can kiss my new job with the Chronicle goodbye. If it was anything else, I'd shine it and be on my way. Can you hold off until the day after tomorrow?"

"Can't you come sooner?"

"I really want to, but I can't. Where are you staying?"

"I don't know where I'll be day after tomorrow."

"Tell you what. I'll meet you in downtown Santa Rosa, at Railroad Square. There's a bronze statue of Charlie Brown and Snoopy. Can you be there at noon?"

"You can't come sooner? I need you."

A pause. "I really want to be there, but I can't. If you'd called about fifteen minutes earlier, I could have, but my editor just got hold of me. I'm all they have. Can you meet me? Where and when I said?"

Tears filled her eyes, clouding her vision. "I'll try."

"Agnes, if you're in trouble, you can call Dr. Leahy. I have her number in my wallet. Do you want me to give it to you?"

"No!" She straightened up in the booth. A familiar feeling crept up her spine.

"Don't be like that. She can help you. You can stay with her until I get back in town."

Agnes looked in both directions and burst into tears. The breathlessness of a panic attack emptied the phone booth of air.

"You have the time and place, right?"

She hunched over, straining to breathe.

"Agnes?"

The next breath came without resistance. She straightened up and pulled it in to capacity. Everything looked crisp, clear. A deep growl-like rumble squeezed through her lips, terminating in a single chuckle.

"Day after tomorrow. Charlie Brown and Snoopy statue. Railroad Square. Got it?"

She laughed a throaty laugh. "Oh, yeah. She got it."

Click.

Jason slammed his fist into the steering wheel. He wasn't lying about the job, but it twisted his gut to put Agnes off like that. He'd promised Bransome he'd set up a meeting in a public place if Agnes ever contacted him. But to hear her voice, hear her say she needed him. It cut into him as deeply as if Lilin's razor had found its mark. He had to do it, though. It was the only way. He knew he could get Agnes to turn herself in, but what if it was Lilin instead of Agnes? Could he handle Lilin by himself, on her turf? The meeting was the best way. But Agnes needed him now . . .

Something about the conversation bothered him, though. He wasn't sure what it was until he tried to replay it in his mind. It was something right at the end. What did she say when he asked if she understood about the meeting? It sounded like she said, "Yeah. She got it." She.

# CHAPTER 29

Lilin opened the door to the motel room and walked over to the bed. Fluffing the pillows, she stacked them against the headboard and fell against them, grabbing the television remote on the way down.

I don't know how you got away from me, but I'm going to make sure you don't do it again. I'm almost done here, and I don't need anymore of your interference.

*Just leave.*

I have two more loose ends to take care of. It's funny. I only had one until that call. I wasn't going to do anything to your Jason. But don't you realize he just set a trap for me? And for you?

*He only wants the best. He's one of the good ones.*

When are you going to realize that you'll never do any better than me? What were you before I came around?  Did you have a man?  Any men?  Had you even had any kind of sex?

*Is sex everything to you?*

No.  Sex is nice, but I can go way beyond nice.  And I can take you with me.  You got a taste of it.  It can be even better.  No man can give you that.  Not unless you do it my way.  That's the only way I can be satisfied by a man like I need to be satisfied.

*By inflicting pain?  By killing?*

Father was a good teacher.  Pain and sex are a powerful combination.  Sex needs an emotional base, or it's just rubbing.  My way, I don't have to worry about any of the baggage that comes with anything more than a one-time event.  Once you realize that, you won't question me anymore.  We can feel the power together.  Anytime we want to.

*If there's no baggage, then why are you on the run?  Why do you need a new identity?  Why do you need to clean up loose ends?*

Shut up.  You turned away from me before.  You wouldn't help.  You left me alone with Father.  And you know what he did.  What he taught me.  You're not going to turn away from me again.  I'm here because of you.  I am what I am because of you.  You owe me.

*You don't understand.  I was a little girl.*

I understand everything now.  I understand what I have to do to get you to unite with me.  To stop questioning me.  You have to go away.  Forever.  And it's happening.  That's why the loose ends aren't merely loose ends. They're more. And you just delivered the most important one to me. And to think I was going to let him go.

*What are you going to do to Jason?*

Don't you know?

*What you want to do? Yes. How you'll do it? No.*

That's because I haven't given it any thought yet. I have to deal with the other one right now. He's not much more than a loose end, but I need to be thorough. Besides, every time I have a man, you have him with me. And you and I become closer to one. A few more and you'll feel the same itch I feel. You'll have the same needs. Then we will unite, and you'll be gone. Forever.

*You kill for the thrill. That won't ever be acceptable. Don't even pretend it's to be thorough.*

Not this discussion again. Okay. I'll humor you. You're right. My juices are near a boil. I have a target. Someone I dealt with earlier. Someone who could talk. Someone who'll give me what I want right now.

*Who are you after?*

You don't know?

*No.*

You'll find out soon. After that, I'll have to find a way to get to your Jason. He's working with the police. I can feel it. He won't be alone at the Snoopy statue. But he will be surprised. I have an idea or two, but I have to think them through. You'll be a good girl. Won't you?

# CHAPTER 30

Jason dialed his cell phone and had to wait only two rings. Detective Bransome's gravelly voice blasted through the earpiece. Jason wondered why some people thought they had to shout into a phone.

"It's Jason. I just talked to Agnes—"

"Agnes or Lilin?"

"It was Agnes."

Bransome's voice faded and then boomed again. "Are you sure?"

"Yes. Does it matter?"

"Lilin might see through it. Agnes wouldn't."

"It was Agnes."

"Good. Did you arrange something?"

Jason switched the phone to his other ear. "I told her to meet me in downtown Santa Rosa. The day after tomorrow."

"Where in Santa Rosa?"

"Railroad Square—"

"Shit," Bransome said. "Where in Railroad Square?"

"Next to the Charlie Brown and—"

"Shit."

Jason waited, but nothing followed the exclamation. "I guess I don't have to ask if you know the place. What's wrong with it?"

"God damn it, it's full of tourists. Easy for a person to mingle, get lost. And a surprise apprehension is tough."

Jason raised his voice to match Bransome's. "You didn't give me any instructions. No suggestions. I wanted someplace that was easy to find. Easy to remember." And someplace safe. With lots of people around.

"We'll have to deal with it. What time?"

"Noon."

"Shit. Shit. Shit."

"What did you want? Midnight?"

"Everyone's out at noon, milling around, eating lunch. Even the locals. You couldn't have found a busier time."

"Won't that make it harder for her to spot any of you? Harder to blow the cover?"

"I don't blow covers. I swear, Powers. If we pull this off, you're going to owe me one hell of a dinner."

Jason nodded, as if Bransome could see him. "I know a McDonald's with an awesome play area."

"They better serve a good T-bone—in a man's size."

Jason thought he heard a chuckle. "So how will it come down? What should I do?"

"There are three possibilities I can see. One, she'll show and walk right up to you. Two, she won't show. In that case, she could just blow you off or stay somewhere in the distance where she can watch you. Three, she could get someone else to come up to you and give you a message."

"Someone else?"

"A stranger. She's a sneaky one, particularly if she's in the Lilin mode. I'm sure she'll either no-show or get someone to talk to you. Probably stand back and watch in either case."

"So what should I do if someone else comes up to me?"

"Do you have a hat you normally wear? Something Agnes may have seen?"

"She's seen me in a Giants baseball hat."

"Good. Wear that. If someone else comes up and gives you a message, take the hat off with your right hand and wipe your forehead with your right forearm. That'll be easy to see."

"Then what?"

"Nothing for you. You just stay put. We'll go in the search mode—everywhere within view."

Jason laughed. "What will you have? An army?"

Bransome's voice rose. "We'll have every available

person from three counties, short of the National Guard. I'd have them as well, but you didn't give me enough notice. We'll have every street and alley covered and re-covered."

"And how will you hide the army of officers? She'll have to walk by at least one of your men."

"We'll all be in plainclothes. Tourist clothes. Business clothes. College student clothes. Maybe even a hooker or two thrown in. You won't know who's who, so how could she?"

"Okay. What if she doesn't show and you don't find her anywhere? Do we all just go home, pop some corn, and put on the TV?"

Bransome snickered. "Pop some extra, because we'll have a tail on you. If she hangs back and follows you when you leave, we'll be right there. So just go straight home. Don't pass Go. Don't collect two hundred dollars."

Jason thought for a few seconds. "If she does show, will I be in any danger? If it's Lilin, she could slice and run."

Bransome laughed so loud the phone blanked for a moment. "I suggest you wear a turtleneck."

"I'm serious. How quickly will you get to me if I need help?"

"We'll have the necessary medical backup. They'll be close enough to save half of your blood."

"Gee. I feel better already. I'm serious. Should I take some protection?"

"You plan to screw her in front of the Snoopy statue?

A rubber won't do much good there." Bransome lost it. His laughs eventually faded in volume.

Jason huffed. "God damn. What's in your coffee? You just went from 'shit-shit-shit' to jokes and hysterical laughter in less than a minute."

"I'm on a high right now. I'm excited about the job, and about covering all bases. I love challenges like this. You won't want to talk to me the morning of the job. My wife stays away when I'm like this."

"I don't know if that's comforting or not. If I hadn't worked with you in Mendocino, I'd back out right here and now."

"Thanks for the vote of confidence. Look. If she's in the Lilin mode, you probably won't even see her. If she's Agnes, we'll get to her before she can finish the hug she'll give you."

"A hug." Jason nearly dropped his phone. A Lilin hug could create all sorts of problems, none with a good outcome.

# CHAPTER 31

Charlie Brown was four feet tall, and Snoopy stood to his chin. A two-foot pedestal brought Charlie's bronze, bowling-ball head to Jason's height. Jason turned away and leaned against the fence that circled the sculpture. The surrounding grass lot gave good visibility in all directions.

Railroad Square was close to the downtown off-ramps of the elevated stretch of Highway 101, which shadowed the dam-like wall of nearby Plaza Mall. Just up the road in a quarter-turn direction was Courthouse Square.

Jason scanned the adjacent parking lot, then spun around to glimpse the brick and stone façades of the businesses that lined the quaint streets, where diagonal parking both increased the packing of cars and added to the antique feel of the old town. This part of downtown was his favorite, even though the 12 percent business vacancy rate hadn't declined significantly through the last twenty years of commissions, urban renewal studies, and unfunded action plans. And despite an infusion of trendy restaurants and shops, the stereotypical one-coffee-shop-per-square-half-mile, and the ubiquitous brew pub, pedestrian traffic dried up every night after the dinner rush, sinking the area into an urban coma. The great debate was over the culprit, argued in city council chambers as anything from parking problems, to the mall and adjacent Marketplace, to the roving bands of teens who migrated between Railroad Square and Courthouse Square looking for ways to satiate their group-wide attention deficit disorders that always seemed to emerge from the congregation of three or more normal juveniles.

On this weekday at noon, the area around Railroad Square was lively. Elderly tourists arrived in buses and General Motors sedans. The statue seemed to slow their sightseeing in favor of nostalgic recollections of how the old days carried a simpler tune. Local businessmen and businesswomen took advantage of the warm weather to grab a bite or to conduct cell phone business on a park bench or patch of dry grass.

Jason chose this area of downtown, and the Snoopy statue, for the openness and the relative quiet. The dull hum of tires on the elevated 101 was muffled and quickly ignored, like the buzz of fluorescent lights in a

Walgreen's drugstore. The homeless preferred the greater expanse of Courthouse Square, so only the odd derelict stopped to pay respects to Snoopy and his master. It was the perfect place for a clandestine meeting, and for a stake-out and ambush.

The mall was too public for the meeting and was without good escape routes. Jason thought it would be too claustrophobic for Lilin. Courthouse Square was too busy and too large. And the deafening, staccato thumping of tires on the faux cobblestone roadway that bisected the park was best tolerated by sensory-dull drunks and groups of young men with dueling boom boxes.

Jason paced in front of the statue, then stopped and leaned against the short fence. His wristwatch read 11:58. If Agnes was out there, would she show up? Probably. If it was Lilin? Probably not. At least not without a disguise.

He spun around and scanned a group of elderly tourists and paused to inspect each of the women, looking for any inconsistency of appearance. It wouldn't be a wig. The hairstyles of most elderly women looked too much like mediocre wigs overdone with wind-resistant curls. And anything could be hidden in the clothing. Including a razor. Jason shivered as he walked to the side of the octagonal fence opposite the herd of picture takers.

He zeroed in on the women's legs, the ankles, and he had to walk back around the fence to get a good view. It would be hard to hide Lilin's shapely ankles. A few steps onto the grass and his pulse picked up to a mid-workout pace. The fence, like Linus's blanket, was a comfort, but more. It was Jason's station in a game of espionage. His safe house. As long as he stayed near it, his people were close, watching.

A step back toward the statue, and a jogger nearly banged into him. She wore a seafoam green, velour running outfit with matching headband. Too much for a warm day like today. And she wasn't drenched in sweat. Probably one of Bransome's recruits. If so, it was a terrible disguise—too unique for more than a single pass through the square.

Now Jason's attention, and imagination, turned to the good guys. Who were the cops? The two men in business suits who sat on a bench at the far end of the grass? One talked nonstop on a cell phone while the other stabbed at the keypad of a Blackberry. The hippie girl next to a small throw rug covered with rows of silver bracelets and earrings? She danced to imaginary music. Was Lilin standing off somewhere, watching, playing the same game of who-are-the-cops?

The warmth of the afternoon burst through Jason's clothing like a soaker hose. Without shade, the sun turned up the thermostat a good ten degrees. His Levi's felt sticky, and a vertical line of sweat stuck his shirt to his back along the length of his spine. On breeze-less days like this, the downtown air had a whiff of staleness. It was the kind of smell that drove most residents west, to the ocean beaches.

The tickle of sweat bubbles ringed the headband of his San Francisco Giants baseball hat. He was a true fan: the hat was fitted, 7 ¼, not one of the generic ones with the adjustable strap in the back. He wanted to lift the hat and wipe his brow with his forearm, like Barry Bonds taking a curtain call from the dugout after blasting a fastball to a splash-down in McCovey Cove. But that was his signal to Bransome's crew. No matter how much the black hat made him sweat, he had to leave it in place until a contact was made. He forced his mind back to the Giants. Like many local fans, he had mixed feelings about Barry's departure. Glad he was gone because of his personality, but sorry to see such talent lost to baseball, chemical enhancement or not.

A bum swaggered toward the statue, his filthy jeans topped with a tattered sport coat, opened to show the front of a T-shirt that had probably been white at one time. Jason's eyes shot to the man's fingernails. The true test. They were long and stained brown, ringed in black like someone had traced their outlines with an eyeliner pen. Definitely not a cop. It was easy to grease the hair, and to make a long beard look stringy. But there was no way to fake the fingernails.

The man had a thick stack of papers folded over his

left forearm. The large photo on the top sheet was of four young men in the non-posed pose of a rock band publicity shot.

The man zigzagged through the throng of people, licking the pad of his right index finger before peeling off the top sheet and shoving it toward the hand of the next person he approached. Every one of his victims hesitated, then grasped the sheet in a thumb-and-forefinger vice. Most swiveled their heads, apparently looking for the nearest trash bin, before looking at what was printed on the leaflet.

The man approached. A bead of Jason's sweat turned into a gusher, rolling down his forehead, around his eyebrow, and onto his cheek. He watched the man's forefinger brush his tongue and grip the corner of another sheet.

The man adjusted the stack of sheets on his forearm before thrusting a sheet in Jason's direction. Not wanting to insult the fellow, Jason accepted the flyer, but dropped his hand to his side without a glance at the paper. The local venue for up-and-coming rock bands, one step up from the garage, was four blocks from the new old downtown, in a direction that changed from quaint to scary within two of the four blocks.

The old man barely moved past before Jason spotted the tastefully decorated garbage can, fifteen feet off to his right. He fell into a single-file line of six tourists, all apparently intent on recycling the derelict's offering. His turn at the receptacle, Jason dropped the sheet without crumpling it, and watched it flutter through the narrow opening.

Two large words, alone in the middle of the clean white sheet, caught his attention. There was no picture, as there had been on all of the other flyers. He jammed his arm down into the bin and grasped for the paper. His hand clamped on several sheets as something wet coated the back of his wrist. He yanked his hand upward and held the handful of papers at arm's length. The top piece had the photo of the band, as did the bottom three. He spread them in his fingers like cards in a poker hand. The second sheet was nearly blank except for something printed in large font, probably 64-point, in the middle of the page.

Jason returned the extra flyers to the can with a disgusted wrist-flip. He grabbed the remaining sheet, one hand on the top, the other on the bottom, as if he was trying to stretch it lengthwise. Two words were perfectly centered on the sheet. "Nice Try."

His right hand shot to the brim of his hat and pulled it straight upward at full arm's length. He didn't bother to mop his brow. Still gripping the sheet in his left hand, he extended the arm with a straight index finger, pointing in the direction of the bum. The old man was halfway down the block, still passing out leaflets to everyone he passed on the sidewalk.

Out of the corner of his eye, Jason saw the two

suited men jump from the park bench and run in his direction. When they came close, he shouted. "The old man. Passing out papers."

The two suits set out in a sprint and Jason fell in, half a dozen steps behind them.

The old man seemed oblivious to the approach of the two men, and he hardly flinched as they each grabbed an arm and dragged him around the street corner. The flyers fell from his arm and landed in a fanned stack, unfettered but stationary in the motionless air.

Jason rounded the corner to find the old man pinned to the brick wall of a corner business. One of the two men shouted at the man, though Jason couldn't tell which one. He panted up to the trio and drew a stern look from the man holding the bum's left arm. "We'll handle this," the suited man said.

Jason didn't pull back. "It was my ass out there. I'm going to find out what's going on."

The suits turned back to the old man.

"Where did you get the flyers? Who told you to pass them out?"

The old man's eyes were wide, and a thin line of spittle fell from his lips as he mouthed silent words. He was trembling from head to foot.

One of the suits leaned close. "Who gave you the flyers?" He pulled back as soon as the words were out.

"S-s-some wo-woman. G-gave me tw-twenty bucks."

"Where is she?"

The old man looked down at the ground as his knees buckled. He dipped, but the two men pulled him back up by his arms. The man's eyes rolled upward, and his head flopped forward. He slumped, limp, in the grips of the two suits. They gently lowered him to the ground.

"Great," the man on the left said.

"Is he breathing?" said the other.

"I'm not giving him mouth-to-mouth."

The man stirred, let out a burp, and went limp again.

The suit with the cell phone brought the phone up to his lips. "Got a problem here. Send a meat wagon. On Third, just off Wilson. And come up the back way. No lights or siren. She's around somewhere, but he didn't say where."

Jason spun around out of reflex, looking for Lilin, even though he knew she wouldn't be on this near-vacant side street. His head went light, and he prayed he wouldn't crumple to the pavement like the old derelict.

One of the suits punched Jason's upper arm. "We've got this now. You need to get back to the statue." He pushed Jason toward the street corner. The second suit was already gone.

Jason rounded the corner, but his stride was slow, shuffling. A memory swirled. When he had reached his elementary school years, his father had graduated from using his hand for delivering spankings to using a stick: a half-inch-thick piece of pine with a crudely notched handle. It was kept in the broom closet just off the kitchen, and his father heaped a psychological swat onto the whipping by making Jason fetch the paddle. The spanking had always been delivered in the privacy of his bedroom, and it was almost a relief after the agonizing thirty-foot walk to the broom closet and back. Dead man walking.

Jason felt the same dread, and anticipation, as he shuffled back toward Snoopy and Charlie. The chatter of people on the sidewalk was loud, but tangled into the "wah-wah" sounds of Charlie Brown's teacher. It had to be Lilin. But where was she? And where were Bransome's men? Were the two suits the only ones? He scanned the area but couldn't find the suit with the Blackberry. He hoped to see the jogger in the seafoam sweat suit, or anyone else who looked like an undercover cop.

He paused at the corner across from the statue and was surrounded by a half dozen close-standing tourists. A wave of panic shot through his spine. He pushed his way to the edge of the group and took an additional step to the side. A car cleared the intersection, and the group moved like a herd of sheep. Safety in numbers and danger in a crowd. The contradiction had barely entered Jason's mind when he noticed his legs were moving, trailing the gaggle into the street.

Halfway across, the tourists scattered, their formation

perforated by a group of young teens weaving through, hurrying in the opposite direction. Jason had to sidestep to avoid a head-on collision. He stopped and turned to watch the teens disappear around the corner.

A car horn spun him back around. He was three-quarters of the way across the street and directly in front of an SUV grill. Two steps and he stopped again. An itch came from his left pinky finger. As soon as it registered, the itch turned to a burn, like it was being prodded with a soldering iron. He pulled his hand upward in time to see a stream of blood produce a steady drip from the fingernail. A red line ran across the width of the finger. It was thin, straight. A razor cut?

Another honk. A car whizzed past in the opposite lane. Jason hurried to the corner and spun around, trying to get sight of her. The SUV squealed its tires through the intersection, temporarily obliterating his view.

His right hand dove into his back pocket and shook the handkerchief open as he pulled it to his left hand. Wrapping it tightly around the finger, he returned his gaze to the pedestrians streaming away on the far side of the intersection.

He rose to tiptoes to get a better glimpse, but the crowd seemed to have doubled. He couldn't see very far in a straight line, and Lilin was short—no more than five foot six.

His eyes flicked left, down the side street, and a hunching figure caught his attention. The right size, the culprit was overdressed for the weather: a long trench coat, at least three sizes too large, hung nearly to the ankles. The coat's collar was upturned. A fedora-like hat was pulled low over the ears, pasting shoulder-length hair to the side of an obscured face.

The traffic had increased, so Jason ran down his side of the street parallel to the path of the mysterious figure. He pulled even at the next intersection and cupped his hands around his mouth. "Hey, you. Stop."

He waited for a car to pass and sprinted across the street short of the intersection.

The hunched figure picked up its pace to the fastest walk this side of a trot and rounded the corner, heading off away from Jason. The road cut in to form a loading zone behind one of the buildings, and the stranger swept in, out of Jason's sight.

Jason rounded the corner to view an empty courtyard. A dumpster to the right stood against a tall brick wall. To the left, nothing but a bare wall and several steel doors. None were open.

He rounded the edge of the dumpster and halted, holding his breath despite the need for oxygen from the run. The small figure crouched, wedged in the corner formed by the dumpster and the brick wall. One hand was held up, covering the face.

Jason pulled a deep breath and blew it out, and then let his breathing free-run. He approached the figure.

"Lilin?"

The person tried to push into the wall.

"Agnes?"

Muscles relaxed and the person's arm lowered, revealing a thick growth of at least a week's worth of whiskers. The man eyed Jason and dropped his eyes. His voice was gravelly. "Don't take me."

"What?" Jason couldn't move. He wanted to run back to look for Lilin, but his legs wouldn't work.

"Don't take me back to the spaceship. I don't know nothing."

"What are you talking about?"

"Don't hurt me no more. I don't know nothing."

Jason stepped back, and the man pushed against the wall again. "I'm not going to hurt you. I thought you were someone else."

The man relaxed.

Jason hurried back around the dumpster and plodded back toward the statue. His cell phone rang. Bransome's voice boomed like he was inches away.

"Where the hell are you? What's going on?"

Jason held the phone six inches from his ear. "I'm coming back to the statue." He decided not to tell Bransome about the cut.

"Don't bother. All hell's broke loose. I'm calling it off."

Jason stopped. "What do you want me to do?"

A heavy exhalation rang from the phone. "I don't

give a damn. Go home. This whole thing's gone to shit."

The phone clicked.

Go home? Right. Lilin was on the loose with a razor, and he was supposed to go home. His thoughts were interrupted by the treble ring of his voice mail. Jason punched a couple of buttons and mumbled to the phone. "The Chronicle. Must have called when I was talking to Bransome."

He punched two more buttons, then hit the one marked "speaker."

"Jason? It's Mary. Where are you? Mr. Franzione wants you to get to the city right away. He's got an exclusive, a terrorist on his way from Oakland. Mr. Franzione's going to call you in fifteen minutes to give you the details. He said you'd better be in your car."

Jason clicked the message off and exhaled. He'd never been so happy to get an emergency assignment. He turned toward Plaza Mall, where he'd parked the Volvo.

The handkerchief was nearly soaked through with blood, so he unwrapped it and peered at the injury. The smooth edges of the slice pulled apart showing pink flesh, now barely oozing. He shook his head. "Needs stitches." He rewrapped the handkerchief, not so tight this time, and started walking.

"No time right now," he said to the sidewalk. The first aid kit in the trunk of the Volvo had a pack of butterfly bandages. That would have to do.

# CHAPTER 32

Lilin thought morning would never come. She was still energized from her meeting with Jason even though it had only been a brief slice of time. Her disguise wasn't much: a baseball hat, sunglasses, and oversized, dowdy clothes. She had slipped past him in the middle of the street amongst a gaggle of marauding youngsters. Her second message had been delivered with a single-edged razor blade, dumped in a garbage bin before she ducked into the bookstore three shops from the intersection. Thirty minutes of browsing and she strolled back to her car undetected.

She'd stayed up all night after the Snoopy affair, first watching TV, then reading through her coverless copy of Dan J. Marlowe's quick read *The Name of the Game Is Death*. The Earl Drake series was her favorite, and for some reason she kept coming back to this one. Maybe it was because Drake wasn't known as Drake yet. This was the story that spawned the metamorphosis. Drake or not, he stood for two things: justice and retribution. He viewed them from a very personal standard. One Lilin found agreeable.

Are you there?

Silence.

Agnes? Can you hear me? Speak up.

Silence.

Good.

Lilin leaned her head back against the stack of pillows. Like Drake, she had a plan. And it was just about to unfold. She needed to be rid of Agnes forever. Especially now. Agnes had disappeared twice. Both times were after satisfying jobs, when Lilin had fallen asleep with an atypical smile on her face. Contentment seemed to be the key to unlock Agnes's cell, and until the key was gone for good, Lilin couldn't savor her own justice and retribution. The victories were hollow without that feeling.

Her mind flipped forward. Jason Powers was the answer. She sensed a congealing, a shaping of a plan that would send Agnes over the edge. The more it took on life, the more perfect it seemed. Agnes would have to kill him—kill the man she loved. And poor little Agnes was halfway there. Lilin had seen the brief flash of anger— of pure emotion—when jealousy had overtaken logic in

Dr. Leahy's condo. That jealousy was the key to mining Agnes's rage. This would be no panning for dust. This vein contained nuggets.

Killing Jason would take away Agnes's final hope, her future. But it wouldn't be easy. Not after Lilin had sliced his finger and slipped into the bookstore across the street. She needed to get him alone, and she needed an hour. Time enough to get Agnes's hand on the razor with hers. Time to turn Agnes's rage loose. On Jason.

And there was more. Jason was the one Lilin wanted to savor. And that savor part would be reserved for her— Lilin. She wouldn't let Agnes in on it. It would drive Agnes over the edge.

Lilin sat forward and smiled. *Killed by her hands but enjoyed by mine. The final guilt-jealousy meltdown. The downfall of all logic.*

Lilin felt a head-to-toe tingle, but it was short-lived. She couldn't believe she had considered letting him go. She thought that knowing he was out there would wear Agnes down. But now she saw it much more clearly. Jason was like her father. He loved his good girl, Agnes.

Lilin took in a maximum breath and let it flow out. *And he wants to hurt me. To kill me.*

A sudden rush of energy propelled her from the bed. She couldn't think about Jason yet. She had another job to do first. The earlier the better. She could use the afterglow of calmness to finalize her plan. And another warm-up would get Agnes better conditioned to the routine. Freedom was close, but first a hot shower and another day on the job.

# CHAPTER 33

Lilin's feet were heavy on the steps: she rarely walked without a purpose. On the fifth step, her heel slipped from the missing lip. Her left hand caught the railing, which wobbled but held. Only the balls of her feet touched the remaining stairs.

She expected a wait. On her previous visit, the place had reeked of marijuana. And the strewn refuse and disorderly stacks of computer equipment suggested he wasn't an eight-to-fiver.

She banged on the door. Silence. Banged again, this time rattling the door in the jamb. A baby cried down the hall, and she thought she heard behind her a door opening a crack and then closing. A shuffle caught her attention.

One more series of bangs, and a thump, a curse, and

a door slam confirmed the occupancy. She waited.

A toilet flushed. She'd have to be careful on this one. Not careful, just quiet. She doubted the neighbors would be the 911 types, and any visitors probably wouldn't want the attention.

The door swung open and a pair of beet red, squinty eyes played a game with focus. She pushed into the room before he could react. The door slammed on his "Oh, shit."

She moved to the one chair in the room and pointed. "Sit." Her right hand was in her purse, and as he moved she stayed within easy lunging distance.

Donnie Powers flopped into the chair. His eyes didn't seem to have trouble with focus anymore.

"What do you want? I have to leave. I have an appointment."

Lilin stood over him. "I have another job for you. This one won't take long, and you have the right equipment here."

"I've been having trouble—"

"Shut up." Her hand twitched in the purse.

Donnie's eyes fell to the purse. They were nearly as round and wide as his mouth. He shrunk into the chair.

*Don't do this.*

Lilin paused.

Hey, look who's back. Come on. You know how it goes. And you're starting to like it. I can tell. We'll do this one together. Just like the car salesman. I'll make the first cut if you want.

*No. Don't kill him.*

Donnie flinched, maybe due to the prolonged silence. His lips moved, as if he was trying to speak, but Lilin waved her left hand in front of his face. He closed his mouth.

*He doesn't mean anything to you. Let him go.*

He's a loose end. And a pretty nice-looking one at that. Good enough for me, loose end or not.

Donnie's lips moved again. "What kind of job?"

"Something needs to be erased."

*No.*

"I can make things go away. It'll cost you—"

"We'll discuss price after." Lilin smiled.

"I like to work it out before."

"After!"

Donnie jumped. His eyes fell to her purse again.

Lilin stepped back a half step. "Stand up. Let's get to this."

Donnie didn't move. "I'll tell you what. Just give me the details and leave. I'll do the job for free. Right after you go."

A husky laugh filled the room. "You're the honorable type. And so generous, too. I'm overwhelmed. Your generosity intrigues me, and when I'm intrigued, I get horny. How about a quickie before you do the job? No charge."

"No." His eyes went to the purse again. "Thank you."

A frown invaded her face in a millisecond, her eyes a

piercing black. "Then get your ass out of the chair."

Donnie didn't move.

*Don't.*

Lilin's face relaxed into a near grin. "You want me out of here, right?"

Donnie nodded.

"Then let's get this job done. It'll only take a few minutes. Then I'll be gone and you can get to your appointment."

Donnie shifted forward in the chair but then stopped. Her left hand was on the purse, holding the edge, her right still in it.

"Come on. I haven't got all day."

*You're not going to do this.*

Lilin chuckled.

Donnie froze. "What's so funny?"

"You ever had one of those little angels on your shoulder?"

He didn't respond.

"Well, this one is wasting her breath. Get up."

He fell back into the chair. "I don't want to." His eyes flicked between the purse and her face.

"It's time."

*No.*

His body shivered. "Please don't kill me. I'm nothing to you. I won't talk. I swear."

Lilin spread her feet and distributed her weight evenly. "Stand up. Like a man."

*Please.*

Now it's please. What happened to *You're not going to do this,* huh?

Her right hand slipped from the purse, the stun gun in her grip.

Donnie pulled his arms over his head. "Please. Don't. We have a mutual friend. Remember? Your reference? Jason Powers."

Lilin's hand dropped back into the purse.

"Jason's my brother."

# CHAPTER 34

Jason tried to shiver the cold, sleepless night from his bones. Frustrated was an understatement. The suspected terrorist, a Middle Eastern man, had turned out to be a graduate student at Cal State, East Bay. He was visiting his brother, a computer analyst in the city, who just happened to have an English-style, formal garden in the backyard of his row house. The trunk-load of fertilizer was purchased and delivered for its intended purpose.

Jason was off coffee after the six cups that had nursed him through the night, and even a steaming plate of scrambled eggs and bacon couldn't compete with his eyelids. The only thing that would out-duel a pillow right now was a roll in the sack with April, but only because the pillow would be right behind it. But she was up in Santa Rosa, and the drive would be a killer. He needed a cheap motel room, even though it was morning. In fact, a room would be perfect. Sleeping would be difficult at his apartment, with Lilin in the area and aware of his activities. And a change of clothes was in a bag in the trunk of his car. He'd been caught too many times in day-old outfits.

He found the perfect place. Close enough to Seal Rock to get the fresh scent of the ocean but far enough to avoid the tourist prices. And a whole step up from a dump. Not good enough for the AAA rating program, but spiffy enough to price out the hookers and druggies. No weekly rates here. And it took credit cards.

The cell phone rang before he could fall out of the car and sleepwalk into the motel office to register.

"Jason? It's Donnie. I have a bit of a problem."

"Not now, big brother. I just pulled an all-nighter, and I want to pass out for half an eternity."

"It's really important."

A shuffle in the background over the phone caught Jason's attention. "Can't it wait?"

"No. It's a life and death—"

The phone made a series of swishing sounds, then clicked. Jason heard breathing on the other end. More like panting.

"Hi, Jason." The voice was husky, vaguely familiar through Jason's fatigued mind-fog. "I have your brother."

He strained to make the connection. "Who is this?"

"Lilin." A muffled exhalation punctuated the word.

Jason's attention shot to midday form. Up until a few seconds ago, he thought he didn't have a pulse. Now it pushed on his temples, rang in his ears. "What do you want with Donnie?"

The husky voice turned sexy. "I don't want Donnie. Not anymore. I want you."

Another heavy exhalation. "I want you here."

"What are you going to do with Donnie?"

"That depends on you. You come here and I let him go. If you don't come, I'll have to vent my frustration . . . and my desire."

"Where's Agnes?"

Lilin laughed. "She wants you here, too. She has something for you. You do want to be with her, don't you?"

"I want to make sure Donnie is all right. Let him go now and I'll drive right up."

Another laugh. "My razor starts cutting in sixty minutes. Sooner if I see or hear a police car. I can disappear in this place faster than a cockroach can squeeze under baseboards. It better be you, and no one else, or Donnie becomes my next lover."

"I want to talk to Agnes."

"Agnes is busy."

"Doing what?"

"Preparing for a long trip. You'll want to say good-bye to her. Fifty-nine minutes now. You may want to get on the road."

A click and the phone went dead.

Jason turned the ignition, and the grinding sound shot through his body like an electric shock. He'd forgotten the car was still running. An hour didn't leave much time to get there. He accelerated out of the motel parking lot. An hour didn't leave much time for a plan either.

# CHAPTER 35

Jason pushed the Volvo beyond its usual nine miles an hour over the speed limit. Good thing the Golden Gate was clear of most traffic. He'd barely missed rush hour, and he was heading in the best direction for the time, outbound from the city. Even so, he'd have to hurry. The gas pedal of the Volvo slapped the floor.

Jason flipped the hinge on his cell phone and brought it to the top of the steering wheel. The number was memorized now. It rang once. He didn't expect a woman to answer.

"I think I have a wrong number. I wanted to talk to Detective Art Bransome. Of Mendocino."

"This is Mrs. Bransome. Art's not here."

"I need to get in touch with him. Can you give me a number?"

"Afraid not. He's doing what he always does before and after a tense job. He's fishing. No phone, no radio. I'm not even sure where he goes."

Jason looked at his watch as he pulled onto Donnie's cluttered street. He'd set his watch timer in San Francisco, and it ticked over to fifty-four minutes with a block to go. Normally, he'd hold out for a parking place in clear view, as close to Donnie's building as he could get. But he couldn't count on an optimal spot on short notice. He nosed the car into the first available space and bailed from the front seat at a near sprint.

Into Donnie's building. His timer read fifty-seven. His Nikes lost traction making a turn in the entryway and he forgot to count the steps, hitting the fifth too close to the edge. His foot slipped downward and he fell forward, hitting his shin first, and then making a two-point landing on his elbow and nose. Each injury, by itself, would tear the eyes, but the combination turned the ducts into faucets, followed by a red gusher from his nose. He didn't have time for this. He scrambled to regain his balance, and hand-and-foot four-wheeled up the remaining steps, leaving a red-dotted slick in his wake. A lunge, and he banged the door with his good arm as the timer hit fifty-nine.

He straightened up at the doorway and waited. Should he pounce when the door opened? Should he step back in case a razor sliced at the air in the doorway? Should he run? Despite the motivation, he was unable to arrive at an optimal plan of action.

The door creaked open, slowly at first, then with a quick swing. A shuffling shadow crossed behind the door, and a flash of clothing stopped at the chair across the room. Donnie was in the chair covering his head with his arms, as if he expected a nuclear blast. Duck and cover. Lilin stood over him, a straight razor held high over her head. Or was it Agnes?

# CHAPTER 36

Lilin's hand twitched on the razor. She looked down at Donnie, then up at Jason standing in the doorway. A slight smile creased her cheeks, and she circled her tongue in an exaggerated lip-lick.

Jason stepped into the apartment and halted six feet from the chair. "Let him go."

*Yes. Let him go. You said you would.*

Lilin's husky voice answered. "Why should I? I've never done it with a pair of brothers. At least not at the same time."

"You said if I came, you'd let him go."

*Let him go. We don't need him.*

Lilin felt her sneering confidence slip a bit. Did she say, *we*? The razor dropped six inches but stayed high. We don't need him?

*We don't. We want Jason. His brother means nothing to us.*

The razor dropped another few inches.

*Let him go. Like we said. We have Jason.*

Jason took a step forward. "Please. Let him go. You wanted me here. You have me."

*We have him.*

Lilin blinked hard and shifted her weight to her right foot. The razor lowered to the side of Donnie's head, then downward to his neck.

Donnie shifted in the chair, squirming away from the blade. Lilin pressed it forward to his neck. Donnie froze.

Jason wiped his nose with his sleeve. His mouth breathing rattled on each exhalation. He palpated his elbow and cringed.

Lilin focused on the blood that ringed Jason's nose. It appeared to be clotting. She felt her heart race. "Have a little accident?"

Jason lowered his arms to his sides. "Let him go."

Lilin giggled. "How do you feel now? Helpless? Not the least bit heroic? Is flight winning over fight? Can you resist the temptation to abandon your brother in the name of saving your own ass?" Her giggle turned to a throaty laugh. "It doesn't matter. I'll find you again."

He blinked a remaining tear loose. "Agnes. Please let Donnie go."

*We will.*

"Agnes isn't in charge. I am." Lilin pressed the razor edge against Donnie's skin again. A slight movement of either her hand or his neck and it would penetrate.

*Take it off his neck. We're going to let him go. Now!*

Lilin's hand flinched, and a red line appeared on Donnie's neck. He let out a loud *whelp* as a drop of blood appeared and then rolled toward his collar.

"God damn it." Jason took another step forward. His face seemed to change. "You cut him again and I'll be on you before you can get the razor up."

*Jason. No.*

Lilin laughed again and pulled the razor away from Donnie's neck. "That's sweet. Your brother's a loser. A dopehead. And you want to risk your life for this waste of human flesh?"

"Put the razor away."

*We will.*

Lilin frowned again. "You'd like that, wouldn't you?"

Jason held his hands out to his sides. "I won't do anything. Just put the razor away."

*Do it.*

She folded the razor halfway and stopped. "Why are you doing this for him?"

"He's my brother."

"He gave you up, but you won't return the favor? What are you, some kind of saint?"

"I'm his brother. Just like Agnes is your sister."

Lilin opened the blade again and put it against Donnie's neck. "You don't want to turn that page."

*I did the only thing I could do.*

Lilin's back straightened. She felt her hand relax a little. It was barely perceptible, but its grip on the razor changed.

Jason's eyes were fixed on her hand. "Agnes did the best she could. She was a scared little girl."

Lilin's hand tightened again. "She left me to him."

*I'm going to take the razor and put it down now.*

"You can't."

Jason's mouth gaped. "Can't what?"

Lilin looked up at him. Something wasn't right.

*I'm going to put the razor down now.*

She pulled the razor away from Donnie's neck, folded it closed, and laid it on the table next to the chair. Donnie's next exhalation went on forever.

*I'm going to let him go, and you're going to let me.*

She stepped back from the chair and raised her hands up to shoulder level.

Jason leaned forward. "Donnie. Get up. Get out of here."

Donnie sat still for an eternal second and then pushed from the chair so fast it scooted back a couple of inches. He ran around Jason and paused.

Jason stepped in front of him. "What are you waiting for? Get the hell out of here."

Donnie sprinted for the front door and pulled it closed behind him. Heavy footsteps faded to silence before the door latch completed its final click.

*Now I'm going to let him go, too. I'm not going to kill today.*

Lilin grabbed the razor.

*I said no killing.*

I'm just putting it away.

She slid the knife into the purse and walked around the chair, toward Jason.

*Put the purse down.*

She slid her right hand out and tossed the purse with her left. It landed on the chair cushion.

Jason watched it bounce once and come to rest. The pearl-like handle of the razor was there, in clear view.

Her shoulders slumped, and her posture relaxed. A different voice spoke. "Go, Jason. Get out of here. I'll be all right."

"Agnes?"

"Go. Please. Just go."

"Not without you."

She stiffened again, and the sneer returned to her face.

Sweet. You're going to do it. You're going to kill him. You know that, don't you?

*I'm stronger than you think.*

She raised her right hand, lunged forward, and the stun gun punched into Jason's ribs.

He jerked sideways as if someone had hit him with a baseball bat. His knees buckled.

"Are you stronger?"

Jason crumpled onto the floor.

*Yes.*

# CHAPTER 37

A warm sensation turned hot. In his shin. Then the pain hit, radiating upward. A sharp tinge shot down his elbow and met the upward bolt, right around the ribs, where another warm spot heated to a scald. Jason's memory cleared: he'd never felt so happy to be in pain. It meant his throat hadn't been slit. His right hand went to his crotch. All intact. No pain there. He exhaled, but nothing happened except a burning pain in his nose. He opened his mouth and tried again.

He didn't want to open his eyes. Lilin might still be there, razor in hand, ready to slice. Or it could be Agnes, with her arms held out for a hug. He opened one eye, then the other. Half of the apartment filled his visual field. No one was there. He turned his head slowly, and a pyre of pain flickered in his chest. No one was in the other half. He was alone.

Curiosity battled relief. Why? Why wasn't he another of Lilin's victims? Had Agnes intervened? It had been Lilin who held the razor. He was sure of that. The look in her eye, her voice, her posture—it was Lilin. Her features were emblazoned in his mind from their earlier meeting, before Imola. But he sensed that Agnes had been in the apartment, too. The actions, the changes in expression, and the strange talk. Agnes must have been in there. Arguing with Lilin? She must have saved him.

Jason's mind turned to his brother. Thank God he ran away, for once without a request for money. But where did he go? Jason rose up on one elbow and immediately regretted it. Where could he find Donnie? He'd never seen his big brother so scared. What Lilin had said about him held some truth, but Donnie wasn't a waste of human flesh. He was family, and Jason needed family right now.

Jason pushed to his feet, and the pain dulled but stiffness moved to fill the void. He grunted. It triggered a flash memory of his father. The old man had said that as one gets older, grunts help whenever standing up or sitting down. They lubricated the joints. The grunt certainly helped him stand up this time.

Jason brushed his clothes straight, and a flash of white caught his eye. It fell from the front of his shirt and fluttered to the ground like a wounded butterfly. A small square of paper landed on the floor between his feet. He leaned to pick it up and gave a double grunt to grease the movement. Three words were written on the scrap, in all caps: "DR. LEAHY, LEVI'S."

Dr. Leahy? April. Was Agnes headed to her place? Was Lilin? The tight sensation of panic pressed on Jason's lungs and constricted his throat. He charged three steps toward the door before his brain kicked in.

His cell phone was in his pocket. He nearly dropped it, and his shaking fingers had trouble pushing the miniature buttons. It clunked and rang. No answer. After seven rings, April's voice mail picked up and a computer-generated woman's voice spoke.

"April. Get out of your apartment right away. Call me when you're gone." He slammed the phone shut and ran for the door.

At the bottom of the stairway, he heard the distant wails of police sirens, coming from two opposite directions, getting closer.

Donnie must have called the police. Jason silently thanked his big brother, then sprinted from the doorway and down the street. He couldn't wait for the police now. He had to get to April's.

The Volvo was intact—no stolen wheels or missing parts—and it fired up on the first key turn. A quick glance at his watch—he'd been out for around fifteen minutes. No sense calling Bransome. He'd still be fishing. Fifteen minutes. Agnes must have left in a hurry.

The police. He could have them check April's apartment. They'd be able to get there before he could. They might find Agnes. Or catch Lilin in the act. He hesitated. Levi's? What did that mean? Was there something at April's that he was meant to see? Or to do? It was a message from Agnes. He'd seen her handwriting before, and the writing on the scrap appeared similar. Maybe Agnes had another message for him or some kind of sign. But she never wore Levi's. Did she? He pressed on the accelerator.

Agnes was close, or rather, he was close to Agnes. That feeling kept returning. She'd saved his life. He was sure of it now. She'd saved him this time. But what about the next meeting? She'd battled Lilin and won. This time. A warm sensation flooded his body, edging through the stiffness and pain. His feelings for Agnes had a familiar tone, and they brought him back to Mendocino, when they'd first met. When her allure was confusing to him, but strong. And it was so different than what he had felt for Eugenia or April. April. His foot pressed down on the accelerator pedal.

Just what was it about Agnes that pulled on him? The sensations were solid, enveloping. His foot backed off the accelerator and then pressed again. They mirrored the feelings he had for Donnie. The need to protect, sure, but it was more. A closeness. A bond. Like family?

# CHAPTER 38

Jason felt a chill that penetrated deep into his body. The door to April's condo was unlocked. He twisted the knob past the catch and pushed, jumping back. No movement, no sound. He inched in, slightly crouched for a quick movement, but he straightened up just inside the door. His throbbing pulse highlighted his injuries. He'd been to too many homicide scenes, and the condo had all of the eerie sensations.

First, there was the quiet. It was complete, as if all small ticks, squeaks, and building noises died with the victim. And it didn't have the echo of emptiness. That was gone, too. Second was the temperature. It was always cold at the scenes. Like the body itself heated the home with energies that went beyond thermal. The lack of human energy drained the place of all warmth.

Finally, there was the smell. It was faint in the front entryway, but it was unmistakable. The putrid, dead-mammal smell of an aging kill. The smell of a fresh scene, up to about twenty-four hours, was almost sterile, but it quickly tuned rancid after that. It more than neutralized perfumes and other fragrances that emanated from a home. Even the grandmotherly smell from an old person's home was sucked away at a death scene.

Jason tiptoed past the kitchen door and the odor hit him hard, immediately realized as a swirling dizziness that went up his neck, invading his brain. He reached out and steadied himself with a hand on the wall, and the lightheadedness passed. This smell was strong—he'd tolerated it numerous times in the past. It didn't make sense. For it to be here, it meant that the death must have occurred well before yesterday, not today. His mind jumped back to his phone conversation with Agnes. He'd told her to go see April. Is that what she'd done? Is that when it had happened? Horror gave way to guilt. Had he set up April's death?

He didn't want to go in any farther. But he had to. He knew what he'd find, and this one was personal.

With his handkerchief covering his nose and mouth, he inched into the living room and spotted a foot sticking out from behind the couch. Its skin was a dull, grayish white. He walked around the couch, and his knees buckled. A lightheaded sensation swept upward through his head again, triggering involuntary gasps. It was April, her throat slit. The wide pool of blood was brown and congealed—the metallic sheen way past jejune. Her severed index finger stuck straight up on her chest, glued by a brownish blob. He stood and stared when he wanted to run. Then the nausea came.

He turned and ran for the sink and stumbled on something, nearly falling over. He grabbed the counter, which stabilized him enough for a quick leap to the sink. He retched. Now his pain was acute: it swirled with his sickness into a whirlwind of misery. And for a moment, he wanted to join April. To check out. He was supposed to be dead, too. But he wasn't. Why not?

Agnes. That's why. What had her note said? Levi's?

He teetered back toward the living room, gaining strength with each step. On the floor, he spotted the object that had tripped him—a pair of Levi's. They were small, the size Lilin would wear. Much too slim for Agnes's taste. Nothing appeared special about them.

For some reason, Detective Bransome's cautions came to mind. Rule number one: don't contaminate a crime scene. Don't touch anything, don't move anything.

But there was no doubt about the murderer in this case. This was open and shut. Jason reached for the jeans but stopped and straightened up. The stench doubled near the floor, the dense air of death forming a viscous layer like the fake fog that bubbled from a chunk of dry ice thrown into water. Was it the smell that fueled his hesitation, or did Bransome's thoroughness intervene?

He kicked at the garment and it flopped over. Nothing significant on that side.

If Agnes had saved his life, she must have been in a battle with Lilin. And she had won. But Agnes could need help. Why else would she leave the note at Donnie's?

Jason gulped a huge lung-full of air, bent down, and held his breath. He grabbed the jeans and straightened up. On his exhalation and his next breath, he found the jeans were permeated with the smell. It was on his hands and rising around him. He fumbled in the pockets—nothing there. He pushed his arms through each leg. Nothing there either. He was about to throw them on the floor when he noticed a bulge in the small change pocket inside the right front pocket. He fished in his index finger and pulled out a folded piece of paper. This one was larger than the scrap left at Donnie's apartment. His fingers twitched violently as he unfolded a handwritten note.

# CHAPTER 39

Lilin stomped through the front room of the trailer, kicked at a chair, and then upset a small table in the corner. She'd driven to Inverness so fast the GTO had nearly left the road three times. She rushed across the living room and swept a lamp from a matching table. The lamp crashed into the wall and fell along the baseboard in a scatter of ceramic shards.

It was late afternoon now, and the day was wasted. Both opportunities to scratch her billowing itch were gone. Maybe for good. She had driven past the apartment of Jason's brother, but there were two police cars outside. Now there was nothing left but to pack up for her disappearance.

She stopped in the middle of the living room and spun around. With a slight bend at the waist, her voice ascended to a near scream. "Are you happy? You fucked everything up. You've jeopardized the future. He'll come looking for you. And for me. He should have died."

She waited, her arms held out in a palms-up query.

"Don't you have anything to say?"

*No.*

"Do you still think you're in control?"

No answer.

"Maybe I should go back and find him."

No voice.

"I could still find a way to get him."

*You won't.*

"How do you know?"

No response.

"Do you want to go to him—to your precious Jason?"

*In time.*

Lilin paced to the entryway and spun around. She stomped back across the room, shaking the trailer with each step. "In time? What the hell's that supposed to mean? You think you have a plan?"

Silence.

She kicked at the ceramic shards near the wall, scattering them across the worn carpet. "I can't believe you stopped me. You don't understand. I need to erase all traces. Eliminate all potential problems. I'm doing this for us. And what thanks do I get? Interference."

*Sounds logical.*

"What's that supposed to mean?"

Lilin stood still. Her hands balled into fists. Her right hand drew back and crashed forward into the wall, cracking the 60s-era walnut paneling. "If you're so strong, why am I here instead of you?"

Nothing.

"Answer me."

Still nothing.

"Answer me, you bitch."

# CHAPTER 40

Jason turned off Highway 1 and guided the Volvo onto the road that circled the terminus of Tomales Bay.

The police were at April's apartment by now. He'd phoned in an anonymous tip. Dr. April Leahy hadn't been seen leaving her apartment for several days. And he'd lied, said there were some strange noises a few nights ago. And now a bad smell was coming from the place. He'd hung up before the desk officer could ask for specifics—and for his identity.

It frustrated him to do it that way. He should have stayed with her body, given her the final comfort of a familiar face until the authorities showed up. Tears clogged his eyes.

In the short time he'd been with April, he'd felt a stirring that hadn't turned his emotions for some time.

It wasn't a category five hurricane, as with Eugenia, but it had progressed from a tropical depression to a tropical storm. Tropical Storm April. She was important to him, but not the way she had wanted. And he felt guilty about it. He never could come out and be honest with her, and now he was glad he hadn't. How perverse was that? He was glad she died thinking they had a chance at something more than the close friendship and the physical love they shared. And what did that make him?

Unfair as it was, April never had a chance. The more she opened his heart to the possibility of forming another loving relationship with a woman, the more she succumbed to the comparative tension of his potential to love. In that way, she was her own worst enemy. The stronger his feelings became for her, the more she helped him realize he was looking for something else. Someone else. But who? There was someone out there, and it wasn't his ex. Eugenia was now just a standard, a bar height. That was April's gift to him. He wiped his eyes on his wrist and noticed it came away moist.

That was the positive spin. Now for the negative. In harsh terms, he couldn't get around the realization that he had used her. It wasn't done in a mean-spirited way. But he should have been honest with her. Eventually, it would have happened. But now . . .

Fortunately, Inverness was close.

He picked up Agnes's note from the passenger seat

and propped it on top of the steering wheel. The note from the change pocket of the Levi's. This was the fifth scan. Or was it the sixth? He didn't need to read it again; he had it memorized.

*About a mile past Father's cabin, a narrow turnoff goes left, through tall bushes. It'll open up to a screen of trees. Follow the road around the trees. I'm in the green trailer. Look for a red GTO.*

Jason tossed the note back on the seat. Was it a setup? The writing looked like Agnes's.

The Volvo slowed as he turned it onto the road to Eddie's cabin. Why would she need a setup? She'd had him incapacitated—a stationary target within razor's reach.

And why would she give the information about the car—a red GTO? Probably because she wanted to be found. Jason pushed on the gas pedal again. She wanted to be found by him. Found or rescued? She had won the battle with Lilin at Donnie's, but had she won the war? What was ahead at the trailer?

And why did he have this single-minded need to be the one to find her? He could have alerted the authorities. He should. He'd be able to see her again back in Imola.

April was right once again. She was one hell of a psychiatrist. Emotion did frequently trump logic.

He picked up the note again. When did Agnes write it? There wasn't time to drop it off at April's after leaving Donnie's apartment. Then how did it get into the Levi's?

They were small, certainly the tight fit Lilin would wear. But not Agnes.

Jason slowed the car. The double-rutted road was up ahead, guarded by high bushes as the note said. He steered the car off the pavement and heard the bushes claw at the Volvo's side panels. He hadn't felt the nervousness of uncertainty to this point, and bringing it to his consciousness didn't ignite the churn in his belly. How could he be so relaxed? Did something happen in the apartment that only registered in his subconscious? Something that let him know everything was all right in Inverness? Something was drawing him here, to Agnes. Or was that part of the trap?

There it was—the churn. And he welcomed it. He needed to be on edge, aware to the precipice of paranoia. Escape systems shouldn't be designed with a hair trigger, but there had to be times when the threshold was purposely adjusted. This was one of those times.

The churn spun off signs of only one color: yellow, the color of caution. Not red, but yellow. Jason pulled the Volvo to a stop short of the bank of trees and cut the engine. A grand entrance didn't fit the situation. He climbed from the seat and pushed the door so it latched with a barely audible tick. His path would be through the trees.

The trailer seemed quiet, peaceful, surrounded by dense foliage on three sides. The red GTO stood sentry next to the front door, backed in as if it was watching for the slightest movement. He mentally slapped his forehead. He should have pulled the Volvo across the road in the narrow arc around the trees. It would have blocked a quick escape. On the other hand, he should have backed the Volvo in, just like the GTO.

He parted the final screen of bushes and walked in a crouch into the opening. His senses porcupined to stand-up alertness. He was ready for anything on a sensory level. On the motor side, his detectors converged to a single output: *run*. His heels hadn't hit dirt since he'd climbed out of his car.

The trailer was way too quiet. If Agnes had left the note, wouldn't she be waiting? Watching? He felt like a trick-or-treater about to knock on the door of a darkened house. No treat. Trick?

He duck-walked the final ten feet, staying below the high windows of the door and the adjacent pop-out addition. What was proper etiquette for such a situation? Knock? Walk right in? Make a noise and see who comes to the door?

He eased upright, peered in through a window of the pop out, and jerked his head down. She was there. In the middle of the room. Just standing there.

He peeked again. She was still in the same position, as if in a trance. Trick or treat? Which was it? Was it the full-sized candy bar or the tarnished penny? The stakes were higher here. This was all or none.

The doorknob was cold to the touch, so cold he

thought his sweat dampened skin might stick to it. It turned without resistance or noise. The doorway had a refrigerator-like seal around the opening, and it let out a quiet sucking sound when it let loose of the door.

He paused. There was no movement, no sound. He pulled the door open far enough to slip in and eased his left leg through the opening. He slid in his hip, then his shoulder. His head followed. She wasn't in view yet. His body shook with his pulse. He pulled in his other foot and stood in the entryway, a short corner away from her. And bent into a three-quarters crouch.

He stepped around the corner, ready to hit the floor and roll away at the slightest stimulus. His focus was sharp. Sharp enough to notice that she didn't even flinch. She just stood there, her only movement a slowly spreading grin.

"Jason. I knew you'd come."

# CHAPTER 41

She walked to him, arms extended wide for a hug.

Jason did a quick scan: nothing in her hands, no bulges in her pockets. But he couldn't see her back pockets. He accepted the hug and felt her arms wrap around him in a tight squeeze.

She pressed her face into his cheek. "I need you. Thank you for coming."

His hands slipped down onto her butt to feel her back pockets. Nothing in them.

She responded with a slow exhalation into his ear.

To him, it seemed like an exhalation of acceptance— or permission. Was this Agnes? The exhalation had a nervous waver. The waver of innocent excitement. Agnes?

He kept his hands on her pockets. She tightened her grip and exhaled again. Her lips brushed his neck.

"I need you."

Her breath was hot, tickling. Every hair on his body seemed to stand straight up. "I'm here."

His hands flinched, and she responded by pressing herself into him.

He tried to think of any other hiding places. The razor was thin. He ran his hands up to the small of her back and around to her hips. All clear.

She responded with another staccato exhalation, this time accompanied by a quiet moan. He thought he felt her lips pucker against his neck. He pressed his hips forward. She didn't object; she held the contact.

His breath was stuttering now but not just from arousal. It was more. This wasn't like Agnes. And it wasn't like Lilin, whose approach to tenderness ran at the speed of a truck driver fresh out of Preparation H.

He had to break the spell. He leaned his torso back, keeping the contact between them with his lower body.

She pulled back in kind and smiled, her eyelids at half-mast. "I need your help. I'm in trouble."

His right hand went to her cheek without any detectable message from his brain. It stroked and then cradled her jaw.

She leaned her face into his hand and broadened her smile. "What should I do?"

He looked into her eyes, searching for any hint of her identity. He decided to be blunt, to trigger a reaction.

"You have to turn yourself in."

Nothing. Which was good and bad. Good because Lilin would have reacted in a millisecond. Bad because Agnes would have reacted, too. She would have been in tears by now. He slid his thumb across her cheek. "I'll go with you."

Her eyes went wide, and he jumped.

"Can we do it in Mendocino? I want to go home. And I know Detective Bransome will be nice to me."

Despite the words, which screamed Agnes, he felt his heart rate climb to a thumping gallop.

Jason pulled his hands away from her. "Bransome." He patted his shirt pocket. The phone was there. "I have to phone him. Tell him what's—"

"No!"

He jerked back and looked for her hands. He raised his arms around her back to keep her arms up around his shoulders. Who was it, damn it?

She brought a hand to the back of his neck. "I'm sorry. I don't want to go until tomorrow. I want to be with you tonight."

Jason dropped his arms around her lower back. "Then let me call him. I want to make sure he'll be there." He looked into her eyes. They seemed bright with hope, not anger. "I won't tell him anything else."

She released her hug and walked into the kitchen. Jason kept his eyes on her as she rummaged through cabinets, cupboards, and drawers.

He was relieved he didn't catch Bransome at home. He didn't want to explain anything. The message he left with Mrs. Bransome was simple: Lilin found me. She's going to turn herself in. We'll be in Mendocino tomorrow afternoon. I'll explain it all then.

She emerged from the kitchen at the same time he clicked his phone closed. Two large, thick candles were tucked under her left arm, and two small votives balanced on her left palm. Her right hand gripped a book of matches.

He scanned her pockets.

She raised her right arm toward the back of the trailer. "There's no electricity in here. And no heat. We'll need these for light."

Her smile looked a little too wicked for Agnes, and the reference to no heat was way too suggestive for her personality. Jason stood still.

She nodded to the west windows and nudged his arm. "Come on. It'll get cold in here fast. We'll have to go wrap up."

He hadn't noticed the amber tone of the light and the long shadows in the room. It'd be dark in less than an hour. It was the first time he'd felt it: the trailer already carried a significant chill.

She nudged again, and he resisted. This time her eyes were different, but still not Lilin-like. There was no anger in them. He'd seen the look before, but he couldn't place it. Was it with Eugenia?

Agnes leaned forward, placed her right fist against his chest, and lightly kissed his lips. "I'll be in the bedroom wrapped in warm blankets. You can stay out here if you want to." She let her fist fall to his stomach and then swept it away as she turned and sauntered out of the room.

Too much data flooded his brain, and a familiar pattern refused to emerge. There was no doubt about where his urges wanted to lead him. It was just all the damn yellow signs. They kept appearing around him, larger with each passing minute. And what about April? How could he hold Agnes in his arms so soon after April's murder? How could he let the hands that so recently slit April's throat caress him now?

He reached in his pocket but pulled out his hand, empty. She deserved more than a coin flip. He wanted to trust her. In fact, he needed to trust her.

But it was more than that. Something stirred in him that pushed all of the past aside. Pushed April aside. He should have seen it coming as soon as he'd opened up to April, as soon as he'd relegated Eugenia's memory to a unit of measure.

It had to be Agnes. He wanted it to be so badly he was willing to ignore all the yellow signs. He wanted it to be so badly he walked to the bedroom in the back of the trailer.

# CHAPTER 42

Jason paused in the bedroom doorway and stared. The shape of her body showed through the tightly wrapped blankets. The bed was a small, the kind that forced intimacy between two people.

He savored her outline. She laid on the right side of the bed, next to a makeshift table—a modified construction crate. One of the large candles sat on the crate, dwarfing an adjacent votive. Her curves pulsated with the flicker of the pale, orange light. Another crate and mismatched pair of candles bracketed the bed on the other side. The candle arrangement was the twin of the one on the right, but it strained to cast a symmetrical glow.

Twins. Jason was ready to curl up with her under the covers until the word came to mind. Now he wasn't so sure. She looked innocent beneath the blankets, a welcoming smile anchoring a look of expectation. But what else could be beneath the blankets? He'd decided to trust her just a few seconds ago, but now those yellow signs were around him again, posted at the foot of the bed. He couldn't keep going back and forth like this. It would drive him crazy.

But he still moved forward into the flickering candlelight. Despite the possibility that it could be Lilin, despite the loss of April to the very hands in the bed before him, he stepped toward her. Why? Why didn't he call the police? Why didn't he run from her?

His hand went to his mouth, covering a deep inhalation. He felt his eyes watering, threatening to release onto his cheeks. And he nodded. It was her all along. It wasn't April who opened his heart to the possibility of loving again—it was Agnes. April was the proof, but Agnes was the motivation, the goal. Agnes's embrace in the other room had introduced the epiphany. Her welcoming presence in the bed confirmed it.

A smile spread on his face. She turned a little in his direction as his knee brushed the side of the bed. His smile faded. On the floor beside the bed, within arm's reach, was her purse. It was open wide. Just sitting there, wide open. She didn't need anything beneath the covers; she had her purse so close by. His hesitation was brief as he brushed the imaginary yellow caution signs aside.

Trust. He had to trust that it was Agnes—a new Agnes. Better yet, the old Agnes with a new attitude. The Agnes he was meant to be with. He stepped around to the empty side of the bed and sat.

She turned farther in his direction and the stretched blankets pulled from her bare shoulders. She rested her head on an uncased pillow and widened her smile.

He rotated his feet onto the bed and lay next to her,

outside the covers.

"You won't get warm like that." Her voice was cozy, but with a hint of sass.

He sat back up and leaned over the edge of the bed to untie his shoes, then straightened back up and turned. She hadn't moved. A tentative giggle escaped her lips.

He pushed the heel of his left shoe down with the toe of his right and flipped it to the floor, then repeated the maneuver with the other shoe. He could face her for the rest.

He peeled to an undershirt and boxers and slipped under the blankets. Skin touched skin.

She didn't move away. Her face was inches from his, and the glow of the candles made her dimples dance. Her soft eyes laser-locked to his. They weren't Lilin's eyes. Or April's eyes. Or even Eugenia's.

A new challenge swamped his brain, emanating from somewhere within his boxers. He felt her bare skin with his knees, his shins, and his feet. But how much of her was unclothed? His entire torso was covered, as was his nether region. He didn't want to grab her. That would be too forward. But he needed to know. He hoped she was naked, but he didn't want to assume it. He struggled to control the physical manifestation of his building need for her. In such a small bed, it could be embarrassing if she only wanted to cuddle.

He half rolled away from her and worked his shirt up from his waist. With an awkward arm cross, he managed to get the garment over his head, but his left arm caught in the fabric. The bed shook with his efforts to get it free.

She leaned over and helped free the shackled arm, and it took him a full second to realize that her bare breasts were pressed against his chest and side. His arms folded around her and pulled her close. They settled together against the single bare pillow.

Her lips reached for his, and the meeting was gentle. She pushed her torso into him, but her kiss was still delicate.

He returned it, just as gently, and felt her lips part and her tongue touch the inside of his upper lip. His tongue met hers.

She pressed firmly into the kiss and emitted what sounded to him like a contented hum. Her nasal exhalations increased in frequency and force, and he detected in them a scent exceeding attractiveness. It was alluring, irresistible. Not a perfumed, artificial odor, but a natural one, a woman one. Whatever it was, he couldn't get enough of it.

She terminated the kiss and pushed her face into his neck and kissed it before snuggling into a hug. A soft moan let out another flume of her aroma.

He wanted to hold her like that forever. This tenderness, this peaceful embrace, was what he had felt with only one other woman. And he knew that whatever happened next would be ratcheted up way beyond wonderful because of it.

Then it happened. The male brain is a joker, and it presses its gags at the most inopportune times. It spun one more challenge to interfere with his tenderness, derailing the immediacy of his actions without changing their direction. Was she wearing anything below the waist? He had to know. Right then.

The joker had control of his movements, and it commanded his right hand to slowly draw a line down her back, to her hip and her right buttock.

But the joke was turned back. Her hands were on the waistband of his boxers, tugging them downward. Her efforts met resistance, and when she ran her left hand down to confront the snag, she whispered with a laugh, "Oh, my."

He helped free the boxers and worked them off each foot with the other. She pressed into him, and their total skin contact spun them into another kiss, this one more forceful and impatient. He heard two long, low moans, one his.

Despite the immediacy of their embrace and kiss, she didn't seem to be in a hurry. Was she like him? He needed to enjoy the intimacy, explore it, find out what made her enjoy their mutual sensations. Find out what made her feel good. There was plenty of time for the ultimate act of closeness, and he felt a stronger bond was formed by building toward it together, slowly, sharing smaller pleasures along the way. Investigating each other for a better understanding, for a better closeness. Most women he'd been with had totally missed it. They wanted to jump to the grand finale. For him, the abbreviated program didn't warrant curtain calls.

His hands moved on her, caressing, while his brain took mental notes of each response. He dwelled on the positive ones, reveling in his ability to give her pleasure. To his surprise, her hands were equally busy and equally adept. Was she making entries in a mental data book of her own?

His right hand slid down the mesa of her stomach, and her legs spread to accept it. It didn't seem like a reflex act, but rather a conscious movement. And it wasn't a jerky twitch of want, but a smooth slide of expectation. He touched her gently, and her response was immediate. No mental notes were needed.

Her lips were next to his ear now, and her breathing was fast and rhythmic. The smell of her filled the room. Her hips fell into motion, mirroring that of his hand. He kept his touch light, steady.

The joker elbowed in. Don't make her wait any longer, it said. You'll lose her. Get on with it.

The joke was a wedge of uncertainty. Was he doing the right thing?

He resisted a change, but brought his mouth near her ear. "Do you want me to keep doing this?"

She exhaled her response, "Yes, please."

And that was the punch line, because her words tickled his ear and enveloped him in her pheromone-laden odor. It made him want her more than ever. And it took all of his self-control to keep her pleasure at the forefront of his intent.

His newfound concentration brought her to within reach of the summit, her rhythmic, openmouthed vocalizations ascending the musical scale. As she reached the top, he felt muscles throughout her body tense. He gently entered her and synchronized his movements with hers, initially keeping pace but then struggling to do so. Her voice filled the room, and her second whole-body contraction vibrated in and out of tetany.

Her arms gripped him tight to constrict his movement, her voice a hoarse whisper. "Wait. Let me get my breath." She finished off a dozen quick breaths with a delicate kiss on his neck. Her hands ran down his back, barely touching it. "Thank you."

He scaled his own mountain in brag-unworthy time and fell against her, trying to catch what little oxygen was left in the room.

He enjoyed their closeness for minutes that seemed like hours. From her steady, calm breathing and her caresses, he assumed she felt the same.

She kissed him gently and pulled her head back a couple of inches, interrupting the mood. "I want to tell you something, and I don't want you to say anything back." Her voice sounded different. It caught his attention. "Promise me you won't say anything back."

His mind took flight. Do women have a joker for a brain, too? He'd never encountered anything like that, anyway.

"Promise me."

He leaned up on one elbow, towering over her. "Okay. I promise."

She took a deep breath and let it out slowly.

He could still smell her odor.

"I love you. I have since before Imola." She pulled him against her. "Don't say anything. Just hold me."

He kept the promise and snuggled against her. He thought he felt the slight hitches of sobs as she burrowed her face into his neck.

He settled into the spiral of relaxation that doomed all postcoital men, when he felt her jerk up in the bed. His faculties were slow.

She leaned over the edge of the bed, and he heard her hand pushing through the contents of her purse. He tried to move, but his muscles were lethargic.

She straightened up and turned toward him.

His sluggishness turned to partial paralysis: he could rise only halfway, but he managed to bring his right hand up in front of his face. All of the yellow signs of caution crowded around the bed, laughing at him. He peered through his fingers.

Something in her hands glinted in the candlelight. She gripped it with both hands, her arms extended. It shook in her grasp.

He tried to move, but he couldn't. His immediate thought was of his background research on Lilith and her demon progeny. How they seduced, then devoured men. He remembered the swipe of Lilin's razor. He closed his eyes. "No. Please."

He held his breath and waited.

And nothing happened.

Then he heard a chuckle. He lowered his hand.

She held a small, white jar out toward him.

"What's that?" His voice came out high-pitched, like a child's.

She laughed. "Carmex. I can't get the lid off. Can you help me?" She thrust the jar into his right hand.

The first two tries were unsuccessful but not due to tightness of the lid. His hands didn't feel like they were attached to his arms. They shook flaccidly like Jell-O salad headed for a picnic over a bumpy road. The lid dislodged on the third try, and he nearly dropped it handing it back to her.

She nodded a thank you. "Whenever I breathe through my mouth a lot, I get chapped lips. I want to head it off."

The logic sunk in, and Jason let out a wheezing breath. Classic Agnes.

She looked at one hand, then the other, and frowned. "You know what?" She twisted the lid back on the jar and threw it across the room. It hit the far wall and fell to the tiled floor. The lid came loose and rolled on its edge toward the door. She turned to him. "I don't need that stuff. I know a better way to take care of my lips." She lunged on top of him and held a strong kiss as long as she could before her giggles broke the seal between them.

Agnes lay awake, propped against the faux wood paneling, cushioned by the thin pillow. Jason's breathing was regular, calm. He was beyond leg-twitching sleep and into full slumber. She wanted to caress him, hold him in her arms, but she didn't want to wake him.

She had dreamed about what happened a little earlier, but her dreams didn't do reality justice. She hadn't known what to expect physically, but she had a good idea of what she wanted emotionally. And Jason carried her beyond her expectations and wants in both arenas. That's why she'd told him. She'd known right then what it was to her. There'd been no need to wait.

A frown crinkled her forehead. She hoped he understood her request. She wanted to hear the three words from him. Desperately. But those words had a history in her world. They were the words of her father, said to both daughters in different ways. If Jason had said them, it would have created a crack, an opening. Lilin was lurking, waiting for the smallest opportunity. And those words sliced two ways.

# CHAPTER 43

Jason stirred, his eyelids flittering at the early morning glow. He rolled on his back and drifted for a moment and then jerked his eyes full open. He searched, in panic, until he saw her.

Agnes leaned down and kissed him. "Good morning, sweetie."

He smiled, started to say something, but stopped until he could turn his head away. "Hi. Sorry. Morning breath."

She pulled on his arms, and he slid to the edge of the bed. He tried to grab a sheet for cover, but she yanked him upright and pulled him across the room to a white-washed chest of drawers. On its top sat a plastic washbasin, half filled with water, two gallon jugs of water, two wash-cloths, and two towels. One washcloth was wet; the other appeared dry. Same for the towels.

Agnes turned to the far edge of the chest and poured coffee from a thermos into a Styrofoam cup. She held out the cup and slid a box of donuts in his direction. She smiled. "I've been busy this morning."

He sipped the coffee, unfazed by his shivering nakedness. "You went out this morning? I didn't wake up?"

"Yes, and no." She laughed and dipped the dry washcloth into the basin. "This is going to be cold." She pressed the cloth to his chest and rubbed a circle before he pulled away, nearly spilling the coffee.

"Jesus." He looked down past his waist as he slid the cup of coffee onto the chest. "That's not going to portray me in the best possible light."

She laughed again. "I saw the best light last night. I can handle this version as long as it isn't permanent."

He grabbed her in a hug. "Any colder and it might be." He kissed her and shivered.

"It's no colder than the air in here."

"Feels like it."

The washcloth headed south.

He grabbed her hand. "About what you said last night. I—"

"Please don't say it." She pulled her hand free and brought the cloth to her target. "Okay?"

"Okay. Okay." He exhaled and immediately pulled in a full shivering breath. "Mind telling me why?"

She pulled close but kept washing. "Last night you showed me. Words weren't needed. I like it that way. So don't tell me. Show me." She leaned back. "Oh, my. I didn't mean so soon."

She pushed him onto the bed and climbed on top, straddling him. Her kiss was hard but not violent. With a final thrust of her tongue, she planted her left palm on his chest and pushed off of him. Before he could react, she slid downward, kissing a path down his chest and belly.

Her scent made him dizzy. His mind caught, but only for a second. This was Agnes. And last night, it was Agnes. No doubt. But it was like a weight had been lifted from her. A trapdoor opened allowing another escape—this one emotional. And she was encouraging him. Daring him. To share.

As his pleasure rocketed, his desire to reciprocate gave chase, and he pulled her upward on the bed, rotating with her until he was on top.

He knelt beside her and peeled her jeans and panties off together in a single slow motion. The smile on her face seemed more a dare than permission.

He grabbed her ankles and pushed them upward and outward, the heels close to her hips, and pushed her elevated knees apart. He lowered himself to her and decided to dispense with any of the preliminary intimacy they'd experienced last night. He sensed her agreement and matched her dare.

# CHAPTER 44

The GTO eased past Eddie Hahn's cabin and made the turn toward Inverness. The morning fog had nearly burned off. Tendrils still clung to the tops of trees, holding on in the building breeze. The on again–off again sun presented a strong case for a clear afternoon.

Agnes guided the powerful car through the serpentine turns as if it were an extension of her mind. She looked over at Jason. "Your car will be fine. No one will even know it's there."

"I could have followed you."

She dropped her right hand from the steering wheel and patted his thigh. "You know Detective Bransome pretty well, right?"

He grabbed her hand and held it. "I know something about him. 'Pretty well,' I'm not sure."

"After the message you left for him, don't you suppose he'd be pretty anxious to find you?"

He shuddered. "Pretty anxious. I may have blown all the headway I made getting on his good side."

"Are you a betting man?"

He looked at her and raised one eyebrow. "Maybe."

"Ten to one says he put an APB on your Volvo as soon as he heard your message."

Jason slumped into the seat. "You know that thing I'm not supposed to say? Well, I do."

Her smile rivaled the crystal bright waters of Tomales Bay.

Agnes pulled to a stop at the junction and cranked down her window. "I love Highway 1. All right with you?"

He looked up at the cloudless blue sky. "Any other way would be a waste."

The growl of the GTO settled into a contented hum.

The road twisted along the Pacific Coast cliffs toward Mendocino, the sea air throwing Agnes's hair backward on the window side. A pair of seagulls dove together, then caught an updraft along the steep hillside and shot upward, past the car. After a few minutes, they reappeared, floating free, expending little of their own energy as they drifted in wide circles and figure eights, riding the air currents.

The GTO rounded a hill-obscured curve and Agnes's foot hit the brakes hard. Jason startled from a daze.

Ahead, on the left, a turnout was crowded with cars. In the center of the mass of machines was a tall white van, plastered with decals of frozen confections. A faint calliope tune tickled the air and bled in through Agnes's open window.

Without a word, she pulled into the turnout, at the extreme near side, and guided the GTO to a stop with its grill two feet from the guardrail. A distant fog bank over the water obscured the horizon and gradually blended its gray tinge into the cloudless blue above. From this angle, looking out over the guardrail, it seemed like she was on the edge of the earth.

She pointed with her right hand; her left found the door handle. "The ice cream man."

"No. Let me." He had his door open first. "You stay here."

"I can come with you."

"No. You stay in the car. Relax. Enjoy the view. What would you like?"

She released the handle and leaned back. "Soft serve, please. Vanilla. Regular cone."

"Stay put." He punctuated the command with an extended, open hand. He smiled and walked to the van.

Agnes leaned her head against the headrest and closed her eyes. The only sounds were the distant whooshes of waves hitting the rocks two hundred feet below and the playful tinkling of the van's music box. The cool air, not still long enough to be heated by the sun, surrounded her. She felt close to heaven. A scent came and went. It reminded her of the sweet smell of cotton candy. Her mind turned to Ferris wheels and midway barkers. The air was suddenly full of smiles.

Her head jerked up, her eyes wide. Her hands gripped the steering wheel, pulling her away from the seat. The dream. She remembered the dream. She was in the car at the ice cream van's turnout, and someone wouldn't let her get out of the car. She hadn't known who wouldn't let her out or why. She hadn't known if the dream was good or bad. But in her dream, she didn't get to have the ice cream.

Her eyes welled with tears as she settled back into the seat. In her dream, it must have been Jason who hadn't let her get out. She must've known about him back then. She wiped her eyes and took a deep breath. He was on his way back to the car.

He walked to her open window and passed the ice cream to her. The ridge of the cone already bulged with molten white fluid. "You better get that before it drips.

I'll be right back. I forgot napkins." He hurried back toward the van.

She flicked her tongue fast. Multiple breaches dribbled over the cone's edge. She looked down. A single white drip splattered her left thigh. She worked the cone, spinning it against her tongue.

*He's coming back. Start the car.*

She froze. Another drop hit her thigh.

*Start the car. And wait until he gets in. Everything we need is in our purse.*

She reached for the doorknob.

*No. Don't get out. We have to stay in the car. Start it. Now!*

She looked over. Jason was halfway back. She turned the key, and the engine fired to its usual growl. This time it sounded mean.

*Good. Now put it in gear. As soon as he gets in, pull away. I'll tell you where to go.*

Jason smiled. The crunches of his footsteps in the gravel were nearly deafening.

*Put it in gear. Get ready.*

She moved the gear lever. Another white drop fell to her thigh.

*Now. Wait until he gets in. Then we'll take off. And hurry.*

Four feet away, his hand reached toward the door handle.

Another drop fell. She looked down. This one was clear. Then another. Also clear.

His hand touched the handle.

Her foot slapped the accelerator to the floor and the GTO lurched. The rear tires threw gravel. The guardrail offered little resistance.

A seagull banked hard left and caught an updraft that carried it skyward, past the windshield. It reappeared, joined by another. Agnes spread her arms and floated with them. No need for wing beats. They were drifting, riding the currents together. She smiled. She was with them.

The sensation was vaguely familiar. She was lighter than air. But that wasn't it. It was on a different plane. She banked with the gulls and closed her eyes. The rushing air tickled her face, her arms.

Her smile released a new stream of tears. That was it. The sensation of flying was the only thing she could feel. And it was all hers. That sensation confirmed it.

She opened her eyes and saw both seagulls fly in close. She could see their eyes, and in them she saw acceptance. She relaxed into the uplifting current. For the first time in her life, she was free.